BEYOND A SHADOW

BEYOND A SHADOW

ALISON KENT

KENSINGTON PUBLISHING CORP.
http://www.kensingtonbooks.com

BRAVA BOOKS are published by

Kensington Publishing Corp.
850 Third Avenue
New York, NY 10022

All Kensington titles, imprints and distributed lines are available at special quantity discounts for bulk purchases for sales promotion, premiums, fund-raising, educational or institutional use.

Special book excerpts or customized printings can also be created to fit specific needs. For details, write or phone the office of the Kensington Special Sales Manager: Kensington Publishing Corp., 850 Third Avenue, New York, NY 10022. Attn. Special Sales Department. Phone: 1-800-221-2647.

Brava and the B logo Reg. U.S. Pat. & TM Off.

ISBN 0-7582-1114-7

First Kensington Trade Paperback Printing: December 2006
10 9 8 7 6 5 4 3 2 1

Printed in the United States of America

This one is for Amy Garvey
Thank you for loving Ezra, Harry, Mick, Eli, Kelly John, Julian,
and Christian (and Tripp after the fact),
and for making sure my words tell the stories I want them to tell.

And to Jamie and Jan
Two women who know the truth about strength in adversity

All human laws are, properly speaking, only declaratory; they have no power over the substance of original justice.

—Edmund Burke, British Statesman and
Philosopher, 1729–1797

Chapter 1

Two inches. Maybe three. That was the distance standing between Emmy Rose Maples and certain death. If she didn't drown, she would *su-ccumb* to hypothermia like her mom was always warning her. She knew that she wouldn't really freeze. The water would have to close around her in a big block of ice for that to happen.

Of course, all she had to do to make sure she didn't die was back up a couple of steps. But she liked standing here and staring down. She didn't even have to move her eyes to see the toes of her galoshes, the edge of the dock, and the rolling green water pulsing from the ocean into the bay. *Pul-sing.* She liked that word. Her mother had used it once to describe the way the waves pushed in through the harbor's entrance.

Pul-sing. That was exactly what her blood was doing now, pulsing through her veins as she looked at the water and listened to it lap against the dock's pylons. The same cold wind whipping her hair around her face drove the waves, making little white caps that crashed into the rocks like the marshmallow foam on hot cocoa.

She probably didn't need to be worrying about drowning or hypothermia. Her mom would be the one to kill her if she saw her down here without her hood. Her mom would think it was bad enough that she was wearing her dad's mackinaw instead of the pink parka hanging in the mudroom on the hook beneath her name. She hated pink. She looked like a wad of bubble gum.

"If I were you, young Miss Maples, I would not stand so close to the edge. Were you to receive an unexpected bump, you would most certainly fall."

"To my death, right?" she asked, glancing over at the man who had spoken. The man she had been waiting for. "You forgot that part. That I would fall to my death."

He considered her for a moment, his dark brown eyes kind of squinting as he swung the duffel bag he'd been carrying from his shoulder to the surface of the dock. He stepped over it and walked toward her. Then he stood beside her, his boots next to her boots, as they both stared down.

"I don't believe you would fall to your death at all."

"Why not?"

"Do you know how to swim?"

She nodded. "This coat is my dad's. It's heavy. It would be even more heavy if it was wet."

"So what would you do? If you fell in wearing the coat?"

"Try to get out of it without struggling."

"Why no struggling?"

"I don't want to get tangled or use up all my oxygen." She shrugged. "But that doesn't mean I could do it, so I might still drown."

"Then you should practice so you will know for certain."

Emmy Rose shuddered. Her heart beat so hard it hurt. "You want me to jump in?"

"What I want is for you to know that you can save yourself. I do not want for you to put your life in danger."

"So," she began, thinking about what he had said. "If I want to practice, I should tell my dad and have him here to help me. And probably have my mom's permission, too. Even though she would never in a million years give it to me."

"Do you think she would rather worry than know you can take care of yourself?"

Emmy Rose scuffed one toe against the dock's wet and salt-crusty planks. "You don't know my mom."

He didn't say anything after that. He just stood beside her, silent and still. Like a statue. She sneaked a quick glance to the side and saw he had his hands down in the pockets of his army pants and his shoulders hunched up in his pea coat against the sharp gusts of wind.

She started to tell him he would be warmer if he wore a hat, but then she remembered that she wasn't wearing one either. Her mom called that "doing what I say, not what I do." And she knew her mom would probably be down here on the warpath any minute to drag her home for supper. She might as well head back on her own.

Before she went, though, there was something she wanted to know. She looked back down into the water in time to see a sliver of silver as a fish swam by. "If I jumped in right now, do you think I'd make it?"

"I know you would, because I would jump in behind you to make sure."

That made her smile. It also made it easier to breathe. "I was down here waiting for you."

"I thought you might be," he said, walking over to pick up his duffel, but not before motioning her away from the dock's edge.

"You know, the water here is a lot colder than where you were born. I looked it up on the Internet in the library at school. I might have to be the one to save you from shock if you jumped in."

He laughed then. A huge laugh out of the middle of his chest that sounded like bamboo wind chimes. "That is quite the possibility, Miss Maples. I am not sure I am looking forward to getting used to the cold."

They started walking up the dock, away from his boat to-

ward the steps cut into the rock of the harbor's natural entrance. He let her go first, and she liked the idea of having
someone behind her to catch her if she slipped and fell. What
she didn't like was the idea of bashing her head open on the
rocks and bleeding to death.

"My mom wasn't sure if you were going to get here before
dark."

"Your mother will learn soon enough that I am a man of my
word."

She didn't figure her mother would have hired him if he
was a liar. Her mother hated liars. "She's cooking a whole
bunch of food for supper. Well, her and Alexa are cooking.
And baking apple pies."

"And you did not help?"

Emmy Rose ignored him for a second while she stepped
from the staircase onto the sidewalk that ran along the edge of
the coastal highway and separated the town of Comfort Bay
from the road. She headed toward the boardwalk and her
mom's candy shop, using the path worn down in the grass instead of the fake bridge tourists used to get there.

"I like to eat, but not really to cook," she finally said, hearing the cold grass crunch beneath her boots.

"Do you know how to cook?"

"Sorta," she said. Her mom bugged her about it enough.
She didn't want him bugging her, too. "It's just with all the
cooking for the stay-over guests and the candy for the shop, I
get sick of everything being about cooking. I'd rather gut a
fish and panfry it over a camp fire."

"Do you build your own camp fires?"

"Sure do," she said proudly.

"Can you do so without flint or a match?"

"Uh, well, no." She wasn't exactly a Boy Scout.

"But you can catch and gut your own fish?"

"Yep." She gave a big nod and kept walking. "My dad's a
fisherman. He taught me everything."

"Did he teach you how to catch a fish with your hands? Standing and waiting as a predator would?"

"No," she said, frowning. "We mostly fish from his boat when I get to go, which isn't very much."

"I see," he said, but that was all.

"What's that supposed to mean?" she asked, stomping against the planks then stopping when she realized she couldn't hear him walking. She hadn't heard him on the grass or on the dock or now on the boardwalk. And so she turned around.

He was standing right behind her, looking down. "It means you will never go hungry as long as you have a baited fishing hook and know how to make a fire."

"Is that your sneaky way of telling me I need to learn how to cook?" She narrowed her eyes. He sure was bossy. Just not in the same way her mom and dad were bossy. They just ordered her around. He made her figure things out for herself.

He laughed again, but stopped as quickly as he'd started. "I believe someone is calling your name."

"I don't hear anything—" But then she did. And she was so glad it was Alexa and not her mom.

This way she could get back into the house without her mom seeing that she wasn't wearing her parka or hood. "We better hurry. Dinner's probably ready, and we'll be in all kinds of trouble if we're late. At least I'll be in trouble. I can't really see you getting in trouble with anyone."

He gestured with the hand that wasn't holding onto his duffel bag's strap and bowed like a gentleman. "After you, Miss Maples. After you."

She giggled, and he smiled, his teeth as bright as the whites of his eyes and shiny against his dark skin. She smiled back, just knowing the Christmas holidays were going to be a lot more fun now that Ezra Moore had come to town.

Chapter 2

Alexa Counsel wrapped her cardigan tighter and huddled deep inside the wool. She hurried down the sloped driveway from the bed and breakfast that was also the Maples' home toward the path that cut across the lawn to the candy store whose business, when combined with that of the B&B, brought in almost as much income for the family as did Danny Maples's fishing tours.

Molly had told Alexa she was certain her daughter had gone down to the docks to wait for the handyman she'd recently hired. Danny's bookings had picked up to the point that he had little time to spare around the house or for the B&B these days, leaving Molly no choice but to pay someone to take care of what had always been her husband's honey-do work. Finding help in the small fishing and tourist community of Comfort Bay on the Oregon coast was an iffy proposition.

With so many of the town's residents self-employed in one of those two trades, the full-timers who weren't retirees had their own work to keep them busy enough to put their teens to work as well. And since many of the part-timers flew south for the winter, that left Molly slim pickings.

Alexa trusted her friend to know what she was doing, but couldn't help but wish Molly knew something about Ezra

Moore. Something as in *anything* besides the fact that he happened to be in the Maple Sugar Shack the morning she put out the "Help Wanted" sign and told her he'd take the job. He didn't ask about hours. He didn't ask about pay.

What he'd told her was that he was taking a sabbatical from a position teaching disadvantaged youths in his Caribbean island home. He wanted a change of scenery to stave off burnout, new experiences to share with his students, broader horizons with which to expand his teaching repertoire. As noble as it sounded in theory, Alexa wasn't easily duped.

That said, she wasn't the one desperate for someone to take over the repairs, maintenance, and odd jobs Danny wasn't able to find time to fit in. And, really, she had no reason to doubt Mr. Moore's claims. She'd come to Comfort Bay five years ago for a similar purpose. She'd stayed because, well, the small community was now her home. Her job was here. She had commitments. She had friends.

And that reminder had her scrambling across the lawn toward the back of the candy shop calling for Emmy Rose Maples to come home, her boot soles slipping on the damp grass, the even damper air kinking her hair around her face. If Ezra Moore was with Emmy Rose, all the better. The trip down would do double duty; on the way back, she could show him around the property for her friend.

If not, then once he arrived he'd have to find his own way to the Maples Inn. Comfort Bay's population of just over twelve hundred guaranteed he could ask anyone he met on the street and come away with detailed directions. Five years later and Alexa, a California girl, was still getting used to that element of small-town living herself.

"A-lex-a!"

Alexa looked up from watching where she was walking and searched out Emmy Rose. The girl had just rounded the side of the Maples' candy shop and waved hugely with both of her arms. Alexa waved back, her mirrored enthusiasm fading as she realized Molly's daughter had, indeed, found the new handyman.

At least that was who Alexa assumed was following on the girl's heels. And even knowing all she knew about Ezra Moore's impending arrival, she had to bite down on her tongue to keep from screaming at Emmy Rose to run.

Even from this distance, Alexa had no trouble discerning that Ezra Moore was a formidably intimidating and dangerous man. He was still too far away for her to see his features clearly. She didn't need to. She stood by her assessment. With every step he took, danger rippled in his wake like rings of water from a smoothly skipped stone.

It was in the way he never stopped soaking in his surroundings, looking over his shoulder as he hefted his duffel bag higher, lifting his chin as if listening to the sounds carried in on the ocean breeze, as if scenting anything in the air he found threatening or unfamiliar.

She had no idea how or why she saw all of that so clearly. She only knew that she did. She was not imagining the tingling at her nape, or the flesh on her arms pebbling from fright more than from cold. All she was doing was watching him, the tension in his stride, the stiffness in his posture, thinking that both of those even more than his skin color would cause him to stand out in Comfort Bay.

And then before she knew it, he was standing in front of her, Emmy Rose a buffer between them. Alexa met his eyes directly and held herself tighter as she shivered anew. She reached for Molly's daughter and pulled the girl close. And only when she felt the small body tucked safely to hers did she hold out her hand.

"I'm Alexa Counsel. A friend of Molly's."

"Alexa's my teacher," Emmy Rose added as Ezra swung his duffel to the ground. "Except at school I have to call her Mrs. Counsel."

"As is proper," Ezra said, his eyes never leaving Alexa's, his cool fingers swallowing hers, the music in his voice continuing to sing in her ears. "I am Ezra Moore, Mrs. Counsel. It is a pleasure to make your acquaintance."

Smooth, dangerous and . . . damaged. She saw it in his eyes, bright and sharp but devoid of emotion, heard it in his words, which were still playing a tune. She felt it most of all in his touch, in the way he took too long to release her, waiting until she hit the edge of nervous discomfort before letting her go.

"It's actually Ms. Counsel. I'm divorced. But the kids knew me first as Mrs., so . . ." Blabbering. She was blabbering. "Please. Call me Alexa."

"Alexa." He took in her hair, her mouth, the line of her jaw before his gaze returned to her eyes. His were nearly black, not so much like coal, more like . . . bottomless. She didn't think she'd ever seen eyes quite so dark, and had yet to look away when he added, "I am sorry for your loss."

Her loss?

"Your husband," Ezra supplied before she could ask. "It was difficult for you, the loss, and I am sorry."

She backed up, straightening her spine and pulling Emmy Rose with her, putting one step between the two of them and Ezra, wanting to put more. "Thank you, but I'm fine." It was the only thing she could think of to say.

No one had ever realized the toll the breakup with Brett had taken. Molly and Rachel, her two best friends in Comfort Bay, had called him a cheating bastard and supplied her with chocolate, doing their best to keep her spirits from falling into a deep dark hole.

They'd fallen anyway, and she'd had to learn not to wear her private face in public. She hadn't wanted them to know the truth of all she'd felt.

But Ezra knew.

He'd looked into her eyes and he'd seen the truth she tried to keep from herself. She had no idea how he'd done it. She hated that he had. She would have to work harder. Reveal less. Find a new trick to use to hide what she was feeling. One that would fool the keen eyes of perceptive strangers as well as her friends.

"I'm hungry," Emmy Rose said, squirming away from Alexa, her interruption breaking the coil of tension binding them, ready to snap. "I'm going home."

Alexa watched the girl scramble up the hill, crossed her arms over her chest to ward off the chill, and followed. Behind her, Ezra hitched up his duffel and then fell into step at her side. "Molly tells me you teach school."

He nodded; she saw it in profile. "Yes. Already you and I have that in common."

Was he expecting them to have more? He had no reason to expect anything at all. He shouldn't have even known she existed. Unless Molly had mentioned her to him. Alexa latched onto the change of subject and asked, "What all has Molly told you about Comfort Bay? Maybe I can fill in the blanks for you. Or answer any questions?"

"You are not from this place originally, are you?"

She avoided glancing over. Too much about him had already set her on edge. She did not need the reminder of his size. Or of his hard strength. She listened instead to the crunch and squish of the ground beneath their boots and wrapped her cardigan tighter.

"I moved here five years ago. From L.A."

"With your husband."

"He wanted to get out of the city and give the quiet life a try."

"He did not find it to his liking."

"He grew tired of it. After a while. Yes." Grew tired of her. Of their marriage, which had been comfortable but never passionate.

"But you did not."

She had, but she'd stayed. She did not abandon friends or treat her commitments lightly. But yes. She missed the energy of the city, the excitement, the environment that stimulated her in ways Comfort Bay could not.

It took her a moment to realize Ezra was no longer walking beside her. She stopped, turned, snagged back strands of hair blowing into her face, but said nothing, waited instead for him to voice whatever he had on his mind, this man who was so very intriguing, so very . . . alive.

He didn't make her wait long. "I was wrong about you, Alexa Counsel. You don't like it here at all."

She shook her head emphatically to disabuse him of the notion that he knew anything about her. To disabuse herself of the notion that he was right. "I have some of the best friends here I've ever had in my life. I love my students. There are so many advantages to teaching in a small district. The teacher-student ratio for one. Of course there's the disadvantage of less funding, but the pros really do make up for the cons."

"None of that proves my assessment wrong."

This had to be the most bizarre conversation she'd ever had with a man she'd just met. "Why are you so interested in how I feel about living here?"

He tilted his head to the side, and she noticed for the first time the jagged scar like a lightning bolt running from his temple to his chin. It was old and faded, a wound from a long time ago, and it started her wondering about where he'd come from, the life he'd lived, how old he was now.

"Because of what it tells me about you." He smiled then, a slight movement of his mouth that revealed the deep groove of a dimple at odds with the intensity of the rest of his face.

She wasn't buying whatever it was he was selling. No dangerously perceptive stranger was going to cause her to start doubting herself. And she was not, she told herself, was *not* the least bit intrigued by the dichotomy of his dimple and that lethal-looking scar.

"You're wrong," she assured him—assured herself as well. "I do like it here. I'm sure you will, too. Oh, one word of warning. If you stick around for any length of time, don't be surprised if you get the sense that you're living under a microscope. Comfort Bay is a very . . . friendly town."

This time when she started walking, he was quicker to catch up. He also moved closer to her side, their shoulders brushing, the breeze blowing the salty scent of the sea from his clothes into her path along with the clean smell of soap.

"That will not be a problem. I am an open book." He lifted his duffel bag higher. "I have no secrets."

She didn't believe a word that he said. She smiled politely, ignoring the prickles of premonition crawling down her spine, prickles telling her that his secrets were ones it might kill her to know.

Chapter 3

His contact was due to arrive at the Maples Inn in ten days. Before then, Ezra had much to accomplish. And this unexpected distraction, this unforeseen knot in the straight line of his plans—if he did not nip it now, if he did not choke it off at the source—was going to get in his way.

Alexa Counsel was a beautiful woman uncertain if she feared him or not. He did not wish to frighten her, or to have her think that he posed any threat. He did, however, need to keep her at a distance, and to convince her that the distance was all her idea. It was a most effective tactic—one he had learned over time—to allow his opponents to believe they possessed a situation's upper hand.

He had, as a child, been taught many of life's lessons by the grandmother who had raised him in their Caribbean island home of San Torisco. It took living to understand her advice, and experience to put her words into practice. And still he faced the occasional challenge for which his childhood lessons and his years undercover left him ill-prepared.

At such times he could only rely on gut instinct, and that instinct told him he needed Alexa to push him away. If his time here was to be lucrative, his focus needed to remain tight. He had to immerse himself in his role, to do what he had to do for himself. He preferred that he not have to make a life or death choice for others who were innocent pawns.

At his side, Alexa laughed softly, the sound a gentle caress that touched him when he should have been immune. "I know all I have is a first impression to go by, but open book is not exactly how I see you. If so, I would only need to turn the page to satisfy my curiosity."

"How do you see me?" he asked, listening intently for what she said as well as the words she left unspoken. He was certain he had given nothing away, and was determined to deflect her scrutiny if he had. He could not reveal himself this early. His entire life's work was at stake.

She grabbed back a handful of the dark curls that had blown into her face. "Well, I only know what Molly told me, but I have to admit I'm finding it hard to reconcile the image I had in mind with the reality."

He found that peculiar. "What was the image you had in mind?"

She hesitated, then shrugged; he heard a soft tinkle from the earrings she wore as the wind caught them. "A school teacher, not a mercenary."

He tossed back his head and laughed. "Did you expect me to arrive wearing an oxford shirt and loafers?"

Her profile showed her smile. "I guess I hadn't thought about you dressing for travel."

"Or about my role here as a laborer?" he asked as they continued their hike.

"That, too."

"Or that I teach in conditions where an oxford shirt and loafers would be a hindrance?"

This time her expression was more of a frown. "What sort of hindrance?"

"The youth whom I teach are not necessarily enthusiastic about education. Most do not believe they will ever see a better life. Were I to dress much differently than they do, it is possible they would consider my show of prosperity an insult. I prefer to remind them we share similar backgrounds and circumstances, and in that way, give them hope."

Alexa was silent after that, and as they made their way to the Maples Inn, Ezra found his thoughts not unexpectedly drifting to San Torisco, to the countless young men who had escaped poverty to what seemed to be a better life, going to work on a neighboring island privately owned by an American businessman.

That the American businessman was the head of the international crime syndicate Spectra IT was a fact only discovered after they'd indentured themselves into his employ. They were not allowed to leave his compound. They were not allowed to contact their families. If they made any attempt to do either, they would die.

A handful rose to play major roles in the organization's kidnapping and prostitution rings, diamond smuggling operations, illegal arms trading, trafficking in drugs. But most did not. They remained slaves. They had food. They had clothing. They had amenities unavailable on San Torisco. But they did not have lives.

Ezra's story about wanting to give hope to the youth of his homeland was true. He did not, however, do that through teaching as he'd explained to Alexa and to Molly Maples when he had spoken to her about taking this job. He did it in ways that he could explain to no one. Ways that made him as malevolent in his own right as was that American businessman, Cameron Gates, in his.

"Many schools in the U.S. have uniforms for that very reason," Alexa then said, redirecting the course of his thoughts. "But since many residents of Comfort Bay rely on thrift stores or charities for their children's clothing, I understand your position. I tend to dress fairly simply for the same reason."

"Even though you could afford more," he said.

She seemed uncomfortable with his observation, guilty perhaps that her situation was not as dire as that of her students, or even that of her friends. "Brett, my ex, owns an IT consulting firm. My divorce settlement was . . . substantial."

He stored away that information. "And no doubt you are extremely generous when a need arises."

She responded with a huff. "What makes you think that?"

"Your hesitation. You prefer your good fortune not be common knowledge." He watched as she shook her head, saw the telling flutter of her hand at her throat.

"It's not a fortune, and nothing about what I went through was good, but you're right that I don't like to talk about it." She laughed, another soft, self-deprecating sound. "Which doesn't explain why I'm spilling all to you."

"I am a good listener," he said. "Even though you do not know me, you sensed that."

"I suppose." She tossed off the comment as if she didn't want to think about what such a link between them might mean. He did not blame her for her reticence. He had not anticipated this turn of events himself.

They had moved from the steep grassy slope to the driveway of crushed shells and stones minutes before, and now she led him down a short walkway to the right of the inn. Moments later, a small peacock blue structure with gingerbread trim appeared among the trees. He'd seen the exterior previously. He had not been inside.

"This is where you'll be staying." Alexa turned the knob and the door swung open. He followed her through. Just inside, she pointed to a hook on the jamb holding a key. "Molly leaves the key here when the apartment isn't being used."

Dropping his duffel onto the stone hearth, he glanced around the one main room separated from the kitchen by a small, jutting bar. Beside it, an archway opened into the bedroom where he assumed he'd find the bath. "Is she not afraid of vandalism?"

"Out here, no," Alexa said in answer as she closed the door.

"The furnishings are strictly functional. You'll find all the antiques in the inn."

There was a sofa against the far wall, no television that he could see, and the radio on the stand by the door included a cassette player rather than one for compact discs. He did not mind. He needed no extra trappings. He would be perfectly comfortable here for the duration of his stay.

The single window on the room's front wall let in very little light. He reached for the switch above the radio. The lamp hanging in the corner above the recliner came on. The glow it cast warmed the room, softening the darkness to one with a tenor of intimacy.

He looked up at Alexa where she stood leaning back against the bar. The first time he'd faced her directly, she'd been fighting the wind and the urge to keep the Maples girl out of his reach. Now it was only the two of them, no wind to whip away their words, no girl child to act as a buffer.

There was only the room growing close around them, the evening clouds hiding the sun. Alexa tilted her head to one side, her earrings chiming softly, but she made no move to leave, to put any distance between them. He sensed her inquisitiveness as well as her fear, and knew he would need to exploit one or the other.

He turned toward the small fireplace and picked up the poker from the set of tools on the hearth. He let his mouth form a smile, though he purposefully kept it from reaching his eyes. "I've never had a fireplace. Where I live there is hardly a need. All the fires I've built have been in the open and used for cooking rather than heat."

Alexa gestured in a direction beyond his shoulder. "There's a shed behind the inn where the wood is stored along with axes, hatchets, and chain saws, plus every tool I can imagine you needing."

He nodded. He'd seen the maintenance shed when he'd interviewed with Molly last week. "I do have a toolbox on the boat, but nothing so extensive. And I definitely have no means for chopping wood."

"I wouldn't think you'd have need," she said, a touch of humor lacing her words. "Not on a boat."

He turned back to her then, still holding the poker, facing her across the room, which was no wider than fifteen feet. "I do have a machete. And a number of knives, but have done little with them beyond cutting away the heads and tails from the fish I have caught."

"Molly told me that you'd been living on your boat for several months," she said, crossing her arms.

That was the story he'd given. That he'd begun his sabbatical sailing the Caribbean, making passage through the Panama Canal and sailing up the Pacific Coast, working odd jobs to finance his trip, but preferring to spend the cold winter months on dry land.

The truth was that he'd been sailing only long enough to search out a location where he could make contact with the Spectra arms buyer unnoticed. He thought back to the things he'd learned from his new employer about her friend Alexa Counsel. "Does Molly tell you everything?"

"We share a lot, yes." Alexa gave him no more than that, turning to walk into the small kitchen, where she flipped the switch for the overhead light and opened the pantry door. "And I can see she set you up with enough strawberry and plum preserves to keep you for weeks. All you need is bread."

"She mentioned a market in the town?"

She nodded, closing the door. "Yes, though you won't have to worry much about food. Molly cooks enough for two dozen armies. She finds comfort in cooking while some of us find it in eating. Oh, but you probably will need to get coffee. If you drink it."

"I do," he said, wondering about Alexa's interest in his well-being. If she was simply helping him to settle in, or if she had a need similar to Molly's to nurture. "I should see what I might need and let her know that I have arrived."

"Emmy Rose has no doubt done that by now. And I told Molly if I found you that I'd see you got settled. Sundays are crazy days for her, getting menus and laundry and everything else ready for the week ahead."

He took a moment to weigh her suspicions. He wanted her to push him away, yes. Instead she seemed intent on distancing him from her friends. He had yet to determine why—if this was her protocol when dealing with outsiders, or if he had tripped her personal alarm. "I think I am well settled. I don't wish to take up more of your time. I will unpack, then walk back to the town for coffee and bread."

"Coffee, yes, but you can get bread tomorrow from Molly. Monday is bread-baking day. Oh, I almost forgot." She reached into the pocket of her sweater, came up with another key. "This one is for the maintenance shed, and that does stay locked all the time."

"I won't forget." When she made no move toward him, he returned the poker to its stand and crossed the room. She remained standing in the center of the kitchen, from where she watched his approach.

He thought she would lay the key on the bar, that she would leave it there for him to pick up once she was gone. But she didn't. She held it. Forcing him to come to her for what he was going to need.

It was a move that signaled a power play, yet he could think of no reason for Alexa to make one. They were not enemies. They were not competitors. They were not even friends, but had only just met. It was a situation which made little sense.

And so he responded to her move as would a player. He stepped into her space and upped the stakes. He did not simply take the key from between her forefinger and thumb. He wrapped his entire hand around hers, and held her still without pulling the key from her grasp.

He did not say a word. She said nothing either. The only reaction he drew from her was the rapid warming of her skin that brought color to her cheeks.

"Do you not believe me?" he finally asked, his own temperature rising, his words causing her to blink and to finally let go.

"No. I'm quite sure Molly has nothing to worry about." She gave him a hesitant smile then ducked around him and made her way to the door, causing him to wonder if she was the one who was worried.

He did what he could to settle her mind. "Thank you for coming to meet me. And for the keys."

She opened the door, lifted her hand in farewell, said, "Not a problem," and then she was gone.

He stood in the kitchen for the several minutes that followed, gripping the key to the shed until the sharp edges cut into his palm. She had put between them the distance he wanted, but it had cost him too much too soon.

Chapter 4

"Your new handyman is very . . . interesting," Alexa said to Molly Maples as the two women stood in the Maples Inn kitchen on opposite sides of the island, Molly readying dough to roll out for pie crusts and Alexa peeling a bowl full of Jonathan apples.

Emmy Rose sat hunkered down on the floor beside Alexa, reaching up every so often to grab the peels as they coiled from the apples and gobbling them down. Alexa laughed. Molly, on the other hand, rolled her eyes at her daughter. "Emmy Rose, you are going to ruin your dinner."

"No, I'm not. And anyway, I'm starving."

Molly let her daughter have her way and glanced at Alexa. "Interesting how?"

Alexa held the paring knife poised over the apple in her hand. She wasn't even sure interesting was a big enough word to encompass all the things she sensed about Ezra Moore, but it would have to do because she couldn't think of another word to capture it all. The fact that he was unlike any man she'd ever met made for the worst sort of cliché. But the fact that he was left her curious, and more than a bit unnerved.

She ended up shrugging. "Don't you think he is? I mean,

how many people have you known to take a true sabbatical? Leaving behind everything to experience more of what life has to offer?" Was that why he intrigued her? Because she wondered if she would ever have the moxie to do the same?

"All that says to me is that he doesn't have the same sort of responsibilities those of us tied to a home and business and family do." Molly dropped a ball of dough onto the island's floured surface and reached for her rolling pin. "I'm sure he'll be anxious to be on his way soon enough, but at least he's agreed to stay until the first of the year.

"If I can get through Christmas and Dan through at least a month of Steelhead season, we can think about hiring someone permanently. In the meantime, I can only hope he remains true to his word and stays."

School let out for Christmas vacation in two weeks. This would be Alexa's third solo holiday since Brett's return to L.A. If this year followed in the steps of the last two, she'd spend a lot of that time at the Maples Inn helping with the overwhelming workload generated by end-of-year vacationers to the B&B.

That meant endless opportunities to run into Ezra Moore, and she hadn't yet decided how she felt about that. "I gave him both keys and told him you'd be baking bread tomorrow. He was going to settle in and find some coffee. I'm sure he'll stop in to say hello, but I did tell him Sundays were crazy for you."

Molly looked up, brushed strands of hair out of her face with the back of her wrist, leaving streaks of flour across one eyebrow. Her dark brown eyes were glazed with the exhaustion that had been her constant companion for too long. "That's why he's here. Dan and I don't have time to show anyone more than the most basic ropes. We decided we had to have someone who could work independently."

"And a man spending a year alone on a boat definitely fills the bill." Even if that man appeared ready to fight a private war. Between his pea coat, his fatigues, and that scar, he looked like a soldier of fortune. "I hope he works out."

"You don't think that he will?" Molly asked, her shoulders bunching as she rolled out the dough.

"He just seems so . . . I don't know. Out of place, I guess." Out of place. Dangerous. Way too perceptive. Intriguing.

Molly laughed. "Are you kidding? I don't think he could be any more out of place. That doesn't mean he won't be able to do something about the toilet that won't stop running on the third floor, or the light fixture on the landing."

Emmy Rose perked up at that. "Mom, I've told you a hundred times. The light's haunted. You don't need a handyman to fix that. You need to hire a ghost whisperer."

"TV. I swear," Molly muttered, shaking her head. "Daughter dearest, get upstairs and start getting ready for tomorrow. I'll call you when dinner's ready."

"But I'm hungry now! I don't want to go," Emmy Rose said, curling her arms around her updrawn knees and hiding between Alexa's legs.

Molly stepped around the kitchen's island and gave her daughter a look. "You need a bath. You need to lay out tomorrow's clothes. You need to clean out your backpack. And you need to make sure all of your homework is done, not just your math worksheets."

"But Mom!"

"Emmy Rose Maples! You have two minutes to get upstairs and get busy."

"But I don't know what to do!"

"I just told you. And if you forget between here and there, it's all written on your wall calendar in the box for today's date. Now go. After dinner, I'll help you with your homework."

"Fine. I'm going." Emmy Rose unfolded from the floor in a fluid disentangling of arms and legs that made Alexa envious of the girl's range of motion.

Between the work she'd been doing on the set for the school's

Christmas pageant and the ongoing remodeling of the cabin she'd bought post-Brett, her body had become an intimate friend with the aches and pains that came from being sedentary and thirty-five years old.

She watched the girl stomp off, head hung low, and couldn't help but laugh. "Have I ever mentioned how glad I am to send my kids home at four o'clock every day?"

Draping crusts over deep-dish ceramic pie plates, Molly countered, "Have I ever mentioned how glad I am to put mine on the bus every morning?"

"At least six dozen times," Alexa said, coring and slicing the apple she held.

"What can I say." Molly shrugged without apology. "She's seven years old and still going through the terrible twos. Who knew it would last this long, or that her father would be too busy to deal with it?"

Alexa looked up from the blade of her paring knife to search out the emotion on her friend's face. She knew much of Molly's exhaustion was seasonal, but lately there seemed to be more to the other woman's swinging moods.

Having suffered the same and recognizing the signs, she feared the Mapleses' marriage had hit a rough patch, and that Molly was losing patience with her daughter as a result, Emmy Rose becoming collateral damage. But prying when Molly hadn't given her a true opening seemed wrong, so Alexa had held off saying anything—though she wouldn't hold off forever.

Molly stopped, took a deep breath, and shook off whatever it was she'd been thinking. She reached for the canister of brown sugar and said, "Now that the little pitcher with the big ears is gone, tell me the truth. Something's bothering you about Ezra."

At the change of subject, Alexa's stomach clenched as if she'd been struck, and it took more effort than it should have for her to toss off a casual, "Not really."

"Dammit, Alexa," Molly said, packing brown sugar into a measuring cup. "I've known you for five years and I've seen you through a divorce that knocked you sideways. Don't tell me you think my handyman is interesting and not expect me to dig for details."

"There aren't any details to find." Alexa reached for another apple. "I'm just generalizing. I can't put my finger on anything specific. It's all intuition, and we know how lousy mine's been in the past."

"With Brett, maybe. But you're not looking at Ezra with the same romantically rosy eyes." Molly froze, her head coming up slowly, a grin of incredibly prurient proportions spreading over her face. "You're not, are you? Or is that why it took the two of you so long to make the climb from the docks?"

Alexa went into denial mode without stopping to examine for whose benefit. "We walked. Uphill. In gale-force winds. I'd like to see you do it faster."

"The wind is not that strong." Molly gestured over Alexa's shoulder toward the window above the sink. "I can see the weather vane from here."

"Your weather vane is mounted on the house and surrounded by trees. Stick it out in the open on the hill and then see how fast that rooster spins."

"That's a weather report, not an answer."

Unfortunately, Molly was right. "What do you want me to say? I talked to the man for twenty minutes."

"That's plenty of time to know if you want to talk to him more."

She did, but she wasn't going to admit it to Molly. She didn't like admitting it to herself, not without knowing why. "If I do, it's just curiosity."

"Uh-huh. The same way I was curious enough after meeting Danny for the first time to want to get to know him better ASAP."

"It's not that kind of curiosity. He's going to be here for a month at the most. I have work. He has work. I doubt we'll see each other more than once a week. That's hardly enough time to become friends."

"And here I thought you believed in all those love-at-first-sight Hallmark moments."

Alexa held up the apple peel she'd removed in one long strip. "If you don't stop, I'm going to wrap this around your neck and choke you."

"An appropriate end considering these pies are about to kill me." Molly stretched her arms high overhead, leaned side to side, and popped her back with a groan. "I wonder if I could pass off Mrs. Smith's frozen as my own. That would free me up enough time to tackle at least a dozen other things."

Poor baby. Alexa wished her own time allowed her more hours to help. She hated seeing Molly in such a miserable bind. "Having Ezra here should make things easier for you and Danny both, yes?"

"I hope," Molly said, tossing the apple slices with the sugar and cinnamon. "The only reference he gave was a Gabriel Corteze in San Torisco, who I was never able to reach, but Ezra was so enthusiastic and I guess charismatic . . ."

"Not to mention available."

Molly laughed. "That, too. I don't know. Hiring him on the spot just seemed right."

"Then let's hope your intuition is working better than mine." It was all Alexa could say. Her reservations about Ezra had no logical basis. And she had no business raining on Molly's parade, when she didn't understand her own feelings.

But that didn't mean she had to sit back and wonder about him when looking into his background wouldn't be that hard. She had his name and that of his reference. She also had a connection . . .

"Besides, an affair wouldn't hurt you, you know," Molly was saying when Alexa snapped back. "Brett's shadow is only going to keep your bed warm for so long."

Alexa nearly shrieked. "An affair? Are you kidding?"

"In a town this small, it's almost impossible, I know. But with a stranger—"

"A stranger everyone will be watching since he'll stand out like a sore thumb," Alexa interrupted to remind her.

Molly waggled one finger. "A stranger most people here would never think you'd be attracted to."

The small town's prejudices aside, Alexa found herself stunned by Molly's suggestion. "You want me to sleep with a man I met for the first time today."

"I'm just throwing out the possibility, not ordering you to strip and climb into his bed. But you can't tell me you didn't find him sexy. Something about that accent, and his eyes. It's like he can see everything you're thinking . . ." Molly let the sentence trail.

Alexa refused to pick it up. "We're not having this conversation, Molly. Not unless you want me to start bugging you about you and Danny."

Molly looked away, her expression closing down. "I need to check on Emmy Rose," was all she said in response.

Motherhood was as effective a way as any to shoot Alexa's prying to the ground. "And that's my cue to get out of your hair." One day, she mused. One day soon. She'd bide her time but she would not sit back and do nothing if it looked like Molly needed bailing out.

"Did you want to stay for dinner?" Molly asked, the offer her way of making amends for any possible slight. "We're having apple pie for dessert."

Smiling, Alexa shook her head. "It's Sunday. I'm meeting Rachel at Vince's."

"Oh, yeah. I forgot you actually have a social life." Molly dusted her hands on her apron and opened her arms for a hug.

"Thanks for the help, sweetie. I don't know what I'd do without you."

"You'll never have to find out," she said, holding the other woman tightly. Molly had been there for her during the worst time of her life, and no one—whether husband or handyman—was going to hurt her friend.

Alexa would never let it happen.

Chapter 5

When Alexa walked into the Gin & Rummy later that evening, she found Rachel already studying a menu in their regular Sunday night booth. Alexa didn't know why Rachel bothered. She would order her usual BLT with cheese fries and a draft beer the same way Alexa would order a cheeseburger and a root beer float.

Along with Molly Maples, Rachel Fine was one of the best friends Alexa had in Comfort Bay. The other woman was a longtime resident of the small coastal town and a talented—and very busy—Jane of all trades.

She worked part-time at the Maple Sugar Shack—Molly's souvenir candy shop on the village boardwalk—owned a small secondhand clothing store that she opened three afternoons a week, and did substitute teaching at Comfort Bay Elementary when needed.

The school was where Alexa had met her, and where the two had bonded over their love of food that was bad for them. They indulged their co-dependence every Sunday night, saving their lives during the rest of the week with grilled chicken and lo-cal dressing on their salads.

Just as Alexa slid into the booth opposite her friend, the overhead lights in the bar flickered. She laughed. "I swear.

Between this place and Molly's, I'd think we were dealing with ghosts if I believed in such a thing."

Rachel's big blue eyes widened. "You should believe. You know the guy who owned the bar before Vince died here."

"From his own cooking?" Alexa teased, though she'd heard the story before.

"Right?" Rachel laughed. "The wiring in this place is barely up to code. Vince keeps saying he's going to get it fixed when he finds the money. He might be good with a gun, but he is so not good with tools."

Alexa started to recommend Vince hire Ezra, but stopped. She had no idea if Ezra was good with anything—even a fire-place poker. Toying with the one in his living room had seemed more about intimidation than getting a feel for the tool.

That was a detail she should have shared with Molly. That, and the way he hadn't seemed in any hurry to take the key to the shed from her hand. Of course, then she'd have to explain why she hadn't wanted to release it, and she still hadn't worked that out for herself.

She shoved away the intruding suggestion Molly made that she have an affair, but doing so wasn't easy. Neither was ignoring the tight coil in her stomach when she thought about his accent and his eyes. As Molly said, there was something about him . . .

Charlene, Vince's waitress, brought over their drinks, and Alexa reached for her root beer float. She was glad for the distraction. She didn't need to dwell on Ezra Moore's long rolling walk, the determination in the motion of his hips, the strength in her fingers, the warm skin of his palm.

She shivered, blamed it on the float. "What do you have going on this next week?"

Rachel threaded her fingers through the handle of her mug. "Tomorrow and Tuesday I'm working in the school library."

Alexa pushed aside her straw. "That's right. Mrs. King's father is in the hospital in Portland. I heard she took family leave and went up for a couple of days."

Rachel nodded. "The rest of the week I'll be working at the candy shop from ten till two, and at Second Time Best from two till eight. A church group in Newton donated two *huge* boxes of clothes last week, and I'm still sorting and washing and pricing it all. There's so much to do, but God, it's going to be great when it's all done."

Alexa slumped back in the booth and groaned. "I swear. Being around you and Molly makes me feel like a bum. I teach school. That's it. No pie and bread baking. No washing and sorting and pricing. Only one job. No volunteer work. Could anyone be more lazy?"

"Excuse me?" Rachel asked, sputtering in her beer. She snagged strands of long blond hair from the corners of her mouth and tucked it behind her ear. "Who's got a whole crew of seven-year-olds building the coolest pageant set ever?"

Alexa looked at Rachel askance. "Think about what you just asked me. Who's doing all the work? I make a great general. Bossiness is in my genes. That hardly measures up to what you and Molly accomplish."

"It's not a competition, Alexa." Rachel grew serious, staring down at her mug and rubbing at the melting frost. "Besides, in this economy, working more than one job isn't a choice for some of us. It's more like sink or swim."

Alexa wanted to bite her tongue. Rachel was single and still needed more than one income to make ends meet. She made do because she had three part-time jobs and shared a small house in town and her living expenses with Vince. Yet still she had to cut corners.

Opening her store only three afternoons a week to save on electricity was one. And since Comfort Bay's residents who shopped with her knew her routine, her sales were brisk enough on those days to make a small profit after she'd paid the store's rent.

Rachel's situation, like Molly's, reminded Alexa that she would always be an outsider. She'd lived here for five years; she could live here for fifty and still be thought of as a newcomer by the locals, who had generations worth of roots anchoring them to the town.

While she fit in easily in so many ways, there were others—ones only the natives were sensitive to—that would always elude her. And for some reason that set her to thinking about Ezra Moore.

From what she understood about the place that he'd come from and the work that he did with the children there, she couldn't fathom how he could afford to take a sabbatical, or for that matter his boat. She would never think of the Maples as gullible, but neither could she sit back while her friends were conned.

So when Charlene arrived with their food, Alexa interrupted Rachel's story about the Newton church charity to ask of the waitress, "Charlene, if Vince has a minute, would you tell him I want to ask him about something?"

"Sure thing, but it might be a while before he can get free."

Rachel perked up at that. "Don't tell me. He's trying to chase down the buggy wiring and kill us all."

Charlene laughed. "It's not quite that scary. O'Malley isn't feeling well, and Vince is doing the cooking."

Both women looked down at their food. Alexa was the first to speak. "It's a sandwich. How bad can it be?"

"Well, he is better in the kitchen than he is with tools, but he's still a lot better with guns."

Alexa was too hungry to wait. She used both hands to wrestle the monstrous burger to her mouth and bit in. She was in hog-and-cheese heaven when Rachel asked, "Is the gun thing what you're wanting to talk to Vince about?"

Guns? God, she hoped not. "No. No guns. I just wanted to see if he could use his connections to check into something for me."

"Something or someone? And why Vince instead of Chief Calendar?" Rachel pulled a strip of bacon from her sandwich and popped it into her mouth.

Bob Calendar ran Comfort Bay's police force more than capably, but he saw little action beyond ticketing speeders from out of town and rounding up truants caught indulging in underage drinking. Vince Daugherty, on the other hand, was even more recently located to the small coastal town than Alexa.

He'd come here two years ago, a detective for the Portland Police Bureau recovering from a gunshot wound suffered while investigating a homicide. When the old family friend with whom he'd been staying had died and deeded him the bar, Vince had decided to retire his badge and make Comfort Bay his home.

Rachel had been waiting tables at the time, and had a lot to do with his decision to stay. Just like she had a lot of input into his business now. Alexa chewed and swallowed, trying to come up with a plausible response that didn't come across like a case of paranoia.

She couldn't help but wonder if she shouldn't just keep her concerns about Ezra to herself and her eyes wide open instead of borrowing unnecessary trouble. But if that trouble kept Molly from getting into more . . . She made up her mind and prepared to confide in Rachel—just as Ezra walked through the door.

Alexa lowered her burger to the paper-lined basket and reached for her float because her mouth had gone dry. She watched as he headed for the bar, where he climbed onto a stool. He'd changed since she'd last seen him. Instead of fatigues tucked into his boots, he wore dark olive jeans that covered them. His pea coat was gone.

In its place was a fisherman's sweater knit in a pattern of black, blue, and green. The lights from the bar showed off only parts of his face. His dimple and scar were clear; his eyes were not. She had no idea if he'd seen her and did nothing to attract his attention. But her focus could hardly be denied, and Rachel noticed.

She turned in her seat to glance over her shoulder, and looked back at Alexa once she was done. "Let me guess," she began, biting into her sandwich and putting together her thoughts. "The something you want Vince to look into."

Alexa returned her concentration to her food. "I'm curious about him, yes. I'm just wondering if I should be more."

"More than curious?" Rachel asked, her tone disapproving. "How so?"

Alexa wondered what Rachel would think about Molly's suggestion of a sexual affair. Though both women had spent their lives in Comfort Bay, Molly's interaction with travelers who stayed at the B&B had exposed her to an encompassing cultural diversity. Rachel, on the other hand, was still suspicious of outsiders—especially, it seemed, of those who were so obviously different as Ezra.

Alexa would have thought otherwise considering Rachel's acceptance of Vince. But then Vince had been law enforcement injured in the line of duty, and had arrived with an unimpeachable Comfort Bay reference of his own.

"He's the Mapleses' new handyman," Alexa finally said. "Molly was never able to check with his reference."

"And you thought Vince could."

She nodded. "His contacts have got to be a lot better than mine. I mean, if I were still in L.A., I'd have more resources. But here I'm so cut off," she said, regretting the words the minute they left her mouth.

Any issues she and Rachel had always sprung from what Rachel called Alexa's sense of entitlement. Alexa argued with her friend that the disparity in their situations made them no different as women, and whatever experience or advantage she might have in one area, Rachel had in others.

None of that stopped Rachel from saying, "No one's forcing you to stay, you know. If L.A. can give you something Comfort Bay can't, then go."

Alexa leaned forward, her forearms braced on the table's edge. "I don't need to be forced. I like it here. I wouldn't stay if I didn't."

"I know," Rachel said softly before frowning and shaking her head. "Sometimes I wonder, though. I really do. You just seem like you'd rather be someplace else."

"That's just because it's been three years since I've had a vacation," Alexa said, thinking back to the observation Ezra had made upon meeting her that she didn't like it here in Comfort Bay at all. She glanced toward him again, and this time she caught his gaze.

She wasn't sure what to do. Not saying hello would be rude. Waving him over without inviting him to join them would be nearly as bad. Making her girlfriend uncomfortable, however, would be the worst. And so all Alexa did was smile.

"Tell him to come over," Rachel said, her words drawing Alexa's gaze. "Vince should be out in a few. You can introduce them, maybe they can talk a bit, then you can get his take."

Alexa frowned. "Are you sure?"

"I wouldn't tell you to do it if I wasn't."

Rachel's logic did make sense. Alexa just wasn't sure she was ready for another Ezra encounter quite so soon. Then she remembered that Molly would be encountering him daily beginning tomorrow morning.

And so she lifted a hand and motioned him over, ignoring the wild zing of sensation beneath the surface of her skin. With each step he took closer, her pulse quickened. The rest of the bar's patrons—all six of them—turned in his wake, understanding nothing of who he was or what he wanted from their town.

She felt all of what they were feeling, and she trembled. Doing so made it hard to smile, but she pushed aside everything she didn't know, and tried to think of everything she did. Except there was so little. His name—was it even real? His story—how was he financing his trip? His reference—did he not have more than the one he'd given?

But then he was standing at her table, and none of that seemed to matter. The only thing she could think about was

Molly's suggestion that she have an affair. It was insane, truly, how fast her blood heated. How the battle between her head and her body was over before it began.

"Rachel, I'd like you to meet Ezra Moore," Alexa finally found her voice to say. "He's working for Molly doing mainte-nance around the inn. Ezra, this is Rachel Fine. She also works for Molly in the candy shop part-time."

Rachel held out her hand. "There is no such thing as six de-grees of separation in Comfort Bay. There rarely seems to be any at all. We're just one big happy family."

"It is a pleasure to meet you, Miss Fine." Ezra shook her hand, but did not linger as he had when he'd held onto Alexa's. He let Rachel go, slipping his hand into his pocket. "I am looking forward to my time here."

"Why don't you join us?" Rachel nodded toward Alexa's side of the booth. "There's no reason for you to eat dinner alone."

"I would love to, but only if Alexa doesn't mind." He turned toward her then, towering above her, his scar doing nothing to dispel her first impression that he came wrapped up in more danger than she'd ever known in her life.

She couldn't tell him that, of course. So instead she scooted over, making room, and said, "No, I don't mind at all."

Chapter 6

Ezra had spent the afternoon thoroughly sweeping the rooms of his quarters for electronic signals—those which would indicate the Mapleses' employ of surveillance devices, and those which would interfere with the equipment he would be putting to use.

He had found the inn's security cameras and determined the frequency of the silent alarm. It was a solid system, but not overly complex, and easily bypassed. He had the keys he needed to the property, but he also needed unobserved access. Not everything he was here to do would be accomplished under the Mapleses' watchful eyes.

Tomorrow he would begin finalizing the details he had needed to be on site to work out. The transfer of the weapons from his boat to the buyer would require additional planning. He had time. He had the property at his disposal. There was nothing standing in the way of his immediate goal, or of the larger one he had been pursuing for years.

Nothing save for Alexa Counsel.

She was the reason he was here, the reason he had chosen to stop in tonight at the Gin & Rummy. He'd wanted to see how she would react to him now following her earlier flight. He wanted to know if her suspicions of him had deepened, if they had grown heavy and dark.

What he hadn't taken into consideration was how he would react to her. He shouldn't have reacted at all. He had spent years living a life of strict discipline, denying himself pleasures he had once embraced, focusing his energies intently on the job. He had done everything required of him. He had never regretted a choice he had made.

Second-guessing his actions would have done nothing to bring him closer to today, to this final task. Only now it seemed that to get what he wanted, he would have to break the code by which he'd lived for so long. Instead of remaining apart and operating on his own, he found himself compelled to use an innocent bystander as cover. Instead of making certain that she continued to keep him at a distance, he was going to become indispensable to Alexa Counsel—and use her to establish his legitimacy as a resident of Comfort Bay.

His hand wrapped around his coffee mug, he felt the warmth from her body seep into his when he slid into the spot she had vacated. His hip bumped hers. Their thighs brushed. He waited for her to move away. When she didn't, neither did he. "Thank you for including me. I have been eating my own cooking for so long that it will be nice to enjoy another's efforts."

"This probably wasn't the best night for you to give the Gin & Rummy a try. The cook isn't up to snuff, and the owner is manning the grill," Rachel said.

Ezra glanced from Alexa's basket of food to Rachel Fine's. "You are both eating."

Alexa laughed. "We are now, yes. Five minutes ago, we were wondering if it was safe."

"How did you decide that it was?"

"We didn't," Rachel said. "We were hungry so we just crossed our fingers."

He brought his coffee mug to his mouth and smiled behind it. "Maybe I will not eat until I see that neither of you become ill. Then again," he added as his own hamburger was delivered, "I believe I will take my chances. I haven't eaten

all day, and will be in good company should we all find ourselves in an emergency room."

Both women laughed, and appeared to relax. He noticed especially the way tension flowed from Alexa's body. Sitting so
near to her, how could he not? She seemed more at ease with
him now that they were no longer alone, which made this time
with her vital. He needed to gain her trust.

"The closest thing we have to an emergency room is Doc
Walker's clinic," she said. "Fortunately, he has a pretty good
reputation for keeping people alive."

Ezra made note. *No E.R. A clinic run by a Dr. Walker.* He set
down his coffee, picked up his hamburger, and took a bite.
"Mmm," he mumbled as he chewed.

"Good stuff?" Alexa asked.

Nodding, he looked to his side where she sat so close. Her
eyes were the color of coffee beans dark roasted, her hair a
shade that was nearly black. Against her skin, which was like
alabaster, the ringlets reflected the bar's colored lights. She
was waiting for him to answer, her mouth smiling, her lips
slightly parted. He would not have noticed had he not been
sitting but inches away. That was the only reason he did.

"Very good stuff," he said at last. "No matter who did the
cooking. As I said, my own is not so pleasing. This reminds me
what I have been missing."

He continued to stare into Alexa's eyes, and he was surprised when she seemed in no hurry to look away. Her
scrutiny was intense, as if she were wondering about other
pleasures he might have forgone while sailing, ones he might
be longing to indulge.

But then she reached for her drink, and it was as if the moment had never happened. All for the best, he thought as she
said, "If you think Vince's burgers are good, wait until you get
a mouthful of Molly's cooking."

Rachel groaned. "I could *live* on her rosemary chicken and
new potatoes."

"How about Thursday's pork chops and apples?" Alexa asked.

Rachel's eyes grew wide. "Or those individual pot pies she makes with ham and cheese and onions."

"And the desserts."

"No, the breads."

Ezra reached for his coffee mug and chuckled. "And all this time I had heard that it was a man's heart that was reached through his stomach."

"This has nothing to do with anyone's heart," Rachel said, signaling for another beer. "This is just me and Alexa moaning about our slow metabolisms. Sundays are the one day each week we give in and eat like there's no tomorrow."

Ezra glanced at the two half-eaten baskets of food. "I don't believe either of you have eaten enough to last you through the night."

The women shared a look, Alexa reaching for her drink and saying, "That's because waking up Mondays feeling like hungover cows is a really crappy way to start the week."

When he sat back and studied her, trying to figure out what she was saying, she added, "We're women. It's a psychological game we play. We give ourselves permission to eat as a reward for not eating, but then we don't eat because we know society will scorn us for our fat thighs if we do."

Another kernel of truth he might use. Alexa conformed because it was expected of her by others, not because she expected it of herself. "Then I am glad I am a man and am able to enjoy a woman's body without concerning myself with what society thinks."

"And that's my cue to grab my own refill," Rachel said, following several ticking moments of thick silence. "Charlene's either forgotten about me or Vince has drafted her into doing even more work. I'll be back in a few."

Ezra watched Rachel scoot out of the booth and head to the bar. Her hair was a dark honey blond that hung straight between her shoulder blades, and she filled out the blue jeans she wore with curves he was certain many women would envy.

But as tight as Rachel's body was, it was the spark of the woman sitting at his side that made hers the body that interested him. He did not wish to remember how long it had been since he had wanted a woman for a reason other than relief, but relief was not why he wanted Alexa Counsel.

The reasons were not simple. Neither were they solely about the part she would play in his assignment for Spectra IT, and that was where the biggest danger lay. He had to be wary. He could not afford to reveal himself. "I apologize. I did not join you with the intention of running off your friend. Especially since I know you would prefer that we not be alone."

Alexa pushed her food basket away and turned in her seat to face him. Leaning into the corner, drawing her knee up onto the bench, she held the handle of her mug with one hand, toyed with her straw using the other, looking at him all the while as if wondering how he'd managed to trap her—and why she wasn't trying to get away.

"Why do you say that?" she finally asked, the mug between them held tight.

There was no reason to put her further on guard, no reason to sidestep the truth. "You were in a hurry to leave my quarters earlier. I can only assume you were uncomfortable in my company."

"We're strangers. Don't you think that's normal?" she asked before she brought her straw to her mouth. She said nothing about the way he'd held onto her hand, nothing about the way she'd tempted him to come to her and take the key.

He wanted to ask her which of their behaviors had bothered her the most. After all, he had only accepted the invitation she had issued. Instead, he nodded his agreement to set her at ease. "What about now? Would you like me to move out of your way so you can leave?"

She glanced toward the bar, where swinging doors led into the kitchen, no doubt looking for Rachel Fine. But then she seemed to settle something inside of herself, and returned her attention to him. "I don't think that would solve anything, do you? We wouldn't be making each other uncomfortable, but we'd still be strangers, and no better off."

He glanced back at his food for a moment to consider what she'd said and the best way to make use of her offer. He didn't believe for a moment that it was anything else. She was curious, and she was not immune. He'd sensed both upon their first meeting, and when they'd been in his quarters, he'd had both proven true.

He had learned much about the town while gathering this mission's intel, but learning about the human element could only be done through personal interaction. Now that he was here he was quite certain that Alexa Counsel could be his ticket in.

He turned his attention toward her again, and watched emotions dance through her eyes as she waited for his response. He gave it, finding great difficulty in keeping his voice steady. "You do not make me uncomfortable, but there is no reason we must remain strangers. We could get to know one another instead, if you would like."

"Yes, I would like," she said after a minute. "I would like that very much."

Chapter 7

A lexa never did have a chance to talk to Vince before leaving the Gin & Rummy. O'Malley's prediction that he'd feel well enough to come into work failed to come true, leaving Vince in the kitchen most of the night, Charlene waiting tables and tending bar, and Rachel pitching in as needed, then sticking around for clean-up and closing.

The bar didn't see much in the way of a crowd on Sunday nights in December, so the ragtag crew of three managed quite capably, and got out by ten. Rachel headed home to the small frame house she shared with Vince just off Comfort Bay's main boardwalk to do more sorting, washing, and pricing before she called it a night.

At eleven o'clock, Vince was on Alexa's front porch with a flashlight and a ladder while Alexa was in the kitchen fixing her coffee pot for a jolt the next morning, and a cup of herbal tea to help her sleep tonight. After what she'd agreed to earlier in the evening, she was going to need all the calming help she could get.

She had no clue what was on Ezra's mind when he'd asked her if she was interested in getting to know him better. She hadn't had time to find out. Rachel had returned before she could, and stayed just long enough to let Alexa know Vince would have her tied up in the kitchen for the rest of the night.

The interruption had allowed the tension binding the breath in Alexa's lungs to ease. She and Ezra had finished their meal with none of her previous concerns rising like brick walls between them. But now, with the physical distance and the time to reflect, the concerns were back, and she headed out to the porch to see what she could do about relieving them.

As long as her suspicions remained, she would never look at Ezra objectively. And she needed impartiality. For Molly's benefit and for her own. That made Vince her best shot at answers.

"You really don't have to do that," she said, watching Vince remove first the cover from her porch light fixture, then the entire fixture itself. She thought about Rachel swearing how he was not so good with tools. "If you're sure it's not just the bulb, I'll get someone out to take a look in a day or two. Or at least let me hold the flashlight."

"Nah, I'm good," Vince said, shining the beam along the wires and into the recessed opening. "Just looking for what keeps blowing your fuse."

It wasn't her own fuse that worried her as much as Rachel's should the other woman find out Vince had been playing with electrical wires while Alexa stood by and watched. What could she say? The former detective turned short order cook looked like a guy who knew his way around a toolbox.

Vince was a man's man. Tough and street smart and hard. Living in Comfort Bay had done little to shave that edge. He wasn't Alexa's type, but she could see the appeal. And right now the appeal was that he please not break her light any further.

"Listen, Vince. The light can wait." At least it wasn't flickering as badly as the lights in his bar—not that that had stopped him from insisting she let him take a look. "I wanted to ask you about something else."

"So Rachel was saying." He set the fixture on the top of the ladder and climbed down. "You want to know about that black guy from the bar."

She nodded, realizing Rachel had been doing more in the Gin & Rummy's kitchen than helping wash up. "He's Molly's new handyman. His name is Ezra Moore."

"And you've got reason to think that he's not who he says he is?"

Did she? Have reason? Or were her suspicions more personal? Was she simply wanting to vet him for herself? Was all that earlier talk of looking out for Molly bunk? "I'm not sure."

Vince shook his head, one corner of his mouth drawn back in a grin that looked more like a smirk. "Is this some sort of women's intuition thing? Because I get enough of that from Rachel, and I can't run an investigation without facts."

She tucked her hands into the pockets of her jeans, huddled deeper into the cardigan she still wore over her T-shirt. "Isn't that what an investigation is? Gathering the facts?"

"Sure, but I need a place to start. I also need to know exactly what it is you want." He braced a biker boot on the ladder's lowest rung, wrapped a hand around one higher. "Jobs he's had. People he's known. Women he's fucked."

Like she would know any of that? "The truth, okay? That's all. Is Ezra Moore his name? Does he teach school in San Torisco? The reference he gave to Molly was a Gabriel Corteze."

"What did Corteze tell her?"

"She never reached him."

"He was unavailable? He didn't get back to her? The contact information was no good? What?"

Alexa shrugged. "I don't know."

Vince rubbed a hand over his chin, his biceps flexing beneath his sweatshirt. Light from inside the cabin spilled through the front window, casting grotesque shadows across the porch. Vince seemed to loom above her ominously; she knew it was nothing but the darkness playing tricks.

Still, she shivered. The night air was crisp and cold, though just shy of causing her breath to frost. The moon was bright where it peeked through arthritic branches that gave a come-hither look.

She'd lived in this cabin for two years. She was totally comfortable here. Yet all she could think of was the sense of danger she felt when with Ezra—a danger that had her looking over Vince's shoulder into the blackness beyond.

"Should I follow up with Molly myself? Or are you wanting to keep this investigation under wraps?" Vince asked, bringing Alexa back to the moment. The way things worked in Comfort Bay, Molly would find out eventually. But for now . . .

Alexa handed Vince the slip of paper she had in her pocket. "This is all I know. This and that his boat's docked in the harbor. And I'd appreciate you not mentioning it to Molly. I'd like to save myself the trouble as long as I can."

"No problem." Vince folded the small note, pulled his wallet from his pocket, and tucked it inside. "I'll make sure Rachel doesn't say anything either."

"Did you talk to him at all?" Alexa found herself asking, remembering how she and Ezra had lingered after their meal, how he'd told her he was going to stay for another coffee when she'd said she needed to go.

"I did, yeah." Vince moved his hand to rub at his nape. "And I've got to say he came across as a pretty straight-up guy. Interesting that he'd end up here out of all the places on the coast."

"I know." That was one of her biggest questions. Why Comfort Bay? "Doesn't that strike you as strange?"

Vince shrugged. "As good a place as any, I guess. Hell, I never thought I'd end up someplace like this."

"But you had a connection to the town," she insisted. "Ezra doesn't."

"You didn't either when you came here, right?"

She shook her head. She hadn't. It was only after she and Brett had fallen in love with the town and relocated that she'd met Molly and Rachel. And it had been a year before she'd been hired on to teach school. She hadn't just shown up one day, walked off her boat, and taken the first paying position she could get.

But then she wasn't doing odd jobs to finance a trip. "No, but this is . . . different."

Vince turned and crossed his arms, backing into the ladder's frame and bracing his backside against it. "We all come from somewhere, Alexa. You from L.A. Me from Portland. Ezra from some island near South America. We all end up finding our place. Fitting in."

"Do you really think it's going to be easy for Ezra to fit in?"

"After talking to the guy? I don't see him having any trouble at all if folks can look past his skin color. He's been through more rough shit than most of us will ever know. He's a tough one. He'll do fine."

Interesting. "So you two did talk."

Vince nodded. "He hung around and drank coffee while me and the girls closed up. Seemed to want the company. Can't say I blame him. It's gotta be pretty dull going days without anyone to talk to but yourself."

Alexa thought back to the months before Brett had left. How they had been two people sharing a house but not conversation. No *how was your day*. No *you look great in that*. No *have you seen my car keys*. There had been nothing to keep her from feeling that she lived alone.

She wondered if Ezra ever got lonely. If that's why he'd stayed to chat with Vince. Or if he had stayed to gather information. Then she wondered when she'd become so suspicious. Why it couldn't have happened earlier. With Brett. When being clueless had kept her from seeing the truth.

She shook off the pathetically mawkish thoughts and got back to Vince. "When have you ever been stuck talking to yourself? Between the detecting and the bartending, I figure you've heard more confessions than a priest."

"C'mon, Alexa." One dark brow went up. The lights shining through the window twinkled in his eyes. "That qualifies as talking about as much as you lecturing second-graders."

He was right. And she knew the difference between feeling lonely and being alone. She just didn't want to think about Ezra experiencing the same. It would make it too hard to keep her distance if she thought of him as vulnerable instead of as a dangerous man.

She sighed. "Speaking of those second-graders . . ."

"Yeah. I need to get going." Vince pushed away from the ladder. "Let me get this put up and I'll get out of your hair."

She waved him off. "Leave it for tonight. I'll see if I can get someone out here tomorrow."

"You sure?"

She leaned forward, kissed his scruffy cheek. He smelled like burgers and fries and sweet man. "I am. Now go home before Rachel sends out a search party."

"She won't send anyone," he said with a growling sort of snort. "She'll come after me herself."

"That's what I'm afraid of." Alexa laughed, and Vince joined in.

"You and me both." He huddled into his sweatshirt, preparing to leave the windbreak provided by the porch. "I'll see you. And I'll let you know if I find out anything about your Ezra."

Her Ezra. *Her Ezra.* Did her wanting to know more about him connect them somehow? In a way she would regret when it was all said and done? Or was looking into the truth of who he was a move so bold it could change her life?

Was that what was bothering her the most? That whether or not she was ready, she had just set into motion an investigation that would turn her world end over end? Shivering anew, Alexa lifted a hand in farewell as Vince jogged down her short drive to where he'd parked his Jeep next to her SUV.

She watched as he made the wide turn onto the road, then

watched his taillights glow like eyes searching through the dark before they vanished. She picked up the flashlight where it was balanced on its end against the porch railing, and climbed the ladder to screw the fixture back into place.

She wanted to blame her sense of being uneasy on reading Stephen King or teaching Edgar Allen Poe or watching George Romero or listening to Rob Zombie. But none of those purveyors of horror had anything to do with her mood.

She'd thought this two-pronged plan of getting to know Ezra better while having Vince run his investigation would ease her mind. She was being proactive. She was moving forward with her eyes wide open. She wasn't waiting around to be blindsided the way she'd been when Brett up and left.

Instead, she felt weighed down with a monstrous burden, certain that going behind Ezra's back would blow up in her face, proving she was nothing but an equal opportunity con artist—and a lousy one at that. But the wheels were in motion, and she couldn't start second-guessing her decision.

She was doing what she had to do—yet the doubt demons lingered. It was a case of wanting to do right by Molly, wanting to do right by herself, and fearing the twain would never meet.

She did not want to have to choose between having her cake and eating it, but feared it was way too late—that her curiosity about Ezra had taken on a life of its own, and would not be easily brought to ground.

Chapter 8

E zra couldn't sleep. Being unable to sleep was not unusual, but he had learned over the years to force himself to relax. Rest was essential for keeping a sound mind, even when sleep remained elusive. Tonight, however, even rest would not come.

He wanted to blame it on the caffeine. He'd been out of coffee for two days before docking in Comfort Bay, and today he felt as if he had consumed two gallons. It was his one and only vice, and as vices went, he did not worry.

He did better saving his worries for other matters—such as deciding what he was going to do about his feelings for Alexa Counsel. Feelings he should not have. Feelings which would make it impossible to accomplish his mission if he nurtured them and allowed them to grow. He could not. He would not. This would end tonight.

Having exchanged the clothes he'd worn this evening for his pea coat, boots, and fatigues, he set out from his quarters, guided by the light from the moon. He did not care if he were seen. He was taking a walk and nothing more. After so much time spent at sea, he needed to feel dry land beneath him in order to get his bearings. He would give no one a reason to think otherwise.

The truth was not quite so simple. Yes, the walk was exercise which he needed. But he also needed to get a feel for the rest of his surroundings. He'd toured the town earlier in the day. Tonight he would tour the forest behind the Maples Inn, scout locations he could use for surveillance should the need arise.

It was Sunday night, and his contact was due to arrive a week from Tuesday. The weapons were secured safely on his boat, where they would remain until it was time to complete the transfer. He was in position. He had assumed his cover. Now he would work to gain the trust of the locals while making preparations for the final step in his plan.

The total annihilation of Spectra IT.

Getting to this point had been a long time in coming. He had given up a real life, a true life, and had lived as an animal no better than the ones who helmed the crime syndicate, directing the illegal activities. To many in the rank and file, he had become the face of the organization, serving beside Warren Aceveda, who reported directly to Spectra's founder Cameron Gates.

Alexa Counsel's suspicions about him were valid—yet in a wry twist of irony, she would never know. She thought he was a scam artist, that he was somehow intent on harming her friends. In truth, if anyone in Comfort Bay were to be hurt by his actions, it would more than likely be Alexa herself.

He reached for the collar of his coat and flipped it up, hunching his shoulders into the wool for warmth. He never overlooked how a location's climate might play into his hands, and was just considering how to use the cold to his benefit when a small cedar cabin came into view.

He stepped from the road to walk hidden along the tree line, slowing when he saw Alexa on the porch. She stood in profile on the third rung of a wooden ladder. Light from the window behind her shone through to outline her body in a haloed silhouette.

He felt his own body react, and he stopped to enjoy the

physical sensation of wanting her. Doing so went against his training and discipline, but he was unable to deny the need. He did not believe he had ever known a woman who feared him as this one did yet who did not run away. Perhaps it was time to test her further. To see how far he could push her before she would break.

He moved away from the cover of the trees and back onto the road, where he would be visible should she look up. He then made the turn onto her drive, walking slowly but with purpose, his hands deep in his pockets, his boots making enough noise to wake any creatures sleeping nearby.

She glanced over her shoulder, searching out the source of the sound, and found him easily with no more than the moonlight that set off his form against the brighter shells and rocks of her drive. He saw the moment recognition dawned. Her body remained tense. Her breathing grew rapid and harsh.

He watched the rise and fall of her chest beneath her sweater as he approached. When he reached the point where her walkway met her steps, he stopped, giving her time to make the decision he knew she was struggling to make. Did she or did she not want him to join her?

"I hope I am not disturbing you," he said. "Even though we agreed to get to know each other better, I did not purposefully seek you out or look for the place where you lived. I could not sleep, and was walking—"

"I couldn't sleep either," she offered quickly, quietly, letting him off the hook while she held a flashlight in one hand and the light fixture from her porch in the other. "And you're not disturbing me."

"Are you having difficulty with your light?"

She nodded. "I thought it was the bulb going bad, but I put in a new one, and it still sputters."

"It must be the wiring then."

"I assume so." She gave a frustrated shrug. "But I'm no electrician."

"Why don't you let me take a look?" he asked, and as she turned to take him in, he climbed the three steps that brought him onto her porch.

He wanted to point out that by fixing her light he would verify the truth of his maintenance skills. But proving that he made a competent handyman would only ease her mind on one count—that he could handle the job he'd been hired to do—and her distrust of him ran much deeper.

In the bar, they had agreed to explore this puzzling urgency between them, but he remembered well the look in her eyes when she'd pulled the Maples girl from his reach. And he would only relieve her of thinking of him as the enemy by convincing her that he was her friend.

When still her silence lingered, he spoke again, keeping the conversation simple, keeping it safe. "Do you have tools? A voltage meter? Wire strippers?"

"I have a screwdriver," she said, holding it up and shaking off whatever it was that had left her mute. "But it's too late to deal with this tonight. Let me put it back together, and I'll call someone tomorrow."

He moved toward the ladder, held out one hand. "I'll do that for you."

"No. I'll do it," she said sharply, holding up one hand. After several seconds passed, she added, "But if you'd hold the flashlight it would help."

"I can do that," he said, and the tension between them began to fade. He stepped in behind her so that her hip was level with his face, so that when he breathed in he smelled the detergent she'd used on her laundry as well as the soap she'd used on her skin, and directed the beam where it would do her the most good.

In so short of a time, she had returned to being wary of him, to wondering how fully to believe in him, to thinking it a wise move to keep him at the distance he'd originally wanted her to keep. Yet he sensed she was fighting against doing so, that she wanted now to keep him close, that he intrigued her enough that she questioned her initial flight response and had decided to stay for the battle.

"You must have been walking for awhile," she finally said, interrupting his musings. "It's at least a mile from here to the inn."

He knew exactly how long he had been walking and exactly how far. "It is closer to a mile and a half, but I was lost in thought so the time passed quickly."

The fixture held against the wall with one hand, she used the other to tighten the screw at the top right. "I'll be glad to drive you back when I'm done here. If you're not up to another long hike."

He didn't want to leave so soon. He wanted a better sense of what she was thinking before he did. "I don't mind the walk. It is rather enjoyable to be able to stretch my muscles after so long at sea."

"Hmm," was her only response, and when she didn't say more, he asked, "What are you thinking?"

"I was thinking you, or anyone really, would have to be pretty happy with yourself to spend so much time alone. All that silence, and no one to talk to?" She shook her head. "The sailor's life is not the life for me."

"Does that mean you are not happy with yourself?" he asked.

She reached for another screw, glanced down and met his gaze, appearing to bite back more words than those which she finally spoke. "It means I'm not cut out for a life at sea. That's all."

He wanted to press, to ask why she chose to live in a community where she obviously didn't fit in. Instead, he found himself turning her observation inward and examining himself as she'd no doubt intended for him to do.

Was he happy with who he was, or had he learned to live with himself in order to do the things that he did? And why could he no longer tell the difference between the two? Had he truly grown that cold and that hard?

His sharp breath caused a burning ache in his chest, so he ended the interrogation and said, "It is not such a bad life. The sea. The solitude. I do enjoy my own company."

She laughed, a soft sound that seemed to be more for her own benefit than for his. "Wouldn't it defeat the whole point of your sabbatical if you didn't? How could you benefit from the time away if your own company was not fit to keep?"

"I suppose I would not, though I have stayed so busy I have had little time to relax. It seems to have become more of a working vacation than anything."

She sighed heavily, shook her head. "What I wouldn't give for a real vacation. Christmas break is coming up, but I set aside that time to finish up the renovations to this place I've been putting off for too long."

He thought back to his earlier assessment that she wasn't happy with her life in Comfort Bay, and knew he'd been right. The fact that she put off such simple repairs as faulty wiring reflected her discontent. "If the upkeep is too much for you, why do you not share your place with a friend?"

"It's not that easy," she said, grabbing another screw. "The people here have roots. They grow up here. They marry here. They stay. I came for the peace and quiet, and had my life turned upside down."

He understood roots. He understood tradition. He did not understand why she remained if being here made her unhappy and restless for change. She did not strike him as a woman to let a failed marriage stop her from living her life.

He watched the flex and roll of her shoulders as she worked to tighten the screw. "What keeps you here then, if you don't have roots? Have you become that attached to the people and the town?"

She turned, angling her body into the shadows and hiding

her face. "I told you this morning. My friends, my students. I adore my job."

The better part of valor demanded he let the subject drop. "I can only hope mine will be equally satisfying. And that I don't disappoint the Maples."

"Well, you get points for being handy with a flashlight. There," she said, finishing with the final screw. "That will do until tomorrow."

"I am not sure how busy I will be in the morning, but I can take a look at the wiring during my lunch break if I have time."

Alexa looked down, a dark brow arching playfully. "You'd better keep that goodwill gene in check. Next thing you know, Vince will have you performing an exorcism at the Gin & Rummy."

Ezra had seen the lights flicker when he'd been in the bar. "Is there no one in town to make such repairs?"

She nodded. "Dale Potter. But he's only one man in a small town that seems to be falling down around his ears with an unfortunate regularity."

"Then it seems I might be your best bet."

"Would you need access from inside?"

"I might."

She glanced over her shoulder at the window as if taking stock of her valuables. "I can leave the place unlocked, I guess. Or you can get the key from Molly."

"If you are not comfortable with me being here without you, I could wait until the evening when we are both finished with work for the day."

"I don't mind you being here, no. But I don't want to take advantage of my friendship with Molly and steal you away when she needs you. I'll go ahead and call Potter's to see when Dale can get out here. If it's going to be weeks, I'll take you up on the offer, okay?"

"Okay," he said, and reached up to help her down.

He had not intended to do anything more than offer his hand, but she turned to toss her screwdriver into the toolbox at his feet, and he grabbed for her as she leaned. It was an instinctive move, thinking she had misstepped and was going to fall, his hands going to her waist to steady her.

But she had not misstepped. And she did not fall. She remained standing where she was, where he held her on the ladder, his hands on her T-shirt beneath her open sweater, her abdomen inches from his face. The screwdriver clattered against the porch. He listened as it began to roll, knowing he needed to release her.

Instead, he slipped his hands lower, finding the small strip of skin where her shirt rose above her jeans and inching his thumbs along the hem, circling one around her navel and breathing her in. The feel of her flesh, her scent . . . It took nothing more. The moment ceased to be about discovering and exploiting any weaknesses in her loyalties. It became, instead, about wanting her.

But he would not force her; he would never force her. And so he bowed his head and prepared to step back. She stopped him. First with a small earthy whimper. Then by cupping one hand to the back of his head and pulling him near. He buried his face against her, gripping her waist, and she held him there as if her want mirrored his.

He felt her skin heat. He heard the rapid beat of her heart. He opened his mouth against her and tasted her on his tongue. His body tightened. His cock began to swell with the rush of his blood. And his reasons for being in Comfort Bay vanished beyond the shadows.

Chapter 9

Alexa had no idea what was happening, what she was doing, what she was allowing Ezra to do. This was insane. Who was he? She didn't know him. Yet reservations weren't enough to make her stop him when he reached for the button and opened the fly of her jeans.

He pressed his lips against the skin he had bared and kissed her. No teeth, no tongue. He used only his lips. They were soft, soothing where his day's growth of beard scratched her. His hair beneath her hand was just as coarse, and she soaked up all of the sensations, wanting to feel more.

But then he hesitated, bowing his head, shaking it where he'd rested his forehead against her. "Your response. It is beyond what I imagined, but I did not come here for this. I did not assume this would happen. This is not why I suggested we get to know one another rather than remain strangers."

She groaned. She couldn't help it. Her body was on fire, and he was backing away. She didn't want him to go. She wasn't ready for him to go. He couldn't go until he'd given her . . . something, anything. Dear God, she'd take a promise that he'd come back for more if that was all she could get.

She placed her hands at the base of his neck and massaged his muscles with her thumbs. "It's not what I intended either.

No one can plan for this. It's impossible. But don't be sorry. Don't ever be sorry."

He raised his head, his eyes regretful and dark. "I am not sorry, but I do apologize. I was out of line to touch you, to presume—"

"You didn't presume," she said, cutting him off as a rush of panic rose to choke her. "And even if you were out of line, it doesn't matter. Not now. Not anymore. I want you to touch me. Please, Ezra. Don't go."

He tightened his grip on her waist, his fingertips gouging her, and lifted her from the ladder to set her at his feet. The fierceness she saw burning in his eyes sent a wisp of fear to sweep through her, but still she stepped into his body, sliding her arms beneath his coat, pressing her fists into his back, pulling him close.

His heat warmed her face. His nearness warmed a deeper, lingering cold. She wasn't afraid that he'd injure her physically or damage her bodily in ways that would never heal. What she feared was the unknown, all the ways he might change her, ways no other man could.

He held her like that for several minutes, and their heartbeats synced, beating between them as one. That was what frightened her, that sense of rightness, that intimate meshing. They were two souls who had found one another in this cold, wintry place where neither of them fit.

"I need you to be sure, Alexa. I can stay. Or I can go." He slid his hands from her waist to her hips then to her bottom, pulling her flush against him. "But you have to be the one to decide because there is but a single choice I can make if you leave this up to me."

"I want what you want," she said, stepping out of his embrace and taking him by the hand, her blood rushing beneath the surface of her skin. She left the ladder where it stood, didn't bother finding the screwdriver or the flashlight or closing up the toolbox. All she did was open her front door and lead him through.

Once inside, she drew the lace sheers over the window and flipped off the lamp on the table beneath, then stepped behind him and pushed him toward the corner chair near the fireplace. It was a monstrous chair, leather with wide wooden arms. And it was a whole lot closer than her bed.

She guided him between the chair and the footstool, tugging his coat from his shoulders before turning him around. He smiled down at her, the scar on his face catching the glow from the candles burning on the mantel, and pulled her arms free from her cardigan. She smiled back, nervous, wanting this more than anything but uncertain what to do next.

He solved the problem for her, grabbing the hem of her T-shirt and sweeping the garment over her head, leaving her in her unbuttoned jeans and work boots and a bra with sheer cups the color of merlot. Her nipples were taut, the circles of her areolas pebbled. She noticed when she bowed her head to catch her breath.

This encounter was unexpected and unplanned, but she didn't want to take things too fast. She wanted to remember it all. She reached for the black T-shirt he wore; he took over, stripping it off so she could discover him with the tips of her fingers.

She walked them over his ribs, counting each one. He was lean, yet amazingly ripped. His abs were like rocks, his skin resilient and taut, the color of bittersweet chocolate, and smooth. Or at least smooth where not scarred.

She touched one jaggedly healed slash that ran from his armpit to the center of his chest. "What happened?"

"It was a long time ago," he said, grabbing hold of her wrist. "I don't wish to remember, or to talk about it."

"I'm sorry. I didn't mean to pry—"

"It was another life. It doesn't belong here now," he said as he brought his hands to her sides.

He cupped her rib cage, brushed his thumbs over her nipples. She held onto his forearms, feeling the flex of his muscles as he moved his hands, and closed her eyes, blindly soaking in the sensations causing her knees to go weak.

The very small part of her that remained sane knew a schoolteacher had no reason to bear this one's scars, but the part of her that only cared about feeling reminded her that she knew next to nothing about the island he called home.

And so she let him touch her, sliding her own hands higher, to his elbows, his biceps, his shoulders, squeezing the balls of muscles there, her fingertips digging in to hold on as he kneaded her breasts, finally dipping his head to draw her into his mouth.

He sucked first one nipple then the other through the sheer mesh of her bra, leaving one side moist and cold while he warmed the other with his lips, his teeth, and his tongue. When he bit her sharply, she cried out, but then he swirled the tip of his tongue over the mark that he'd made, and the cry quickly became a whimper.

She shivered and she shook, and he slid one hand down her stomach into the open fly of her jeans. He didn't ask what she wanted. He didn't take it slow. He wasn't polite or particularly gentle, and she didn't even care. She wanted exactly what he was giving her. Sex, pleasure, hot and thrilling and wonderfully raw.

He found the elastic band of her panties and pushed his way beneath to cup her sex with his palm. She wiggled against his hand, wanting more, and he wasted no time in giving it to her, thumbing her clit, crooking his middle finger and sliding it deep inside.

She thrust into his hand, lost in the sensation as her arousal took on a life of its own. Her thigh muscles burned, her lower back ached. She didn't care. Nothing mattered but what his hand was doing between her legs, what his mouth was doing to her chest.

He teased her, bit her, fingered her gently then roughly, as if he knew when she needed it soft and when she ached to be done hard. And then she came. She'd been wanting it, waiting for it, working to find it, but still her orgasm hit her like she'd never known a thing.

When her knees buckled, he wrapped an arm around her to keep her upright. He stayed with her through it all, pressing where she needed the pressure to finish. And when he finally pulled his hand from her pants, it was to grab them and take them all the way down.

She bent to get rid of her boots, then stepped out of her panties and jeans and reached for his zipper. He raised his arms overhead, lacing his hands at his nape and watching her work. She felt the full impact of his grin without ever looking up into his eyes.

"What's so funny?" she asked, her mouth going dry at the flex of his biceps, triceps, and pecs, and the flat, flat plane of his stomach that came into view when she pulled down his pants. He wore black boxer briefs and filled them out frighteningly well. She paused, taking a deeply appreciative breath.

"I am not smiling out of humor," he said, as still as a statue and putting her completely in charge. "What I am feeling is about pleasure and joy."

The pleasure she understood well. Figuring out what gave him joy would have to wait because she had slipped his last bit of clothing over his backside and was now easing the elastic and fabric over his erection.

His cock was a beautiful thing to see. Thick and engorged, the skin covering the head tight and slick. She wet her lips and leaned forward, sucking him into her mouth and trying to enclose his shaft in the ring of her fingers.

He hissed back a sharp breath and shuddered, his hands coming down to hold her head and guide her. He filled her mouth; she ran her tongue over the seam beneath his glans and around the ridge, admittedly surprised at finding him cut.

But he stopped her from further thought by covering her hand on his shaft with his own and pulling free. He said nothing more. All he did was take a step back and sit with his legs spread, patting his thighs in invitation.

She climbed on and straddled him, her legs sinking into the leather cushion on either side of his hips. His cock rose up between her legs, pressed against her belly. She lifted and lowered her hips to feel the slide of his powerful heat against her skin, grinding against the base until she swore she was going to come.

He stopped her with a quick slap on her ass. "Get up."

She braced her hands on his shoulders and balanced on her knees, looking down, biting at her lip as he held his cock like a piston in his fist and slid the ripe head through her folds. He spread her moisture until they were both glistening, his cock thick and dark between her pussy's pink lips.

And then he was there, pushing inside and saying, "Look at me, Alexa. Into my eyes."

She did, holding her breath as he entered her, as she lowered her hips to take him in. His eyes were dark, nearly black, catching the flickering flames of the mantel's candles and reflecting the light. When he hit bottom, she gasped, and he placed a finger against her mouth, soothing her with softly whispered singsong words she didn't understand.

And then she began to ride him, sliding so high that only the head of his cock remained inside of her before lowering her hips in a rolling motion that had him hitting all the right spots. She rode him hard, measuring his level of control by the tic pounding in his jaw and the vein at his temple that throbbed.

She wanted him to let go, to lose it, to be as rough and dirty as he wanted to be, and so she teased him, releasing her hold on his shoulders to pinch her own nipples, tugging and playing, catching her tongue between her teeth until he reached behind her and tore the hooks from her bra.

She skinned it off, cupped her breasts, pressed them together. He buried his face between them and bruised her with hard sucking kisses that he bathed with his tongue. He was doing everything right, everything for her, and she was teetering on the edge of coming apart.

And so she stopped him, pushing him back in the chair with a hand in the center of his chest. He sat there breathing hard, his abs contracting, his cock straining where he was buried deep in her sex. When he would have started again, thrusting into her, she shook her head.

"You're making this all about me." She moved her hands to his chest, flexed her fingers against his pecs. "I don't want to be the only one here having a good time."

"I am having a very good time, one that is made even better by the pleasure I give you." His voice was soft, melodious, and rumbled deep in his chest. The vibration tickled her fingers and she shivered. "You are a very beautiful woman, Alexa. You are very passionate, too. I am enjoying you immensely. Don't think that I am not."

"But I don't want you to just enjoy me. I want you to enjoy yourself."

"Ah, I think you do not understand that they are one and the same. Here. Let me show you." He placed his hands in the crease where her hips met her thighs, and captured her clit with his thumbs. She shuddered and moaned, but she also felt his cock swell. "You see, when you respond, I respond. Your pleasure becomes part of mine."

He continued to toy with her clit, and she let him, closing her eyes when it became impossible to do anything but feel. Bracing her hands on his knees, she leaned back while he brought her off. She burst until she couldn't breathe, until she swore her heart couldn't beat any harder.

And then she squeezed him, milked him, gripped him firmly and worked her sex up and down and around his cock. Even after she had finished, after her head had stopped spinning and the ache in her chest eased, she continued to move, to rub, to pull him deeper, to swivel her hips.

When his legs began to tremble beneath her, she opened

her eyes and captured his gaze, parting her lips and reminding him what she could do with her tongue. His eyes grew hot and heavy-lidded. His nostrils flared. His chin came up and he groaned, clenching her thighs so firmly she knew she'd be colored black and blue for days.

He came then, and the sound he made was brutal, a harsh, growling cry that was more animal than man. She rocked against him, swayed back and forth, pumped up and down, never stopping or letting him go.

He stayed hard for so long that she began to wonder if she hadn't imagined that he was done. But then he smiled, and his eyes grew sleepy, and she realized that no matter how well-endowed and skilled, he was only a man.

A man she knew nearly nothing about at all.

Chapter 10

Emmy Rose Maples hated Mondays. Mondays meant another week spending all her time at school and never seeing her dad. It wasn't fair that she was stuck with her mom so much when she wanted to go fishing and hang out with him.

He'd told her he'd take her up the river on her very own Steelhead trip when she was off during Christmas break, but she would probably never get to go. It wasn't fair that even on vacation she had tons of chores to do at home.

Cassie O'Malley never had to do anything except watch TV or play with her PlayStation. Emmy Rose didn't have a PlayStation. Or a computer. Her mom said she was too young and didn't need to be on the Internet or waste her time playing video games. It just wasn't fair the way her mom ruined everything and her dad wasn't around to rescue her.

Emmy Rose swore that if she lived long enough to grow up and have kids, she would never tell them they were too young for anything. What did parents know anyway? They hadn't been kids for so long that nothing about it was the same.

Besides, kids grew up fast these days. She'd heard her mom even say so to Mrs. King one day in the library. So if she was growing up so fast, how come it felt like it was taking forever to get there? She was going to die before it happened. The stress of being a kid would kill her before she even made it out of elementary school.

She took a deep breath and stared down into the pail of brown paint she was using to paint the cutout of one of the extra reindeer for the play about the one who ran away. And that gave her a really bright idea.

She should run away. Maybe if she did then her mom would finally notice that she wasn't a little kid who needed to lay out her clothes and clean out her backpack all the time, and that she was old enough for a PlayStation. Maybe then she'd get to spend more time with her dad.

Didn't anyone understand that she was going to die if she didn't get to spend more time with her dad? She leaned forward on the drop cloth covering the stage, rocking back and forth on her hands and knees and watching the ends of her hair skim over the paint in the pail.

And just when she thought about dunking her whole face into the can, a pair of black army boots came into her view. "That is a very fine representation of a reindeer. But he does not look like he is happy."

She didn't answer right away. First she sniffed to clear her throat. Then she wiped her cheek on her sleeve. "He's not happy. That's what the whole play is about."

"You are presenting a play about an unhappy reindeer?"

"They're all unhappy because one of them ran away."

"Why is that?"

"Because he had to leave his home and face certain death before anyone would notice he exists."

Ezra dropped down to squat beside her. He smelled like the sea, and she thought of her dad. "That does not seem like a story to excite an audience looking for Christmas cheer."

She sighed. How come he knew everything? How come he was so smart? She tapped her brush on the edge of the pail. "It's not really about facing certain death. But he does have to leave home."

"For what reason?"

She glanced over, saw him frowning while he looked at the section she'd painted. "He doesn't think Santa needs him since there are so many other reindeer to pull the sleigh."

"Ah, does he not understand that not all reindeers can have the same job?"

"Well, yeah. He learns that at the end. It's . . . what do you call it? The moral of the story," she said, dipping her brush into the paint. "That's what Mrs. Counsel says we're supposed to pay attention to. The lessons the reindeer learns."

"Mrs. Counsel is a wise teacher," he said with a really soft voice. "Many of life's lessons can be learned through legends and fables."

"And fairy tales? Like Aesop's and Grimm's and Walt Disney?"

He nodded, a smile on his face as he propped an arm on his knee. "When I was growing up, my grandmother shared many tales with me that I still remember today."

"What kind of tales?" she asked, leaning forward to paint on the reindeer's hide, wishing her dad was home more often to tell her stories, or that her mother wasn't always so tired at bedtime.

"I will share with you one of my favorites," he said, sitting cross-legged on the cloth beside her and picking up the extra paintbrush Mrs. Counsel had given her to use. "On the island where I was born, we have many tropical creatures. Birds, reptiles, amphibians. Insects, too."

"Like in *The Jungle Book*?"

"Somewhat, yes. You will find monkeys and big cats, but no elephants or bears."

"I've seen bears when we've gone camping, but just from a long way away. Mostly here all I see are fish. And whales. But not up close." She sighed, feeling sad. "My dad has seen them up close."

"I have not yet met your father. Only your mother."

She watched Ezra stroke his paintbrush over the reindeer's back leg. He was being very slow and *pre-cise* the way Mrs. Counsel wanted all of them to be, but Emmy Rose had seen the big mess Cassie O'Malley had made because she was so busy talking about her new iPod.

"My dad isn't home very much," was what she finally said. "How come you're here at school anyway? Did you already fix the light on the stairs?"

Ezra laughed. "I have noticed that many buildings in your town have problems with lights."

She nodded. "My dad says that's because so many buildings are old and out of code, or something like that. When you lived on your island, did you live in a hut?"

"I did not, no. My ancestors lived in rudimentary conditions, but my grandmother, who raised me, had a small frame house."

"Was it in the jungle?" She frowned, trying to remember if she knew what *ru-di-ment-ary* meant. "Or did you live in a town like this one?"

"It was similar in size, though we lived inland on a river rather than near the sea."

"I'll bet the water there is really warm, isn't it? It's too cold here to swim much."

"Our waters are quite warm most of the year. San Torisco is very near the equator."

"We learned about climate in geography this year." She dipped her brush into the paint again and slapped a big blob onto the wood, then smoothed it very *pre-cise-ly*. "But I'm pretty sure I'll be stuck here in the cold wearing my stupid pink parka until I die."

"Is a pink parka so bad?" he asked, helping her paint the reindeer's stomach. "If it keeps you warm and dry?"

She shrugged and leaned forward onto her free hand and knees. "No one else has pink. I look like a big fat piece of bubblegum."

Ezra didn't say anything for several seconds and she wondered if he even cared that she felt all chewed up and spit out. But then he began to talk. "There is a frog which lives near the river where I grew up. It is a very bright pink, and it is unable to camouflage itself by simply hiding in its surroundings."

"See, that's what I was saying!" she exclaimed. "Pink is just gross."

"Not when you use it to your advantage," he said, sounding very wise.

"How am I supposed to do that?"

"Much like the frog learned to do. You forget that you are wearing pink, and everyone else will do the same."

"That doesn't make any sense." She shook her head and frowned. "How can I forget that I look like a wad of gum?"

"You do so by being true to yourself. You see, every evening on my island when the sun descends in the sky, the crickets begin to tune their instruments for the farewell they play to the day. Their song is enjoyed by all the creatures in the jungle. But it has not always been that way."

"Why not?"

"The crickets do not know how to begin playing at the same time or in the same key so that they sound like a true orchestra. If one plays before the others and the rest try to catch up, the result is a lot of screeching that does not sound like music at all."

"They need a conductor."

"They have one. They discovered him quite by accident."

"How did they do that?"

"One day after the jungle council explained to the crickets that they would have to leave if they did not learn to play as one, the frog decided to share his opinion even though he had always been ignored. After all, it was his jungle, too." Ezra dipped his brush in the pail to get more paint. "Before he spoke, he cleared his throat. The sound was very loud and very deep. No one had expected such a sound to come out of a creature who was such a frivolous color."

"What happened then?"

"The council called for another vote, and all the creatures in the jungle agreed that the frog's voice was too valuable not to be heard. They also agreed that his bright pink skin would serve as a beacon for the crickets' nightly gathering. From that day forward, his existence was just as important to the jungle as every other creature living there."

Emmy Rose thought about the story for several minutes while Ezra continued to paint. "That was a fable, wasn't it? With a moral and everything."

"What do you think the moral was?"

"That just because someone makes a lot of noise and gets a lot of attention doesn't mean anyone really wants to listen to them," she said, thinking about how Cassie O'Malley always had to have something to say about everything.

"And?"

"And just because you stand out wearing a pink coat doesn't mean you aren't important and smart."

"Anything else?"

"Yes. That being different doesn't mean you can't find a way to fit in."

"I believe you are right."

She continued to watch him paint for several minutes. She liked having him here. He made her feel warm, which was silly, and that made her laugh. "That was a really dumb story, you know."

"Yes." Ezra laughed, too. "Yes. It was."

Chapter 11

"I came to make sure that you are all right," Ezra said, forcing Alexa to look up from the papers in her lap. She was sitting on a small stool tucked into a corner of the stage, supervising her second-grade painting crew while reading the paragraphs they'd written for English today.

She could not remember a Monday ever sucking so bad. At least twice during the day she'd been snapped out of a skin-tingling fantasy by a student's question, and it had been harder than she wanted to admit to come back to the real world after those stolen moments spent alone with Ezra in her mind.

And then to look out over the small auditorium minutes ago and find him walking toward her? At first she'd thought she was seeing things, that her imagination had conjured him up yet again. But he was too real and too vibrant to be anything but alive, and so she'd sat as still as she possibly could, hoping he wouldn't see her in the shadows as he settled in beside Emmy Rose.

The way he'd talked softly to the girl, the way he'd held her attention when the other kids had been chattering aloud about him, the way Emmy Rose had hung on his every word as if no other adult had ever given her the time of day, was almost more than Alexa could bear to witness. Her chest had grown painfully tight.

She didn't want him to possess a compassionate soul. She didn't want him to have an empathetic heart. She didn't want him to be truly selfless and kind because it made her decision to have Vince dig for the truth seem so petty.

She swallowed hard, wondering what she had stooped to. Not trusting a man's word because Brett hadn't kept his? Was she doomed to spend the rest of her life judging men by the one who had left her?

She didn't believe that about herself, no. But she did know that she wasn't ready to see Ezra face to face. Not until she had a better handle on what she was feeling beyond the intuition telling her she was in over her head.

And not until she'd chastised herself fully for being so incredibly stupid. So what if she hadn't had sex since Brett had walked out, and at least six months before that? Horniness was no excuse for losing her mind.

"Alexa?"

Ezra's voice, deep and resonant and musical, sent tiny charges zinging over her skin, reminding her that he was waiting. As if she could ever forget. "I'm fine. Just multitasking my little heart out so I don't have to take these papers home tonight. Home repairs await."

She still hadn't looked up at him, but had kept her eyes on the sheets in her lap, so he dropped to his haunches in front of her, forcing her to meet his gaze. She lifted her chin slowly, uncertain what to expect, not at all prepared for what she saw in his expression.

His tone should've warned her, but she didn't think any warning would have readied her for the lines of worry fanning from his eyelids to his temples, the concern, the fear that she was hurt, that he was at fault. How in the world did he convey all of that with his eyes?

It was just sex, she wanted to scream at him. *It was nothing but sex*. But she wasn't a very good liar, so she asked, "What are you doing here?"

"You were not answering your cell phone."

"You tried to call me?"

He shook his head. "Molly was trying to reach you. She is unable to pick up Emmy Rose, and asked if you could drive her home once you are done here for the day."

"Sure, but why didn't she just have you pick her up?"

"I am on my way to Newton for supplies. I will not be back before it is time for the girl to share dinner with her parents."

"Oh," was all Alexa could think of to say. She needed more time. Looking at him now, remembering what they had done . . . Heat flushed her skin, her breasts tightened, and she had never been so thankful for the dark.

"Alexa, we have to talk."

"I have these papers." She shuffled them uselessly. His voice. Dear God, his voice. "And there are several students still here whom I'm responsible for." Too bad she didn't seem to feel the same sense of personal accountability. "Can't this wait?"

He shook his head, shifted further into her space. He smelled like the wind from the sea. "I will speak softly, and I will not distract you but for a moment or two."

She wanted to laugh. He'd been distracting her since she'd first seen him yesterday afternoon. "Fine, though I don't understand why we can't do this later."

He faced her without blocking her view of her students, so out of place that it was hard to believe she'd found a man like him in her world. He was wearing clothes similar to those he'd had on when he'd first arrived. Combat boots, olive-colored fatigues, a long-sleeved T-shirt in black.

Yet what she saw was his bare body, his skin softly bathed in candlelight, his thick erection opening her in ways she'd never known. She shuddered. Her heart began to race. And all she could do was stare at the papers in her lap, wishing he would go away.

"The reason we cannot wait until later is because I need to be sure you are not worrying. You have no need."

"Worrying?"

"We were intimate without discussing birth control or other matters of a sexual nature."

"I know. I was there." And she'd been kicking herself ever since. "It was a very stupid thing to do."

"It would not have happened if I had thought it a stupid thing to do," he said, his words causing her to look over and meet his gaze.

His eyes flickered brightly, intently; his expression demanded her attention while leaving her confused. What was she thinking? Everything about this man left her confused. "I don't get it. How can you say that?"

"Because I know myself." He leaned closer, the scar on his face seeming to bisect his cheek in rigid relief. "And I allowed myself to lose control because I had no concerns over the physical consequences."

"Of course not. You're not the one with the womb." She still couldn't believe she'd been so stupidly human to take such a risk.

Ezra shook his head sharply. "I knew a long time ago that my life was not the sort I wanted to share with a child, and I took the necessary steps to see that it would not happen."

What was he saying? How bad could his life possibly be to make it unsuitable to share? "You had a vasectomy?"

This time, he nodded. "I have also had testing done for diseases. Living where I do, it is more of a practical matter than anything."

Was his taking all the responsibility supposed to make her feel better? On one level, she did find a sense of relief. On another, she found she was still reeling from her reckless behavior. "Then as long as I'm clean, neither of us should have regrets. Is that what you're saying?"

He reached up and placed his palm on her wrist, wrapping her small bones in his much larger fingers. "I don't regret anything, Alexa, except that we did not have more time. It was the end of a long day. We were both tired. The sex was physically satisfying, but it wasn't enough."

"I'm not sure that helps, but thanks. And you have nothing to worry about as far as, well . . ." She hated this. Hated it. "Let's just say that the only thing you could possibly catch from me would be abstinence."

His mouth quirked to one side and showed off his dimple. "Then I am flattered to have been chosen to put an end to your celibacy."

"I'm not so sure there was any choosing involved," she found herself admitting, though it was the last thing he probably wanted to hear, sounding as it did of karma and fate when it was more about convenience and hunger. Except it wasn't, and she knew that.

There had been something shimmering between them since their first encounter on the hill leading up to the Maples Inn. It had grown larger during the time she'd spent showing him his quarters. When he'd come close enough to take the key from her hand, she'd barely been able to breathe.

But last night on her porch . . . Oh, that was something. The heat of his fingers scorching her skin. Just a tiny grazing of his hands to her stomach, his thumb toying briefly, slightly, with her navel. Thinking about it now . . . She closed her eyes. It was all she could do.

"I believe that is called chemistry," he said, and before she could find the switch between her brain and her mouth she responded with, "At the very least."

"You believe it is more?"

"I don't know what to believe, or to think, or to feel. I've never in my life done . . . *that* with a man I don't know."

"Perhaps that is because you feel I am a man whom you do know."

No, no. She shook her head, glanced up to check on her students. "But I don't. And you're as aware of that as I am. We

met for the first time twenty-four hours ago. It doesn't make
sense that we . . ."

She couldn't even finish her sentence because narrowing
down her arguments was impossible. And she didn't like facing what she didn't understand.

"Alexa, listen to me."

She was reluctant to return her attention to him, to look into
his eyes where she saw things about herself that she didn't expect to see. Like the bold truth of how much she wanted to
sleep with him again.

"Life doesn't make sense, Alexa. But do I believe for a moment that had Molly hired another man you would have reacted the same to him?" He shook his head slowly, his eyes
unusually piercing and bright.

He was a hard man to ignore, or even to look away from, but
she managed to tear her gaze from his and stare across the
stage at her class. "What do you want me to say? I've already
admitted that whatever this is, it's a first."

"That is exactly what I want you to say. That there is something here. What I don't want is for you to walk away because
I have frightened you."

Walk away? From him? Frightened or not, she didn't think
that was possible. And besides, if she had been frightened by
anything, her own actions topped the list. "I'm not frightened," she told him. "And I'm not walking away. But I don't
think that whatever we have here can possibly matter."

"Because of the different colors of our skin?"

She rolled her eyes. "Did that stop me last night?"

He grinned. "It did not."

"It's not a racial issue, Ezra. It's an issue of me living here
and you hanging out for a month. What good is that going to
do either of us?"

"I believe the answer to that depends on your expectations.
Are you looking for a true romance?"

"Of course not." She answered before she could stop herself, hating being put on the spot. "I don't know that I'm looking for anything. Last night just happened."

"It happened for a reason, Alexa. You were looking to explore the connection between us."

Which made her, what? A woman in need of a sexual partner? An affair with no strings attached?

He tightened his hold on her wrist. "What I want to know is whether or not you would like to continue this exploration with me?"

She pulled in a deep breath, searching for clarity. "How am I supposed to answer that?"

"With a yes or a no."

"It's not that simple."

"It can be if you allow it."

Was he right? Could she turn a blind eye to all her unanswered questions about who he was and why he was here? Could she do as Molly had urged her to do and give in to the attraction without a second thought?

She gave him the only answer she could, the only response that was honest. In the end, all she could say was, "Yes."

Chapter 12

Ezra's trip to Newton was a welcome distraction, one provided by Molly Maples's inattention to matters of repair at the inn. She had no idea what tools, equipment, or supplies were stocked in the maintenance shed.

It was equally apparent that her husband's occupation as a fishing guide caught up in the Pacific Northwest's Steelhead season kept him too busy to notice what was happening in his home—including things that concerned his wife and his daughter.

It was not Ezra's place to judge the way a man juggled his work, his life, and his family, but Daniel Maples's method had created a disaster of mismanagement that cleared the way for Ezra to easily maneuver things.

He had free reign of the Mapleses' property, of their phone lines, the dish used for the inn's satellite television—even the computer on which the reservations and financial records were kept. Today he'd checked on the confirmed arrivals dating into next week.

Davis Brown, his contact, had added a second room to his booking but had given Mrs. Maples no additional name. More than likely the man would be accompanied by an associate. This did not mean a wrench had been thrown into Ezra's plans, but it did leave him unsettled.

Whatever the reason for the change, he did not like being kept in the dark. His superiors had to know he would discover that Brown was not traveling alone. Whether or not—and how—he questioned the reasons for Brown's actions would prove his position with Spectra.

Try as he did, he could think of nothing he had done to raise the suspicions of Warren Aceveda or Cameron Gates and warrant a test of his loyalty. And since he could not, he would acknowledge the modification without questioning the basis for the change—and then wait.

To do that, he had two options. Use the equipment on his boat, or make his way far enough south for his cell phone to pick up a new signal. Since he was already on the road for Molly, the latter made the most sense. He parked the Maples Inn pickup in the lot of the hardware store and dug his phone from the pocket hidden in the placket of his coat.

Once the service that scrambled Spectra's calls responded, Ezra left a brief message in code. The connection lasted twenty seconds. It was the only step he could have taken, but it left him feeling as if he had not done enough.

For one thing, he found himself thinking about the effect his mission would have on Alexa Counsel. He had bedded her after knowing her for less than twelve hours, no thought for anything but the relief his body was seeking and the smoke screen she would provide.

She was lending authenticity to his cover. He had to protect her for both of their benefits. And as unlike him as it was to admit, he would owe her safe passage into a new life once all here was said and done.

He turned off the truck and reached for the door handle, then paused, thinking of a number he'd committed to memory years before. A number he had never had occasion to use but which served as a safeguard—a safeguard that seemed the only option available with Alexa involved.

He considered the ramifications of using it now, in this situation that was a matter of life and death for so many, a matter of long overdue justice for all.

He lived alone, worked alone, slept alone, killed alone, yet this final mission was bigger than any assignment he'd undertaken before and he didn't wish to fail because his arrogance made him assume he could succeed on his own.

Reaching into the same pocket, he set the device which would insure that no one listening in could decipher a thing he said or the number he dialed. Once he had, he listened to the faint clicks as the call was routed and rerouted into an untraceable loop before it was answered in an engineering office in Manhattan.

"Hank Smithson, here. State your business."

"My business is annihilation. One of great interest to you. I believe you know of the party involved."

Hank Smithson cleared his throat, and Ezra pictured him rolling the stub of a cigar from one side of his mouth to the other and chomping down. "I do indeed, son. I do indeed. What help should I be sending, and where?"

"I do not require help, and this call will be my only contact."

Hank sputtered into the phone. "What in blazes do you mean, you don't need help? Ezra, son, has that hair of yours finally choked off the blood supply to your brain? Of course you need help."

Ezra couldn't help but smile at the picture the old warrior's words painted. "I no longer wear my dreadlocks, and my brain is in good working order. I do, however, fear that if anything happens to me the truth will never be known. And there is a woman here. One who does not know how deeply I have already involved her in my quest."

"Hells fuckin' bells. Where exactly are you, and what nonsense have you gotten yourself into?"

Ezra took several minutes to briefly explain the arms deal, his cover, his location, the fact that he had nine days to work out the last of the details, and Alexa. "I am sharing this information for one reason only. Should I fail, I will not be alive to make another attempt. And I would like to be returned to San Torisco for burial."

"You're getting ahead of yourself here. Let's talk this thing through."

"There is nothing that needs to be said. If I am successful, I will remain in my current position until the first of the year. If you do not hear from me after that . . ." He let the sentence trail. He could not finish the thought. He could not consider his failure.

"I'll personally see that you get home," Hank said, clearing his throat. "We're all soldiers here, Ezra, and we leave no man behind."

Chapter 13

"Before you yell at me or tell me what a moron I am, just understand that I've already called myself every name in the book. And done so repeatedly in a very loud voice."

"What in the world are you talking about?" Molly straightened from where she'd been tucking in a clean sheet on the far side of the third floor guest room's bed. This particular room was soft and feminine, done up in a palette of cream and country blue in florals and stripes, solids and plaids.

After the other parents had picked up the members of her second-grade painting crew, Alexa had driven Emmy Rose home and come looking for the girl's mother. After all, it was Molly who had gotten her into this mess, talking about affairs . . .

"I slept with him."

Molly's jaw dropped. "You did? When?"

"Last night."

"So soon?"

"Why let a good thing go to waste?"

Molly snapped the comforter into place. "How good was his thing? Oh, and is that trunk-of-an-oak-tree rumor true or false?"

Alexa only glared.

"Okay, okay. Start at the beginning, please? I've had two last-minute bookings today, and I've been running myself ragged getting the rooms ready and adjusting meal plans. I didn't even get all my bread baked before they started calling."

The beginning, huh? That was easy enough. In fact, it was the only part that was. "I had sex with Ezra."

"I got that part. I'm still waiting for the part where I'm supposed to start calling you names."

"I had incredible, multi-orgasmic"—here was where she paused—"and completely unprotected sex with Ezra."

Molly blinked like an owl. "Unprotected sex? You didn't use a condom?"

"Nope. I didn't have one to use, but didn't even think about it until after the fact, moron that I am."

"And the pill? You stayed on after Brett?"

"Nope." Alexa felt herself cringe. "Complete moron. Go ahead and say it."

Molly lifted a brow, got back to work with a cloth and a feather duster. "I don't need to say it when you've already said it to yourself. But I will ask you if you talked at all. About your histories. Your partners."

"Not until today," Alexa said, finishing with the pillowcases and shams before replacing the liner in the small wicker trash basket. "When he came by the school to tell me you needed me to give Emmy Rose a ride."

"And?"

"He said I'm safe. From disease and pregnancy both."

"Do you believe him?"

"I'm inclined to because it makes me feel better about my moronic self. But yeah. I do. He was sincere. And . . . convincing."

"That was nice." Molly fluffed the bed's throw pillows. "Not to leave you wondering and worrying. As long as it's true."

Alexa felt as if she should be doing more than she was to help, but Molly blew through the room like the wind. "Yeah. I expected him to abdicate all responsibility for any life we might have created."

"No." Molly waggled a finger. "That would've been what Brett said."

Alexa snorted. "He seemed so nice and normal when we got married. Who knew he was such a skunk?"

"So now what?"

"He wants to see me again," she said, leaving out the part about having already said yes.

"And why wouldn't he?" Molly asked, strutting as if she'd made the match of the century.

Alexa wasn't feeling quite so cocky. "Right? Who wouldn't stick around for wild uncomplicated sex?"

"I wasn't talking about the sex."

What else was there to talk about? "Molly, we jumped into bed without knowing anything about each other besides the fact that we wanted to have sex."

Molly shrugged. "He cared enough to come set things straight with you."

"Unless, of course, all he cared about was getting his next fix," Alexa said, hating that she hated what was probably the truth.

"Is that what you really think?"

"I honestly don't know what to think. Any affairs I had before marrying Brett—and trust me, there weren't many—were nothing like what happened with Ezra last night."

Molly set her basket of cleaning supplies outside the door, then bent and gathered up the ball of dirty sheets and pillowcases. "This conversation calls for tea or coffee or something with cream and Godiva Liqueur."

Laughing, Alexa followed her friend down the hallway and three flights of stairs into the kitchen. Molly headed for the laundry room where she dropped the linens, while Alexa headed for the freezer where she found the dark blue bottle and plenty of ice.

By the time she turned around, Molly had the blender ready to go and was pouring in cream and what coffee was left in the kitchen carafe. "I'm doing pot pies for dinner. Thank God, because all I have to do is pop them from the freezer into the oven. Cooking tonight would be the last straw."

"That bad of a day?" Alexa asked, dumping ice cubes into the creamed coffee mixture then pouring way too much of the chocolate liqueur on top.

Molly secured the blender's top and punched the button for frappe. While the ice crushed and swirled, Alexa found two tall glasses bearing the insignia of the Maples Inn.

"Last-minute bookings can't be a bad thing, right?" Alexa asked, reaching for her glass once Molly had poured. "Good for the bottom line and all that?"

Molly stared down into her drink as she leaned against the counter. "I'm starting to get resentful, and that's not good for any line."

Alexa frowned. "Resentful? Of?"

"Too many things to list." Molly shook off the thought and took a drink. "Mostly that I have no home life. My daughter is gone eight hours a day. My husband is gone at least twelve or fourteen. My own days consist of keeping house and cooking for people I don't even know. Forget watching television or reading a book or playing a game with Emmy Rose or ever having time to make love with Dan."

Molly sighed, and Alexa remained silent, uncertain if there was anything she could say to make Molly feel better, hoping that being here and listening was enough for now.

"You know what I want to do more than anything?" Molly lifted the blender from the motorized base. "Take this entire pitcher to the master bathroom, fill the tub with bath salts, and stay there until I'm a prune."

"Go," Alexa insisted, waving in the direction of Molly's bedroom. "I'll put in the pot pies. I'll wash the sheets. I won't bake the bread, but I can manage the rest."

"No, no." Molly shook her head. Strands of ash blond hair escaped the confines of her headband to tumble into her face. She pushed them back. "Give me the lowdown on your sex life. Maybe that'll be enough of an oomph to help me make it until bedtime."

"I hate that you're having such a hard time," Alexa said, giving her friend a sympathy pout. "And I hate that I can't do more to help you out."

"Right now you're not even doing the one thing I've asked you to do," Molly said as she climbed onto a stool at the kitchen's island. "Sex. Give it to me."

Now Alexa felt even worse for her friend than before. If things with Molly were so bad that she needed the distraction of Alexa's sex life to get her through the day . . . "It was incredible. Amazing. Beyond amazing. I know, I know. I sound like some reality TV show contestant, but I promise not to start talking about the journey."

Molly arched a brow. "What journey would that be? The one from the door to the bed?"

"We didn't even bother with the bed. Vince was over—"

"A threesome?" Molly nearly choked on her drink. "Wow. This is getting better and better."

Alexa glared at the other woman as Molly began to giggle. "Vince was over trying to fix my porch light."

"Are you kidding me? Why would you have Vince try to fix anything? Just use Ezra. Have him bill me the hours."

She had used Ezra. Ruthlessly. That much she didn't mind having Molly know. But she was going to have to step carefully so as not to reveal why Vince had been at her house in the first place. "He's going to take a look at it if he gets a chance. If not, I'll just call Potter's."

Molly polished off her drink and snickered. "C'mon, Alexa. Potter's can't possibly provide the same quality of service as Ezra."

And if *that* understatement and a half didn't scare the hell out of her . . . Wouldn't it be easier to give him up now than later? Come January, wouldn't she be too used to having him in her bed? And in her life? Would the agony of the future be worth the ecstasy of the here and now?

"What are you thinking about?"

At Molly's question, Alexa looked up. "What happens after the first of the year, Molly? What do I do when he's gone?"

Molly's sympathetic expression spoke volumes, but her words were simple and plain. "You'll only have one choice. You'll have to call Potter's."

And at that, both women dissolved into peals of mad, snorting laughter as only best friends can do.

Chapter 14

It was almost nine o'clock when Alexa finally turned into her driveway. The day had been unforgivably long and tiring. Mondays often were, but today she'd had the added sex hangover to deal with, as well as the residual fear and self-loathing caused by her reckless lack of common sense.

Mental flagellation wore a woman out, and Ezra's assurance that she had no reason to worry about physical consequences only went so far in easing the stress that had settled like steel bands in her shoulders and neck. That stiffness guaranteed she would get nothing done around the house tonight.

She'd purchased the small cabin two years ago after her divorce, unable to see herself living alone in the larger oceanfront home she'd shared with Brett. Not only were the memories of the place not so good, who needed twenty-five hundred square feet of hardwood floors and Pacific-facing windows to clean?

That house, while newly built and suffering none of her cabin's obvious flaws, had no personality. Coming here at the end of the day was truly coming home. She was surrounded by the forest, tucked away from the town's prying eyes, able to live her private life privately—at least most of the time.

Having Ezra show up today at school had been the worst

sort of public fodder. Even if he'd come on orders from Molly and not just to see her, the parents of two of her students had responded to her introductions with a chill, making ice cubes out of the knots of nerves in her stomach.

Parents and students aside, she'd tried to convince herself that she was only a postscript, that Ezra's dropping by to talk to her was common courtesy and nothing more, but she had a hard time believing any of that.

The conversation they'd had was too intimate and too critical to be off the cuff. His consideration had surprised her, enough so that she was looking forward to a quiet evening home alone to decide if she was comfortable accepting his invitation to go forward with this affair.

Her first indication that her night wasn't going to be any more relaxing than her day was the fact that she could see her porch light through the army of trees standing guard between the road and her door. Ezra had been by. She wondered if he'd fixed it before or after he'd stopped at the school, before or after he'd put in a full day's work at the Maples Inn, which included a drive to Newton.

And then she wondered why it mattered, knowing it didn't, but feeling . . . special, she guessed. It was nice, having someone she barely knew—having Ezra—go out of his way to repair a light she was rarely home long enough to use.

She parked, climbed down from the SUV, dropped her keys into her purse, and gathered up the rest of her things. Against all odds, she'd managed to finish grading the papers she'd been working on after school. And with her light in working order, she could turn her attention to the kitchen cabinets in desperate need of being stripped and then sealed with new varnish.

Except as she began the climb up her porch steps, she saw the silhouette of a man move past her front window. Her first thought was that Vince already had news, but then she realized the body she saw did not belong to the owner of the Gin & Rummy. It was that of the man who'd asked her today if she'd like to continue the affair they'd started last night.

She paused for a moment, hitching her tote bag close and holding tightly to the strap, as if doing so would somehow help her make up her mind. What was she going to do? Open the door and tumble into the waiting maelstrom of physical bliss? Was that what she wanted? A wild and explosive sexual affair that she knew would only last for a month?

Or did she want to mark up last night to the heat of the moment, and stave off any residual desire until a more suitable man came along? And wasn't that a ridiculous sentiment, considering it was a suitable man who had up and left her when she no longer suited his needs.

And so she reached for the brass handle, pushing the door open to find Ezra just inside, tightening the screws on the faceplate covering the switch.

"You didn't have to do this, you know." She closed the door behind her, doing her best to ignore the way her belly had begun to flutter when she'd seen him not five hours ago. "I was going to call Potter's tomorrow. I just got too busy today."

"I wasn't too busy, so I saved you the phone call and the cost."

"You can't do my repair work for free. And I won't let you bill the time to Molly." Alexa circled behind him to drop her purse and tote onto the table in front of the window, deciding then and there that denim jeans had nothing on the fit of fatigues. Mmm-mmm-mmm.

He cut his gaze toward her, fighting a smile. "Did Molly suggest I do that?"

Cocky man. "She's always insisted I call her maintenance man or even Danny if I need something done that I can't do myself."

"I thought she might be giving you and I her approval."

"She has. Or she did." Alexa turned to lean against the table, her hands curled over the slick wood surface at her hips. "We talked about you when I dropped off Emmy Rose."

He pulled a small pouch of tools from his back waistband

and tucked the screwdriver inside before rolling the pouch closed. "Should I be concerned over your conversation?"

"Were your ears burning?" When he frowned, she explained. "If your ears are burning, it's supposed to mean that someone is talking about you."

"Ah, well." He stepped away from the wall, crossing his arms as he faced her, the biceps beneath his T-shirt bulging, his feet planted firmly on her hardwood floor. "It's not my ears that have been burning today. Does that mean someone has been thinking about me in another way?"

Yes. She had been thinking about him in another way for what seemed like twenty-four hours. She lifted her chin. "Does that bother you? Does it make it seem as if I only want you for your . . . ?"

She couldn't say it. She wasn't a prude, but talking about his cock just seemed so wrong. The man had come to the school today to set her mind at ease. He had used his personal time to take care of her home repairs.

But the sentence she couldn't complete began to take over the room, growing larger and swirling around them like an ever-tightening spring. Ezra walked slowly toward her, tossing the pouch of tools to slide across the table before he leaned forward, bracing his hands on either side of hers, locking her in place, his lips and his eyes only inches away.

"I want you to enjoy my cock, Alexa," he said, and she felt her face color. "I want you to enjoy it as much as I enjoy sliding it deep inside your beautiful cunt. But don't think for a moment that my cock is all that I am."

She shook her head, a rapid denial of his words and the apprehension climbing her spine. "I don't think that. I don't think that at all."

"Are you certain?" he asked, covering one of her hands with his, slipping his fingers between her own. "I will be glad to demonstrate if you have already forgotten what I can do with my hands."

She closed her eyes, let her head fall back on her shoulders. "I haven't forgotten. But you can show me anything you like."

The sound he made was as much a growl as it was a sinister laugh. "It will be my pleasure to do so."

She didn't care what he said. She was quite certain no pleasure he received could possibly match what anticipation and his fingertips were doing to her. He was leaning so close that he tickled the hair curling at her temple when he breathed.

She shivered, her nipples growing hard, and she wished she wasn't still wearing her heavy sweater so he could see. She wanted him to know what he did to her, the pleasure *she* felt, that she had not come lightly to this affair, but had given in because this thing between them was too big to ignore.

Neither could she ignore the movement of his palm from her hand to her thigh and higher, to her hip, and to her stomach, where he finally turned his fingers and slid them down between her legs.

She gasped, her breath caught in her lungs as he found her clit beneath the fabric of her pants and toyed with the knot while pressing the heel of his palm to her mound.

She couldn't move. She had nothing but the table to keep her steady. And even that was beginning to shake now that his mouth was at her ear, his teeth nipping at her lobe, his tongue darting out to touch the skin beneath, then that of her neck, which he bit.

And he did it all while a soft buzzing sound hummed deep in his throat. The vibration raised gooseflesh all over her body. She felt it between her legs where his questing fingers had dipped lower, where he'd wedged them between her lips while still rubbing her clit with his palm.

"I told you that I have more to offer you than my cock."

She nodded, breathless.

"I have my mouth," he murmured against her skin.

She groaned and shuddered.

"I have my mind, Alexa. I use my ears to listen. I can give

you things you have only imagined before you saw me walking up that slope, before I saw you standing there at the top, wrapped tightly in your sweater, your hair whipped wildly by the wind."

She cried out, shuddering, reaching between her legs to hold him in place as she came. The flood of sensation was endless, rocking her until she let go, her hand flailing for purchase. He pressed up, pushed up, ground against her hard.

She knocked both her purse and his tool pouch to the floor. The vase of flowers followed. By the time she finished, she wasn't sure her legs would be able to hold her. But she knew without question that she was on board for this ride however long it might last.

Chapter 15

Later that week, at six-fifteen on Wednesday night, Alexa parked in front of the Gin & Rummy. She was meeting Ezra for dinner at seven and had come early, hoping for a chance to talk to Vince without Rachel around, knowing the other woman would be tied up at Second Time Best until at least eight.

Yes, Rachel knew that Alexa was having Vince do a background check on Ezra. And it was quite possible that Vince had already shared any information he'd uncovered with his girlfriend, though Alexa hoped otherwise.

Not that she knew for sure he had news; it had only been three days, after all. But if he did, she wanted to hear it without any commentary from Rachel. Alexa's friend had already made her feelings about Ezra clear.

And if she were to learn that Alexa had spent the last three nights having the best sex of her life, well, no doubt her friend-approval rating would plummet.

No, it was just easier to deal with Vince one-on-one. Keeping things all about business meant Alexa would be less likely to give away any of what she felt.

She climbed onto a stool at the bar and had Charlene bring her a beer, wishing instead for a cocktail. Having an endless variety of food and drink to choose from was one thing she definitely missed about L.A. Comfort Bay offered up little more than burgers and beer, or seafood with French fries and salads of iceberg lettuce.

Most of the time she didn't mind. She ate a lot of Molly's home cooking. But there were times she would kill for a plate of chicken enchiladas smothered in tomatillo sauce. Those were the same times Molly would promptly point her to the shelf of cookbooks in her kitchen, or the inn's office computer with Internet access.

"Vince said give him five," Charlene called out as she circled the end of the bar carrying a tray piled high with bags of chips, sandwiches, burgers, and fries. "He's got something to give you."

"Thanks, Charlene." Alexa reached for her beer, her heart thudding. She glanced at the Olympia Beer clock hanging over the kitchen door, glanced at her watch to make sure the time was right. Ezra would be here in thirty-five minutes unless, like her, he came early.

She was busy praying Vince's five didn't turn into ten or twenty when he pushed through the swinging doors. He glanced at the long row of booths then toward the end of the bar, and headed that way, having spotted her.

"I don't have much time," he said, wiping his hands on a towel before slinging it over his shoulder. "Damn O'Malley's still down with some shit."

"I don't have much time either. Ezra is meeting me at seven for dinner."

"Well, I hope you guys won't be wanting more than a bowl of cereal because I am fresh out of patience with that grill."

Alexa forced a laugh. As much as she wanted to rush him, she didn't want to let on how desperate she was to hear what he had to say. "Charlene said you have something to give me?"

Way to not be desperate.

"Oh, right." He reached into his back pocket and handed her a folded sheet of paper. "I got this from a guy at the Portland Bureau who's got a military contact. Your boy went to the Naval Academy. Twenty years back. Don't know yet what he's been up to since, or how he got from the Caribbean to Annapolis, but he started out on the right foot."

Alexa unfolded the paper, her hands suddenly damp, and didn't say a word. Not thanks. Not wow. Not a single word. If her life had depended on her finding her voice in that moment, she was pretty damn certain she would have died.

She hadn't expected this. She wouldn't have been the least bit surprised if Vince had come up with a rap sheet—and what did that say about her—but this? From the United States Naval Academy? How did that make any sense when combined with the things that Ezra had told her?

"I'm floored," was what she finally got out. "This is the last thing I thought you'd find."

"Yeah, but I can see it," Vince said with a pensive nod.

"How?" she nearly screeched. "He's a schoolteacher from an island in the Caribbean. That doesn't jive at all with this."

"Just because he teaches school now doesn't mean that's what he's always done." Vince grabbed for his towel and wiped a circle of condensation from the surface of the bar. "Or maybe he doesn't teach at all."

"So why would he say that he does?" She could think of reasons she didn't like, but was having trouble with reasons she could live with.

"Because he doesn't want you to know how he really makes his living." Before Alexa could say anything else, Vince waved at Charlene, who was signaling him to the phone. "Look, I've got to get back to work. Check with me in a couple of days and I might have more to give you. And don't start jumping to conclusions. Just let things simmer for now."

Simmer? Was he kidding? There was no way she'd be able to tuck this away for a couple of days without going totally insane, and Vince had to be mad to think so. She watched him slam into the kitchen before she looked back down at the information she was supposed to let simmer.

Ezra's face returned her gaze, though this wasn't her Ezra at all. The Ezra in the photo couldn't have been more than twenty years old. His hair was shorn close to his scalp. His expression was determined, righteously so, as if he knew he had it in him to make all the difference in the world. That wasn't a whole lot unlike than what she saw in him now, except now his eyes were even harder, and beneath his polite and proper veneer, she often sensed a seed of bitterness desperate to grow.

She ran a finger over his lips, thinking how soft they looked. How soft, in fact, his whole face appeared. Young and untried and innocent. Dear God, he looked as if he had never seen corruption or depravity in his life. And his scar was gone. Or wasn't there. Hadn't yet been earned. Was it in battle? A military conflict? Had he been honorably discharged? Was he in the navy even now and didn't want anyone to know because he was covertly deployed?

Really, she was grasping at ridiculously thin straws, but this information left her reeling. She didn't know how she was supposed to react; did she tell him what she knew? She'd been prepared for the worst, prepared to find out Ezra had reformed after an unsavory past. And it made no sense at all that she had been ready to deal with that scenario yet had no idea how to react to this one. To the unexpected truth.

She chose that moment to take a deep breath and look up— and was so very glad that she did. She was just in time to see Ezra pull open the door. She dropped her hands to her lap and folded the paper, quickly stuffing it into the bottom of her purse sitting on the stool beside her. She had time to do that, but no time to compose herself afterward, and was flushed and breathless when he reached her.

His smile faded. "Are you not well? You look feverish."

She gave a quick shake of her head. "I'm fine. I was just talking to Vince."

"And he had bad news?"

That depended on what one considered bad, she mused, now didn't it? "Only on the food front. His cook is still out. We're stuck with chips and beer."

"Hmm. I do not believe that chips and beer will hold me."

She forced a laugh. "I was thinking the same thing. We can try someplace else. Or we can see if Molly has any leftovers."

"Or I could cook for us both." When she didn't immediately respond, he added, "Of course I have only a tiny galley on my boat, and an even smaller kitchen in my quarters."

He smiled at her, and she swore her heart stopped beating. "I take that to mean you want to use mine?"

"I would need to stop at the market first. Unless you have chicken and pineapple and chilies?"

Her stomach began to rumble. "I don't have anything but tomato soup, Cheetos, and diet soda. Would you like me to come with you? To shop? I need to pick up coffee anyway. For some strange reason, I've almost run through the pound I just bought."

"You have discovered my only true vice." He reached up and tugged loose curls away from her face. "Or it was my only vice until meeting you."

Why? Why did he have to make her feel like he was who she'd been looking for all of her life? "Are you saying that I'm bad for you?"

"Only because you are like an addiction, and I am beginning to wonder if I will ever get enough."

Chapter 16

The late trip to the market on Wednesday night had been successful in more ways than Ezra finding workable—if not first choice—ingredients for dinner. It had given him the chance to be seen publicly in Alexa's company, and in a place other than Vince Daugherty's bar.

Even better was the fact that it had been Alexa's idea and at her request. When she'd made the suggestion, he had immediately started thinking about how best to capitalize on the opportunity—whether to interact with her as a friend, as her lover, or simply play the role he'd taken on of the Maples's handyman.

He need not have wasted his time. Being out in the open with Alexa was as naturally comfortable as were their hours spent in private. She'd treated him as someone she was proud to have the few friends she ran into meet.

They had laughed, flirted, groaned at the cost of tomatoes. They had argued over buying a whole chicken or only the breast. And yes, they had received the disapproving looks he had expected, but they had received more. Looks that were kindly curious, if hesitantly accepting.

It had been so long since anyone had looked to him for more than a clean killshot, that he had allowed himself to briefly indulge in the fantasy that he and Alexa were real. That this was the town where they lived, the market where they shopped. That these were their friends. It was a dangerous mental and emotional risk, but he took it. He wasn't so far gone that he couldn't still separate fiction from fact.

The few hateful whispers he had heard were hollow. He didn't need to win over the entire town. He had been seen with Alexa, and word would get out. He was a member of the community now, a handyman working for a family whose many businesses contributed largely to the local economy. And he was dating a schoolteacher adored by all.

The charade would cost him nothing while gaining him much in the way of good will. Once he was gone, it would be Alexa left to pick up the pieces. Alexa forced to deal with the I-told-you-so's and what-was-she-thinking's. The possibility existed that she might be forced to forfeit her job, losing the respect of the parents whose children she taught, and the favor of her peers.

He had put her into an untenable position as required by his own, just as he'd done to others so many times in the past. Except this time wasn't like the others at all, because this time a choking burden of regret weighed him down.

He had tried to shake it off all through dinner that night. She had sat at the bar sipping wine while he baked a dish of spicy chicken smothered in a sauce of tropical fruit. They had laughed about having to use canned pineapple and orange juice concentrate instead of the real thing, about the impossibility of finding fresh mangoes or papayas in such a small town.

In the end, the food had been wonderful, her company sublime, the night's mission accomplished, his conscience clear. Keeping it so was the only way he could operate, the only way to guarantee he would survive. And Alexa was strong. She would survive, too. Of that he had no question.

During the days that followed, Ezra found himself too busy

to do anything beyond the odd jobs Molly Maples had hired him to do. He realized his work at the Maples Inn was a vital part of his cover, but his chores had kept him from getting down to his boat until late Friday night.

The delay wasn't truly an issue. Settling into the community mattered more than checking on what chatter the bugs he had installed had picked up. He didn't expect to hear anything more interesting than gossip about his affair with Alexa, but he'd been playing this game long enough to prefer being safe to being sorry.

Tonight his most pressing errand was to act on any communication received from Spectra IT in response to the message left Monday. He still had not been able to determine the identity of the guest traveling with Davis Brown. He hoped to find the answer tonight; the pair would be here in less than four days.

Securing the cabin door behind him and dousing any lights visible from outside, he pulled down the fold-up seat facing the navigation station—and the computer console hidden behind a small panel on the center shelf. Once in place, he tugged his headphones on and flipped the power switch, the one that activated the satellite antenna, and the one set to queue up the digital recordings.

He had positioned several voice-activated listening devices throughout the week. One in his quarters, one in the Gin & Rummy, one in the maintenance shed behind the Maples Inn, one in the inn itself, one outside the police chief's office, one at the school, and one at Alexa's cabin—each maintained by his boat's cutting edge surveillance system.

Comfort Bay was small, his circle of involvement even smaller. Those locations were the ones most likely to capture conversations relevant to his presence and community standing—especially now that Alexa had been well established as his second pair of eyes and ears in the town.

Before settling in to scan the recordings using keyword triggers to filter the noise, he logged into Spectra's secure contact server. Curiously, he found nothing there but an index acknowledging his call. He shouldn't have been surprised to have received so little. He rarely received more.

He operated independently, willingly involving himself in the syndicate's criminal activities, and doing so without sanction or the auspices of any nation's government. The annihilation of Spectra IT was his endgame; he was prepared to pay any price for the things he had done as long as the syndicate came crashing down.

He had thought to crumble the organization from within, take it apart one brick at a time. He had allowed one of Spectra's henchmen, Benny Rivers, to make contact with the Smithson Group—Hank Smithson's team of rogue undercover operatives—instead of taking him out as ordered, thereby gaining SG-5's limited trust.

He had assassinated Oliver Shore, who brokered many of Spectra's Sierra Leone diamond deals. He had blasted from the face of the earth a compound in Mexico housing a major smuggling and prostitution ring. He had released two interlopers who had stumbled onto the bunker in New Mexico housing Spectra's headquarters for western U.S. operations.

And though he had documents in hand capable of destroying Cameron Gates personally, all of Ezra's efforts had barely shaken the workings of the organization, leaving him no choice but to topple it from above. First to go would be Warren Aceveda. Then, finally, Cameron Gates.

Cocked back in his chair, his feet propped on the saloon's padded bench, Ezra was so lost in thought that he nearly missed the current recording's reference to the Naval Academy. When it hit him, he sat forward with a jolt, his feet slamming to the floor as he reached out and hit reverse, backing up several minutes worth of the track before starting it again.

He noted the time, date stamp, and identifying markers on the playback screen, realizing he was listening to Alexa and

Vince in the Gin & Rummy on Wednesday night. She'd pur-posefully arrived before he had in order to talk to Vince. And it was Vince that Ezra had heard speaking.

"I got this from a guy at the Portland Bureau who's got a military contact. Your boy went to the Naval Academy. Twenty years back. Don't know yet what he's been up to since, or how he got from the Caribbean to Annapolis, but he started out on the right foot."

Ezra's military records weren't sealed. Though he had made sure no one would have reason, anyone with the right contacts could discover the truth of those eight years. The fifteen years since, and especially the last five, were the ones he had taken steps to keep under wraps.

But the bigger concern was why Vince was digging. And it took less than a minute for Ezra to find out.

"I'm floored. This is the last thing I thought you'd find."

"Yeah, but I can see it."

"How? He's a schoolteacher from an island in the Caribbean. That doesn't jive at all with this."

"Just because he teaches school now doesn't mean that's what he's always done. Or maybe he doesn't teach at all."

"So why would he say that he does?"

"Because he doesn't want you to know how he really makes his liv-ing."

Alexa. Ezra's military service was the last thing she thought Vince would find. Meaning . . . she had the former detective looking. Why?

Again Ezra listened to the conversation. Vince seemed mat-ter of fact, relating what he'd found, serving up suppositions based on the evidence. All straightforward. Nothing personal.

Alexa was the one who was emotional, the one asking ques-tions he could tell she didn't want answered. He heard shock, disbelief, and denial—and ignored even more. But none of those came close to the fury boiling red and unchecked be-hind his eyes.

It was an irrational response. He couldn't say where his

anger was directed—at himself for a carelessness he couldn't remember, or at Alexa for being there to pick up whatever clues he had dropped.

He thought back over the past week but was unable to pinpoint any particular moment, any possible slip, any place where he had not been true to character. He was not surprised when he was unable to think of one. Living the life he lived required he not make mistakes.

And that left him only one conclusion to draw. Alexa's investigation had less to do with the success of his immersion in his role than with her perception of the part he was playing. For some reason, she hadn't bought into his story. He thought back to their first meeting and how she had questioned his physical appearance then.

He thought, too, how later she had wondered about his feelings in keeping no company but his own. She had seemed uneasy when inviting him to join her and Rachel Fine for dinner, but nothing in her response had triggered a warning that he felt compelled to heed. And her display of nerves when he'd visited her at school he had chalked up to the previous night's unexpected intimacy.

The question then was what had sent her delving into his past? And was whatever it was the same thing that had drawn them together the moment they'd met?

In order to do the things that he did, he had long ago ceased factoring the human component into his decisions. There was nothing human about the men he worked for or the deeds he perpetrated on their behalf. But that same reasoning was getting him nowhere in defining Alexa.

If she were to continue serving her purpose as his shield in Comfort Bay, he saw no option but to step outside of his usual—and proven—method of operation.

Instead of maintaining a connection that was purely physical, he would need to dig into her psyche in order to convince her that he was not a threat to anyone, that neither she nor her friends were in harm's way, that he had, indeed, served in the military and held dual citizenship, but that was information he suppressed for the same reason he did not wear oxford shirts and loafers.

Alexa taken care of, one other thing was certain. He needed to give Vince Daugherty something to think about besides digging into his past. Something to keep him busy for the next few days while Ezra conducted Spectra's business as well as his own with Davis Brown. He thought back to the compound in Mexico that he'd taken out with one blast.

It had been a glorious sight, all that power and fury wiping out an immeasurable amount of evil with one properly timed fuse. This time he wouldn't need to employ the same lethal force. He would use an opportunity that had already presented itself

The Gin & Rummy's defective lights.

Chapter 17

Alexa cut her SUV's headlights before coming to a complete stop, and did that in the Maples Inn parking lot rather than driving up the short road to Ezra's. She wasn't sure why she didn't want him to know she was there, or why she thought the element of surprise might work in her favor. He was hardly the type of man one surprised.

She didn't think her hesitance to park at his place was an issue of propriety or not wanting to be seen by anyone passing by. For one thing, no one had reason to pass by the small house that sat alone at the end of the road. For another, she really didn't care if she was seen. Besides, she'd been seen with him already and more than once.

The issue of propriety aside, she had to figure out what to do with the information Vince had shocked her with—which led her to wonder if she was intentionally keeping Ezra at a distance because of it. She hadn't seen him since then, since they'd shopped together as a couple, since they'd spent the evening after dinner cuddled up in her big leather chair in front of a crackling fire—one Ezra had built.

She hadn't gone out of her way to avoid him, but neither had she made an effort to look him up. And it was madness that she was even stressing about their separation when she'd only known him six days—even if they had been as intimate as two people could possibly be the very day that they'd met.

Obviously her subconscious had been telling her to take a break and step back, to give herself time to gain perspective on what they were doing and on the Naval Academy revelation, but until she'd parked and cut her engine, she'd convinced herself that not seeing Ezra had been a case of being too busy—when the truth was she'd been no busier the last two days than the previous four.

But there was another truth, too. One bothering her more than it should have. A big fat question that she didn't want to ask and wasn't sure she wanted to have answered. Why hadn't *he* come to see *her* since leaving her bed Thursday morning?

Not wanting to seem pathetically desperate even to herself, she had until now avoided putting the thoughts flitting through her mind into words, but as soon as she opened her door, they rushed in. Was he tired of her already? Had she been too clingy and driven him away? Did the sex just plain suck?

She tucked her keys into her jeans pocket and headed down the drive. It was late. She had stayed after school till six working on the pageant set and meeting with the parents on the costume committee. After that, she'd gone home, showered, changed, made a sandwich that she'd zipped into a plastic bag and refrigerated because, Naval Academy or not, it had been long enough. She had to see him again.

The spotlight on the outside corner of the house was on, but she could see none of the lamps inside burning. She knocked softly, and when she got no answer, she tried the door, honestly surprised to find it unlocked. She'd told him he had nothing to worry about from vandals, but he still seemed the type to take precautions—unless she had it all wrong and he didn't have anything to hide.

But he did. The paper she had wrapped in plastic and stored in her freezer was proof.

She stepped into the darkened front room and heard the

shower running in the back. She headed that way but stopped on the near side of the bedroom and called, "Ezra?" Surprising him was one thing. Walking in on him while he was wet and naked in the shower was another. "Ezra?"

"Alexa?"

"It's me."

"You can come closer. I do not bite."

He did bite, but that was neither here nor there. "I'll wait in here," she said, turning back into the main room and hearing the water shut off.

He opened the door to the bathroom and walked out, switching on the bedroom's overhead light. "You do not have to wait anywhere, and I would like it very much not to have to raise my voice to be heard through the house."

The house was small enough that they didn't have to raise their voices much at all, but she wanted to see him, he wanted to see her; why argue? She walked farther into the bedroom, and since the room had no chairs, sat on the foot of the bed and watched him dry off.

He wore nothing but a towel wrapped around his hips, and used another which he'd draped over his head to squeeze the water from his hair. He had both arms lifted, his chest exposed, and before she could stop herself she found herself prying. "That scar. On your chest. How did you get it?"

His arms still raised, he tucked his chin to his chest and looked down, finally running his index finger from the point where the jagged slash began in his armpit to where it bisected the center of his chest. "That was a machete, I hate to say. And a very innocent accident."

Like the rest of his body, there was nothing about that scar that brought the word innocent to mind. She thought back to the first time she'd seen him, how she'd pegged him not as a schoolteacher but a mercenary. She stood by that assessment even now, especially knowing what she did about his military training. "What sort of accident?"

He swiped the towel under one arm then the other. "It happened during a building project in which my students were involved. One of the boys was swinging the blade to cut a wide swath in an exceptionally thick growth of kudzu. He stepped around the corner of the small house just as I stepped out of the door. It could have been much worse."

And it could be a lie. He had told her before that the scar was nothing, that it belonged to another life, that he didn't wish to remember or talk about it, yet his story of an accident contradicted the impression he had given her that the injury was one surrounded in pain.

He was so smooth, so casual; if he was lying, he was doing it well. She swallowed uncomfortably, hating that she thought of deception before even considering that he was telling the truth. But knowing things about him now that she hadn't known before . . . She couldn't help thinking there were many levels of reality when it came to Ezra Moore.

She cocked her head to the side and briefly held his gaze before studying the jagged lightning bolt scarring the side of his face. She nodded, indicating his cheek, and asked, "What about that one?"

This time he wasn't so quick to answer. He frowned instead, considering her the same way he might consider any necessary evil, and the tension around them began to simmer like a cauldron of poison. "Why are you asking me about my scars, Alexa? Are you wanting to know more about my past? Do you think my scars will tell you the whole story?"

"Of course not." Not when she could only see two of the physical ones, and she knew how deep internal scars could damage. "It's just seeing you naked—"

"You've seen me naked before."

"I've seen . . . parts of you," she said, her chest tightening on the words. "Most of the time we've been naked together in the dark."

"Then you haven't seen this scar, have you?" he asked, whipping the towel from around his hips and turning.

Alexa sucked in a hissing breath at the three-pronged wound that resembled a pitchfork turned on its side. One slash cut into the muscle above his right buttock, while the other two stood out like welts on the cheek itself.

She rubbed her thumbs over the pads of her fingers, trying to remember the feel of that jagged ridge. Surely she'd touched him there? When urging him deeper into her body? But she shook her head, because it wasn't familiar at all. And then she cringed, realizing she'd caused him to expose a part of himself he wasn't ready to reveal.

"I'm sorry." She held her knees pressed together tightly and twisted her hands in her lap. "I'm sorry I asked. And I'm sorry for whatever has happened to you. I just . . ."

"You just what?" he prompted, his tone harsh, before walking away to jerk open a bureau drawer and pull on a clean pair of boxers.

"I just want to know more about you." She was trying to keep this simple, innocent, a bit breezy. She did not want to give him reason to wonder how far she would go to get the information she wanted.

"Do I pry into your life?" He snagged the towels from where he'd dropped them and spread both out to dry on the shower curtain rod. "Asking about your divorce or other things that you don't wish to tell me?"

He hadn't asked her directly, no. But he had sensed a dissatisfaction she had never admitted to anyone and pointed it out only moments after they'd met. Still, her curiosity wasn't about his personal relationships or any discontent he had with his living conditions. It was about getting to the center of what she feared was a tangled web of deceit.

She reached into her pocket for her keys. "I won't ask again. And I apologize for hitting what is obviously a sore subject. Again."

He stared at her from the bathroom doorway, his forearms braced on either side of the jamb, one ankle crossed over the other. He was clean and barefoot, wearing only his underwear, his skin a gorgeous chocolate brown. Yet the circles beneath his eyes appeared dark purple and deep.

She didn't know if he was tired from the week's worth of work and lack of sleep, or if he was worn out by the direction of this conversation and the memories it brought to mind. Even if he had been slashed accidentally by a hard-working student, it couldn't be something he enjoyed talking about.

But then she wondered if it was keeping secrets that was wearing him down. If whatever had brought him to Comfort Bay under the guise of a handyman was eating away at his calm and collected exterior. She thought again of Vince's comment that Ezra might not be a schoolteacher at all, and that he might not want Alexa—or anyone—to know what he did.

Why? *Why, why, why?* If he were a government operative, she would never expect him to reveal secrets or out himself. But that didn't make it any easier to deal with the unknown. Not when she didn't even have a clue as to what side of the law he was on. And not when her best friend remained at the center of Ezra's game.

"Alexa, please, I do not want you to apologize. What I want is for you to understand that there are things I am unable to tell you."

"I know that. I do." She threaded her keys through her fingers, squeezing the sharp edges as she thought. She didn't want to bring Brett into the mix, but her treatment at the hands of her ex made a strong case for her aversion to being left in the dark. "I'm just not real big on secrets."

Ezra hung his head as if centering his thoughts, then pushed off the door and came toward her, his steps silent, the motion of his body like that of a panther, graceful and determined and defined. "I will not blame you if this changes things. And I do not want to put you in an uncomfortable position. You deserve better than that."

She couldn't help but be moved by his consideration, then realized that in the scheme of their involvement, her questions were not much more invasive than what he'd just said. She raised an inquiring brow. "Are you sure you know me well enough to know what I deserve?"

"You told me before that you were not looking for true romance," he said, leaning over her, his fists pushing into the mattress on either side of her hips. His smile, when he finally let go, took her apart. "Since that is the case, I believe I know exactly what you deserve."

Chapter 18

He didn't want to make love to her. He was still seething over his discovery of her investigation, and still wired from the last hour spent at the Gin & Rummy. He had hoped the shower's hot water would pummel the anger from his head as well as from his muscles, which had tightened like fists. It hadn't worked. He had been standing under the stinging spray for thirty minutes when he heard her call his name.

He knew he had not imagined hearing her the first time she spoke, but had waited for her to speak again in order to identify the source of the jolt that had charged through his heart—whether it was the surprise, or Alexa herself. When it happened the second time, he had his answer, but he did not have an understanding of why she caused such a reaction, or of why the response she elicited diluted much of his ire.

If he cared for her emotionally, if they were involved in a romantic way, the distraction of Alexa would be believable. But they were not, and it was not, yet here he was leaning over her, enjoying the rush of blood through his body and the swelling sensation of his cock.

"Tell me something, Alexa. Do I know you well enough for what we have?" He nuzzled his cheek to hers, spoke close to her ear. "Is there something you would like that I have not given you?"

She shook her head, wisps of her curls tickling his cheek. Her hands came up to touch his chest. "You have given me everything. I was afraid I had asked for too much."

"Why would you think that?"

"I didn't see you yesterday."

He chuckled. She was not supposed to make him feel better. He was not supposed to lose the hardened hold he had that guaranteed his survival. Laughing with her, feeling with her, feeling about her . . . This was his time to learn who she was and dig in, not give up whatever weaknesses he had.

He pulled back far enough to look into her eyes. And he did not lie. "You didn't see me because I was in the attic most of the day working on the wiring."

She pushed her hair out of her face, glanced away with a short soft grin. "I told myself you were busy. And that I was worrying for nothing."

"It is not nothing if it causes you to worry." He motioned for her to scoot from the edge of the bed to the center, then crawled up over her and forced her onto her elbows. "I was going to come to your house last night, but it was late . . ."

"You should have." She leaned to one side, wrapped one arm around his shoulders, then wrapped him in both and pulled him down onto the mattress beside her. "I wouldn't mind if it was late, or mind to have you wake me."

"I had no one to wake me," he said, draping his thigh over hers while admitting a weakness he hoped made him more human. "I fell asleep in the recliner without even changing my clothes."

She moved one arm, brought her hand close, brushed the pad of her thumb across his brow in a soothing motion he enjoyed more than was wise. "I don't know what I'm doing here. I should go and let you rest."

He shook his head. "I closed my eyes while I showered."

She gave him a crooked grin. "If that's your idea of rest, no wonder you fell asleep in the chair."

She continued to stroke his brow, and then along his hairline from his temple to his ear. He let her, and he enjoyed it, when he should have done neither, and distracted himself by going to work on the buttons of her blouse, baring her bra and her skin to his gaze.

Her blouse was white with black pinstripes to match her pants, and her bra was another with sheer mesh cups. This one was nearly the color of her skin, and her nipples brought to mind black cherries, making him hungry, making him hard. He opened her blouse fully, pushing the two parts down at her sides before splaying his palm the width of her stomach above the waist of her pants.

"You are wearing too many clothes," he told her, well aware of how easily he'd made her come previously when she was fully dressed.

She shivered. "I wouldn't be wearing anything, except you've got me pinned to the bed, and that makes it hard to maneuver."

He slid his leg higher, pressed his knee to the V between her thighs, rubbing her there until her eyes rolled back and closed. "Then maybe *I* should finish undressing you."

"I vote yes."

Laughing softly, he moved his hand to her waistband and freed the button. Then he lowered her zipper. Her panties were the same transparent mesh as her bra, and her dark bush of hair tempted him to touch the flesh beneath.

"Lift your hips," he told her, and she did. He worked the piece of clothing down her legs. She toed off the loafers she wore then wiggled out of her blouse. That left her wearing nothing but knee-high silk stockings the same color and transparency as her lingerie.

He closed his eyes for several long seconds because he felt himself falling into a place he didn't want to be, a place that meant more than the moment, a place he had no business thinking about. When he looked up again, centered, controlled, it was to find Alexa staring at him, her own eyes mirroring the emotion he'd banished, and he couldn't deal with what he saw, not tonight, not with her.

Growling, he rolled over her, climbed above her, captured her legs between his and slid down her body, burying his face between her breasts, breathing deeply of her scent before he sucked her nipple into his mouth. She whimpered, squirmed, pushed up against him. He grabbed her wrists and used one hand to pin both of hers over her head.

He held her completely captive and rubbed his erection on her mound, his hips grinding into hers as he lifted one breast from the cup of her bra to play, pinching her nipple, rolling it with his tongue, teasing the areola and the surrounding skin which was soft, the plump flesh.

Her breasts were gorgeous. He wanted to press them together and slide his slick cock between them, but later. They had time. They had all night. He needed her with him, all night, tonight. And so he used his lips and teeth and tongue to arouse her, used his fingers to pinch and pull, to tease, his palm to knead her and shape her for his mouth.

Moaning softly, she arched her back, and he slipped his hand around to release the bra's catch, slipping the garment lower, turning her toward him and massaging the muscles along her spine. After a moment, his hand slipped lower still, beneath the elastic of her panties, where he cupped the swell of her bottom and eased his fingers between her cheeks.

He toyed with her there, playing with the rim of her ass, and playing deeper, finding her sex wet and swollen, and spreading her moisture to ease the way of his hand. When she tugged to free her leg, he released her, and she hooked her knee over his, opening herself further to his questing hand.

He took full advantage, pushing his thumb into her once before pushing it through her folds to rub and flick and fondle her clit. She rocked her hips, moving side to side, moving up and down, masturbating against his thumb and his fingers when he slid them inside to stroke her.

And so he masturbated against her, sliding and grinding his cock over her thigh, growing harder, his sac gripping his balls. But it wasn't enough, this playing, this pleasuring. He knew how to take his time, how not to rush and enjoy every moment spent in bed. Right now, however, all he wanted was to fill her, to sink into her, to use the base of his cock against her clit to get her off.

He released her hands and got to his knees, shedding his boxers while she watched, while she rid herself of her remaining clothes, while she smiled, her eyes warm and dreamy and welcoming. He wanted her to want his body, that was all. He didn't have time to deal with any expectations, or the involvement of her heart and mind.

This was sex. Convenient sex that relieved his physical needs. Convenient sex that gave credence to his relationship with Alexa and his reasons for being here in this town. His mind was protected. His heart was not engaged. He did not need to remind himself of what was so obviously clear.

He bowed his head, avoiding her gaze as he climbed over her, as he lowered his body on top of hers, feet to feet, chest to chest, his weight on his elbows where he braced them on either side of her head.

"Is this what you want?" he whispered into her ear. "Do you want to feel me like this?"

She curled her fingers into the blanket at her hips. "Anything. Everything. I want to feel everything."

What she didn't want was to lie still, to wait, to savor, to anticipate. He knew that she wanted none of that because she couldn't stop moving. She squirmed beneath him, parted her legs and drew up her knees, holding them close to her chest.

He started to tease her about her impatience but found himself short on humor. Neither would ambivalence come, no matter how hard he searched to find it. In the end, all he could do was feel.

He reached between their bodies, ringed his fingers around the head of his cock and pierced her, pushing in, pushing deep, sinking his body into hers and stepping outside of his mind—or so he tried to do, to forget this was Alexa, to forget that she caused him to care.

When she groaned, he stopped, asked, "Am I hurting you?"

"No. God, no."

"If I were, would you tell me?"

Her eyes had been closed, but she opened them then, opened them and stared up, curious. "That's a very strange question to ask."

He pushed her hair from her face. "I want you to enjoy this as much as I do. I want you to be selfish. What I don't want is for you to give yourself to me simply because I want you."

"That sounds all well and good and very adult, but it doesn't quite work that way," she said, tightening her legs around his waist. "I can't separate the wanting from the wanting to give."

There should have been something for him to say. A contradiction for him to make. A denial. But there was nothing. Nothing. He could not respond with words. He could not smile, or even look away.

All he could do was move. His hands into her hair. His mouth over her breasts. His cock in and out of her cunt. He devoured her with a ruthless, reckless hunger, driving into her, thrusting as if unable to stop.

She held on tight, gripping his arms, her feet hooked over the backs of his thighs, and pushed up when he pushed down, matching the pace and the rhythm he set. The tingle and burn at the base of his spine quickly became too large to contain. Try as he might, he was unable to wait.

She came with him as if his semen were a trigger, and the ride they shared was fierce and brutal and stunning in its power. He shuddered and she followed. She gasped for air and he found himself unable to breathe. It was a completion rare in its intensity, and the aftershocks lingered.

Several minutes passed before either of them could move,

and then he did little more than pull free of her body and tuck her close to his side.

He remembered nothing more, coming awake hours later to hear her ask, "Do you hear that?"

"What?"

"Sirens. It sounds like the town's siren."

Chapter 19

One thing Alexa had found most appealing about Comfort Bay was the lack of crime. Chief Calendar and his two deputies were kept fairly busy writing traffic tickets on the coastal highway where travelers failed to reduce their speed at the edge of town. Once in awhile they had to deal with a domestic incident, or a drunk and disorderly.

But the town had no murders, armed robberies, assaults with deadly weapons, gang violence, or the muggings and home invasions that had driven her and Brett from L.A. And so far during the five years Alexa had lived here, the town had never seen a fire to rival the one now burning the Gin & Rummy to the ground while half the residents stood and watched, still wearing their nightgowns and pajamas beneath their coats, shocked awake by the siren as Alexa and Ezra had been.

The volunteer fire department was hard at work making sure the blaze didn't spread to the forest behind the bar or to the businesses across the street. Alexa stood clutching Ezra's arm while Molly stood at her side with her arms wrapped tightly around Emmy Rose. No one was saying a thing.

No one could. It was one of those situations where words were meaningless and only got in the way of the unfolding horror. Closer to the cordon of police cars and pickups, Rachel stood behind Vince, her arms wrapped around him, her face buried between his shoulder blades.

Vince faced forward, his stance radiating the anger he couldn't keep contained. He was wearing nothing but a T-shirt over his jeans, his arms crossed over his chest, his feet planted shoulder-width apart, his knees locked. It was as if he was braced against being bowled over, as if expecting another cruel blow.

Rachel's sobs didn't move him at all, but they broke Alexa's heart until she couldn't breathe, and when she did inhale, all she tasted was heat and soot and smoke. She wanted to go to her friend, but this wasn't the time. This mourning, though very public, was still a very private moment between the two, one Alexa had to respect.

But that didn't stop her from shuddering where she stood. Ezra pulled his arm from her grip and enfolded her in his embrace. He brought her close to his body, and she nuzzled her face into the dip of his armpit, wrapping her arms around his waist, lacing her fingers on his other side.

He was so solid, so strong, and having him to hold onto right now meant everything. All the worries she'd had earlier lost much of their threat, and she thought again that she was falling too hard and too fast because this couldn't be real when it was only expediency, when he was here as a shoulder for this moment and nothing more.

And then she felt even worse because she'd given little thought to Molly and Emmy Rose as the flannel-clad pair watched the flames devour the building that had been a constant in Comfort Bay for decades, watched as those same flames licked around the volunteers fighting the furious, disrespectful blaze, watched as tendrils of fire reached out to tease and torture Danny Maples.

Alexa straightened, turned to her friend. "How are you doing?"

Molly shook her head, glanced over. Her eyes were wide and wet and terrified. "He'll be fine. I know he'll be fine. He's trained for this. He knows what he's doing. But, God, I don't want to think about how old that building is. It's going to crumble. I don't want him to be inside."

The look on Molly's face . . . Alexa couldn't even look at Emmy Rose. "No one was inside. He won't have to go in. They're not trying to save it, just control it."

All Molly could do was give a brisk nod and press her daughter's head to her belly when Emmy Rose turned and grabbed on. "How do other wives deal with this? When their husbands do this for a living? Danny only volunteers . . ."

Alexa reached for Molly's shoulder and squeezed, cutting her off. "Most wives don't see their husbands at work. They hear about it later, if they hear about it at all. Not all of their men want to talk."

"Alexa is right," Ezra said, stepping closer and surprising Molly, her daughter, and Alexa, too. She wasn't aware he'd been listening. "I understand you wanting to be here, but doing something at home to prepare for her father's safe return might take away some of your daughter's fear."

At that, Emmy Rose lifted her head and searched out her mother's face. "What is everyone going to do for breakfast tomorrow?"

Molly frowned, shook her head, her focus taking a minute to catch up with her daughter's. "I don't think our guests will mind fruit and cereal tomorrow, sweetie, considering what's going on tonight."

"It's already tomorrow," Emmy Rose insisted. "And I wasn't talking about the guests."

"Sweetie, I'm sorry. I can't—"

"Mom!" Emmy Rose shoved backwards out of her mother's embrace. "Everyone eats breakfast on Saturday at the Gin & Rummy! Everyone! Chief Calendar and Dr. Walker and Cassie

O'Malley and Mrs. King." She stopped then, breathless, as if she couldn't think of another single name.

"You're right," Molly said, several long tense moments later, a new determination in her voice. "After tonight, we need to make sure everyone has a place to go and something hot to eat."

Emmy Rose nodded with huge enthusiasm, her pink parka hanging open over her Portland Trailblazers pajamas. "And Dad will be there and the other firemen, and all this work means they'll be starving!"

Ruffling her daughter's hair before pulling up the girl's hood, Molly glanced at Alexa then Ezra. "You're right. I need to stay busy. For both of our sakes. Thank you."

"Do you want help?" Alexa asked. "I can come help. I'm not doing anyone any good out here."

"Sure," Molly said. "Emmy Rose and I would love your help. Wouldn't we, sweetie?"

The girl nodded, holding tightly to her mother, her gaze sliding from Alexa to Ezra. "Thank you for fixing the light on the stairs. I'm not so scared anymore that it might really be a ghost."

"Emmy Rose?" Molly cupped her daughter's chin in her hand and lifted her face. "You didn't tell me you were scared. I thought you were having fun pretending we had a ghost."

The girl shrugged. "I wasn't really so scared, I guess. Dad said it was the wiring, but then I thought if it was the wiring he'd be able to fix it, and since he never did I wasn't so sure anymore."

Alexa met Molly's troubled gaze, wrapping an arm around her shoulder because here in the middle of the night, with the forest surrounding them and the sky above pitch black save for the shower of firefly sparks, and the only light that from the fire, holding her friend seemed the best thing to do.

But Ezra did more. He squatted in front of Emmy Rose and

put out one hand, waiting quietly, patiently, until she placed her fingers in his open palm. He closed his over hers, but only lightly, never threatening or firm.

"Your father is using his skills here tonight," he said, his voice low, musical, like wind chimes. "This week, I used my skills to repair your home's lighting. We each have our own unique strengths, and ways to contribute to those who are most in need of our help."

"Like the pink frog."

Ezra nodded. "Exactly like the pink frog."

Alexa caught Molly's gaze; the other woman mouthed, "Pink frog?" and Alexa gave a shrugging shake of her head.

"So what is the best thing for you to do?" he asked, rubbing his thumb over the back of Emmy Rose's hand, so small and white in his.

She stared down to where he held her as if it made it easier to think. "Help my mom make some food."

"I'm sure that would be very much appreciated by every-one here who has been working so hard." Ezra released the girl's hand and patted her shoulder before he got to his feet. "And I think your pink parka is very nice."

Emmy Rose giggled, then grabbed both of her mother's hands, spinning her and tugging her in the other direction. "Let's go, Mom! We have to make biscuits and muffins and get out a big ham."

Arms outstretched as her daughter pulled her, Molly stumbled briefly then leaned over and kissed Alexa's cheek, whispering, "She'll be out like a light before we measure our first cup of flour."

Alexa laughed, feeling strangely lighter. "I'll be there in a few."

Once the mother/daughter pair was out of earshot, cuddled up and matching footsteps as they hiked their way back to the Maples Inn with Molly's flashlight illuminating the way, Alexa hooked her arm through Ezra's again and snuggled close.

Her eyes followed the volunteer firemen dousing the blaze. "What was that about a pink frog?"

Ezra shrugged off her question. "It was a story I told the girl the afternoon I came to the school."

Well, that answered next to nothing. "I wondered what you two were discussing so intently. I didn't think you had come to paint just for fun."

"She is very concerned with her father dying."

What? Whoa! As the sucker punch pounded, Alexa pulled back, heart hammering, to look into his face. "What? Is that what she told you?"

He stared straight ahead, watching the fire. His eyes reflected the flames like ribbons on glass. His profile blended into the dark. "She has told me enough."

Strange. This was so very strange. And making no sense at all. And making Alexa angry. "I didn't know you were that close to Emmy Rose."

"It is not so much that we are close, but that I listen to the things she does not say when she speaks." He glanced down at Alexa then, his eyes less intensely focused. "She misses her father immensely, and she is too focused on death for a child as young as she is."

"I don't understand." She stepped away, releasing his arm and shaking her head. "I've never picked up on anything like that from her."

He arched a brow. "Do you talk with her about things other than her schoolwork?"

She couldn't believe they were having this conversation in the middle of the night while a Comfort Bay landmark burned to the ground. "Nothing as serious as that, no. At school, we work. And when I'm at Molly's, she hangs around like one of the girls. I've never done counseling with her."

"I am not blaming you. She is not your daughter."

"Wait a minute," she said, bristling. "That sounds like you're blaming Molly."

"I am blaming no one, Alexa. I am telling you what I have seen, what I have observed." A large section of the building's wall crashed inward, the sound ominous and deadly, and he looked away again, distracted again, his voice coming from far away instead of from where this conversation centered. "I am a bystander, nothing more."

"You're an awfully intuitive bystander." It was hard to believe he'd notice what neither she nor the girl's parents had seen when he'd known her less than a week.

She watched him blink, then watched him give a quick shake of his head and inhale, as if returning to the present from another time and place. It was a surreal thing to witness, and it left her wondering if this was possibly the same man who only hours ago had taken apart her body.

But then he turned to face her, squeezing her shoulders before sliding his hands down her arms until he held only her fingers, much like he'd held onto Emmy Rose. "I am who I am, Alexa. An impartial observer. Often those closest to the issue are blind. Please do not take what I've said as a slight against your friends, or as gospel. There's always the chance that I'm wrong."

She pressed her lips together, twisted her mouth, enjoying the soothing way he touched her. "I have a feeling that's very rarely the case."

Pulling her close to his side, he turned away from the fire and started them both walking back to the inn. "I am right more often than not. It serves my purpose to be so."

"And what is your purpose?" she asked, wrapping an arm around his waist, wondering what it took to have this man's confidence.

"Making certain that the work I undertake is done well."

She smiled to herself. "That's it? You don't have some supreme life-altering goal?"

He was silent for several minutes as they walked, rubbing his hand up and down her arm as if to warm her, or to warm himself. She couldn't be sure, and she wondered if he was even aware of doing it. He seemed lost again, distracted.

But just as quickly he shook it off, saying, "I believe there is something to be said for living day to day."

She didn't answer, but she couldn't have agreed more.

Chapter 20

It was mid-Saturday before the arson investigator could get to the site. Chief Calendar had called him in at the request of the volunteer department's head firefighter, Billy Mooney, who wasn't happy with the look of the wiring that had started the blaze. And it was Sunday before the insurance company's investigator made it to Comfort Bay.

Dozens of volunteers with pickups, trailers, shovels, and wheelbarrows had gathered both days to begin the cleanup, but had been put off by the red tape that couldn't be broken. Ezra had waited with them, part of the group though at a distance, listening to the conversations around him without letting on that he heard a thing.

"Arson, shit. I would've taken hundred to one odds that the fire was electrical."

"It was electrical. It just had a little help getting electrified."

"Does that mean Daugherty's insurance won't pay out?"

"Yep. He's gonna have to eat the whole thing."

"It'll pay if they decide he had nothing to do with it."

"How the hell are they supposed to decide that?"

"That's what investigators are trained to do."

"Criminal investigators, maybe. Not insurance or arson."

"Yeah, well, they'll be out next."

"Why would anyone want to burn down Vince's place?"

"Considering the bar was a fire waiting to happen, he should be glad. If it burned because he hadn't kept it up to code, he'd be shit outta luck."

"If they think he's the one who did the arson, he's shit outta luck anyway."

"Well, he didn't and he ain't. It'll all come out in the wash, and he'll be back in business."

The talk had varied little from one day to the next, leaving Ezra satisfied that he had done his job well—the very work ethic he had explained to Alexa.

Vince would have time for nothing but arguing with the multitude of investigators and clearing his name, meaning the fire had accomplished the first part of its purpose—taking him away from Alexa's investigation. With the site cleared for cleanup, the second part commenced now. The part where Ezra waved his community colors.

He had driven to the site today in the Maples's pickup, bringing with him two wheelbarrows and two shovels—all marked with the inn's logo. He had stationed himself toward what had been the rear of the building, scraping the edge of his shovel across the foundation before scooping up debris.

He didn't expect to find anything linking him to the scene, an expectation made almost nil by the investigators' fine-tooth combs. But as always, he was operating in better-safe-than-sorry mode. And though he was intently focused on his search, he was not so preoccupied that he did not see the burly fisherman walking toward him.

"Afternoon, fella." The man propped his shovel blade-down on the ground and crossed his wrists over the handle. "Name's Tommy Mooney. Brother Bobby's the fire chief here."

Ezra dumped the detritus from his shovel into his wheelbarrow and held out his hand. "Ezra Moore. A pleasure."

Tommy shook his hand then pointed up the road, nodding

toward the Maples Inn. "You're that new guy working for Danny Maples."

It was a statement, but Ezra knew Tommy meant it as a question. "I am, yes. Molly said she could spare me for the day as my help might be needed here."

Tommy bobbed his head, slowing the motion as he finally said, "Well, we appreciate you pitching in. It's not often we have visitors make themselves at home. Nice to see."

Visitors. It seemed Tommy wanted to be clear that Ezra was a temporary resident. He was, but found it interesting that the other man insisted on pointing it out—and doing so in front of the others.

"I doubt I will stay long beyond the first of the year. I had thought to sail down the coast in January and find another location to spend a few weeks." Ezra scooped up another pile of charred debris.

Tommy pulled his logo cap from his head, wiped his forearm over his brow even though Ezra had not seen him do enough work to break a sweat. "I'm figuring you'll have to be getting back to wherever it is you're from before too long."

Another questioning statement. Another reminder that he had no reason to settle in permanently. Ezra straightened and stretched, deciding defensiveness would get him nowhere, that acquiescence was the better part of valor. "I will be taking up my teaching duties again next year, yes."

"Teaching, huh?" Tommy scooped up a shovel full of trash, tossed it into the wheelbarrow. "I guess that's why you've been seeing so much of Ms. Counsel. Both of you being schoolteachers."

The hair on Ezra's nape began to bristle. "We do have that in common, and I do enjoy her company."

"From what I hear, you've been enjoying her company more than anyone else around here ever has," Tommy said with a laugh that was not the threat he thought it could be, but was of an attitude that fueled gossip. "Pretty strange with her living here alone and being divorced all this time."

Ezra filed away the nugget of information on Alexa. The tone of Tommy's voice he fought to ignore, as well as the implication that he had stepped in where he was not wanted. The town was small, available females few and far between.

That Ezra had arrived for a month's worth of employment and acquired one of the most desirable single women could not have gone over well with any bachelor seeking a mate. It had obviously not gone over well with Tommy Mooney.

Ezra would have been wise to consider the human component, the emotional component, the territorial markings of the Comfort Bay male, and lust. He had not, however, and was now forced to offer up a defense. "Perhaps our shared circumstance as outsiders brought us close quite quickly."

Tommy snorted. "Yeah, I'd say close."

"I am sorry." Ezra felt his breath turn to fire, felt the shovel turn to a weapon in his hand. "What was that?"

"You know. You've been pretty cozy with her." The other man slung another load of debris into the wheelbarrow. Half of it hit the side, sliding out and over and onto Ezra's feet. "Spending a lot of late hours at her place."

Her place was off the main road. It was not a place anyone drove by to notice who was there any hour of the day or night. And if someone had driven by, he and Alexa would have noticed. The only person Ezra had seen there was Vince . . .

He searched out the owner of the Gin & Rummy in the crowd, and found his anger rising to settle at the base of his skull. "It is my business where I spend my time. And it is that of whomever I am with."

"Sure. I'm just saying. Lots of folks around here were surprised to find her taking up with someone from outta town." Another scoop of trash barely made it into the wheelbarrow, and Tommy had trouble hiding a sneer.

Ezra watched as a front-end loader crawled up the road and

onto the scene, drowning out the sound of the distant conversations while making Ezra's with Tommy discreet. He hefted his shovel into one hand, wrapping his fingers around the wooden handle as he circled the wheelbarrow.

Tommy looked up at his approach, straightened, narrowed his eyes. Then he backed a step away. "I didn't intend any insult. No need to take it personal."

"When you are talking about my life, it is personal. It is personal to me. And in this case, it is also personal to Alexa."

"Lighten up, buddy. It was just a comment."

"No. It was not just a comment. You know that as well as I." Ezra moved closer to the other man, stopping only when Tommy Mooney would not possibly be able to misunderstand his meaning. "It is foolish of you to insult a man about whom you know nothing. You do not know how I might react. Neither do you know how I might retaliate. Fortunately for you, I have no need to do either."

Tommy cleared his throat. "Hey, like I said, no harm, no foul."

Ezra slammed the sharp edge of his shovel against the site's concrete foundation. The sound rang like that of a guillotine blade coming down, echoing shrilly above the rumble of the heavy equipment. "You are wrong. There is harm. There is harm to Alexa. She does not deserve such disrespect."

"I didn't mean the lady any disrespect. She's well thought of here. She does a good job with the kids she schools."

"Then I do not understand why you would concern yourself with her personal life."

Tommy shrugged. "It's like I said. She hasn't showed no interest in anyone around here. And then you come along. It's gonna raise some eyebrows, you know."

He did know. But he had not thought he would have to defend a woman he was using as a cover. He had misjudged, misstepped. He wasn't sure where or when. "Do not speak to me of Alexa again."

"Whatever, guy. I don't need your permission—"

Ezra stepped forward, eye to eye, the center of his chest fighting the crushing weight of an anvil. "If you say another word about her, you will need my permission to draw your next breath. I do not make threats lightly. But I will not discuss Alexa Counsel with you. Do you understand?"

Tommy did nothing but blink. So this time Ezra spoke in a voice the man would never forget. "Do you understand?"

"Yeah, yeah. Sure thing." He glanced off to where a larger group of men had stepped back to give the front-end loader access to the site. "I'm gonna go see if I can lend the boys a hand. Nice talking to you."

"It was my pleasure," Ezra said, turning his back on the other man and driving his shovel into the refuse, tossing load after load into the wheelbarrow, a machine in motion. He could not consider all the gained ground he had relinquished. He could not think of the suspicions he had raised.

All he could do was lash out against the heavy constriction, the pressing, choking sense of violation aching in his gut, making it impossible to draw a clean breath. It was a pain he didn't know or recognize, one he wanted to run from, to escape. He wanted to fight but flailed instead, and struggled to stay afloat. He thought of Alexa . . . Alexa.

And the anvil crashed all the way through.

Chapter 21

Alexa waited until Sunday night to talk to Molly, letting things settle, letting Dan get home safe, letting Emmy Rose enjoy what quiet time she could with her dad. It just seemed the thing to do before stirring up more worry for a friend who was elbows deep already.

It was pie night again, only this time instead of peeling pounds of apples, Alexa had been assigned to stir the ingredients from Molly's recipe into freshly cooked pumpkin and pour the cinnamon-and-clove-scented filling into the shells waiting to be baked.

With the inn's breakfast room having become the center of the town's morning rush, she had since moved on from the army of pies to muffins in bulk—and gained a new respect for all the work Molly did. But now it was time to broach the subject she'd been putting off since the fire.

"I know you have to be getting tired of hearing about my thing with Ezra—"

"Is *thing* the new word for relationship?" Molly asked, her hands buried up to her wrists in cinnamon roll dough.

Alexa measured flour into a bowl of dry ingredients that would be parceled out, mixed with the wet, and turned into fruit muffins—blueberry, orange cranberry, banana, and apple walnut. "It's not a relationship. If it were, I probably wouldn't feel so weird talking to you about it."

Molly's brow went up. "Are you going to regale me with more of your sexcapades? Please?"

Alexa smiled but refused to be distracted. "Not this time, no."

"Then what?"

A deep breath and . . . "After you left the fire the other night? Ezra told me that Emmy Rose is afraid that Danny is going to die."

"What?" The ball of dough hit the floured surface hard enough to send Molly's rolling pin rolling. She grabbed it before it skittered off the island to the floor. "Did she tell him that?"

Alexa turned her concentration to the teaspoon she held and avoided meeting her friend's gaze. "Not in so many words, no. I guess it was more a case of putting two and two together."

"What a crock," Molly said as she got back to kneading, and kneading. And kneading some more. "I spend time with her every day, and I've never put that particular two and two together. I can see her missing Danny. Hell, I miss Danny. But why in the world would she think he's going to die?"

"I don't know." And that was the honest truth. But Ezra's conviction was so very real, it was hard for Alexa not to give it credence.

"Oh, God." Molly's head popped up. "I just remembered something."

Alexa frowned. "What?"

"The lights. The ghost. I mean, it wasn't a ghost, but she always said that it was. I thought she was pretending, you know. But then she told Ezra"—Molly shook her head, blew a sigh heavy with disbelief into her feathery bangs, then pushed them out of her eyes with her wrist—"she told Ezra that she'd been scared."

At the fire. Alexa remembered.

"She never told me that she was scared. Why wouldn't she tell me? Why would she tell him? She hardly knows him. I'm her mother." Molly's questions were rhetorical, her declarations statements of the obvious. Her need to vent was equally so.

Alexa let her friend stew because nothing she could think of to say would make things better. She had quickly come to understand that knowing Ezra had to be experienced; it couldn't be put into words.

Molly hadn't had the time or any real reason to interact with him beyond their working relationship. But Emmy Rose and Alexa had both been witness to a side of him that had nothing to do with his handyman skills.

What they had learned was how intuitive he was, how perceptive, how easily he explained away fears and doubts, and how willing—and patient—he was when doing so, how easily he put a mind at ease.

But she wasn't sure telling all of that to Molly was such a good idea. At least not now when, knowing the other woman as well as she did, Alexa had no doubt doing so would add another level of stress to the load under which her friend already staggered.

So all she said was, "I hesitated mentioning it, but it seemed like something you should know. It could be that he's reading too much into what Emmy Rose said. I just . . . thought you should know."

"Oh, I'm *glad* you said something." Molly dropped the ball of dough into a ceramic bowl to rise, covering it with a dishcloth and setting it on a baker's rack away from foot traffic and drafts. "Maybe I've been cruising for a bruising sort of wakeup call. This was obviously it."

Alexa cocked her head to one side. *Cruising for a bruising sort of wakeup call?* "Molly, dearest. That was bad. Really, really bad," she teased, but her friend was having none of it.

"No, what's bad is that I have totally lost touch with my daughter. I feed her. I make sure she has clean clothes, clean sheets, a clean backpack. I make sure her homework is done, but I don't know who her friends are at school or anything anymore about what's happening with her. Oh, get this." Molly reached into the fridge for eggs, milk, and a colander of fresh blueberries.

Surprisingly, she got all of it to the island in one piece and one trip. "So, Danny gets in from the fire around six on Saturday morning, right? He showers, changes, and heads out for a scheduled charter. He did the same thing today." She stopped and made sure she had Alexa's full attention. "Emmy Rose hasn't seen him since the fire."

"You're kidding," Alexa said, gathering up empty eggshells for the garden's compost pail.

"Nope. She's seen every other Tom, Dick, and Bobby Mooney coming through for breakfast the past two days, but not her father. Not even for ten minutes. He comes in while she's sleeping, leaves before she gets up." Molly raised her voice above the whir of her mixer. "It's insane, Alexa. What are Danny and I doing with a child when neither of us has the time she needs given to her? Hell, I'm beginning to wonder why we even call what we have a marriage."

The mixer blades clattered against the sides of the ceramic bowl, causing Alexa to wonder if the noise was an echo of the doubts slamming around in Molly's mind. She wanted to say something clever, something supportive and pithy and smart. But who was she to offer advice? Her own relationship had not been the stuff of fairy tales.

The most she could give was encouragement. So she did. "You're just going through a rough patch. These things happen in every marriage."

"They've never happened in ours. Ever. God, Alexa. Do you realize how long Danny and I have known each other? We met in junior high when his family moved here from Seattle.

The day he checked into school, every girl old enough to know that boy cooties weren't so bad went on the make. But he chose me, and I chose him, and neither one of us ever looked back."

Molly stopped, laughed softly, her eyes misty with memories. "God, does anyone still say 'cooties'? Or 'on the make'? When did I get so old?"

Alexa offered up a sympathy groan. "You can't be old because that would make me old, and I am a spring chicken."

"You just said spring chicken. That makes you old," Molly said with a snort. "Is it too early for a drink?"

"Normally, I'd say no." Alexa glanced around the kitchen with a knowing eye. "But with as much work as you have left to do tonight requiring sharp objects and a hot oven? Yeah. It's too soon."

Molly waved her off. "Stop being so practical. If you're going to be practical at thirty-five, what excuse do I have at forty for living on the edge?"

"The edge?" Alexa tried not to laugh. Tried, and failed miserably. "Is that what you're doing here?"

"I know. Pathetic, isn't it?"

"No. God, no. Why would you say that?"

Molly lined up her muffin pans on the counter and began to grease and flour the cups. "Maybe because my idea of a good time is a hot bath and a glass of wine?"

"Sounds good to me," Alexa said, peeling bananas to mash.

"It sounds good to me, too, but it's all I know. What if there's something better out there, but I'm stuck here kneading bread dough and washing sheets," Molly said, her voice rising with what sounded like panic. "And let's not even talk about the candy, and forget keeping my bedroom skills honed. How will I ever know, huh? Answer me that."

Alexa circled the kitchen island, taking Molly by the shoulders and turning her around. "You are an amazing woman,

Molly Maples. Look at all you manage to do with running the businesses and being a mother and wife."

Molly cut off Alexa as if she hadn't said a thing. "Let me ask you something. As a professional. And this is not an insult to your abilities as a teacher."

Uh-oh. "Sure. What?" she asked, letting Molly go.

"Do you think Emmy Rose would get a better education someplace else? Someplace where everything isn't about fishing and tourists and the latest gossip? Someplace like Portland or Seattle or L.A.?"

"You think L.A. isn't about the latest gossip?"

"You know what I mean. A bigger city with more advantages, more opportunities. I don't want to see her end up married to someone like Tommy Mooney."

Alexa shook her head. "The man is such a lech."

"Tell me." Molly shuddered. "I felt like getting out the disinfectant the minute he left after breakfast. But seriously. What do you think?"

"About Emmy Rose growing up in Comfort Bay? Didn't you grow up in Comfort Bay?"

"Yeah. Forty years ago. In the stone age," Molly said with a harsh laugh. "And with two parents who were around to do more than make sure I was clean."

"You do more than make sure Emmy Rose is clean."

"Sure. I also clean the dishes, the bathrooms, the linens, the floors . . ." Molly sighed, shook off the thought, and moved on. "Thank goodness Rachel's coming in a couple of days this week to help out with all the extra guests."

"Good for you. And for her." Alexa returned to the bananas. "With Vince losing the Gin & Rummy, I know she's got to be worried."

"Hey, if it comes down to it, they can move in here for awhile. Maybe he and Ezra could work on converting that space in the attic to another room."

"I don't think so," Alexa said, and laughed. "That would require Vince using tools."

"You're right. What was I thinking. Well, maybe he could hold things in place and let Ezra swing the hammer." Molly finished doling out the blueberry batter and set the bowl in the sink. "Listen, Alexa. You're with Emmy Rose way more than I am every day. You will tell me if you see anything going on with her, right?"

"Of course I will. And not just because I'm your friend," she added, pointing one finger. "It's my job."

"God, I've got to talk to Danny," Molly said, moving from one subject to another the same way she did with her tasks. "I don't care if he has to cancel a charter, he's got to spend some quality time with his daughter."

"Maybe with Christmas break coming up?"

"He's promised, and he had better stick to it. Not only because I need her out from under my feet, but because he needs time with her. And she needs time with him. Especially if she has this fear of him dying. I can't imagine where she got that idea."

"Television? A book? Maybe someone at school said something to her?"

"She's been reading *Harry Potter and the Half-Blood Prince*. Again. That could be it. With the Dumbledore thing."

"Sure. That makes perfect sense," Alexa said, remembering how devastated the girl had been at the old wizard's unexpected demise.

"Well, all I can say is that I'm glad Emmy Rose is comfortable talking to Ezra. If he wasn't here, who knows if I would ever have found out what she's feeling? I almost can't help wondering if he was sent here for a reason, as New-Agey crystals and candles as that sounds."

Actually, it didn't sound that way at all. Alexa had been wondering much the same thing herself.

Chapter 22

Monday afternoon, Emmy Rose got off the school bus and climbed from the bottom of the drive to the top of the hill, where she headed for her back door. Usually she went inside right away for a snack, but today she had something else she wanted to do first.

She set her backpack on the steps so her mom would know she was home, and she kept on her parka so she wouldn't get in trouble, and then she skipped down to the maintenance shed. She didn't know where Ezra Moore was working, but she thought he might be there.

And then she knew he was because she heard someone chopping wood, and her dad had left early this morning before she'd even gotten out of bed. She stopped for just a second to snug her hood into place and tie it on tight, then fix her hair to cover her left eye and cheek.

She found Ezra behind the shed swinging an ax to split a log on the chopping block. She stood way back out of his way like her dad had taught her to do. She didn't want to get hit by pieces of splintered wood, or by the ax head if it came flying off the handle. If it hit her skull, it would slice through her brain, and she'd fall down in a pool of gory red blood and die.

"Ezra Moore!" she called, waving both arms overhead. "It's me, Emmy Rose."

He stooped to pick up the pieces of wood and toss them toward the pile waiting to be stacked in the shed. Then he turned and motioned her closer, watching her skip toward him, frowning when she got right up next to him. "What happened to your face, young Miss Maples?"

Ugh. Her hood had come off. She reached to pull it back up but then realized it didn't matter anymore. He'd already seen her black eye. "Do we have to talk about it?"

He looked down at her, and his dark eyes reminded her of a wise old owl's. "Isn't talking about it why you are here?"

She hung her head, nodded. He always knew everything. She reached up and touched the tender spot on her cheek. "Mrs. Counsel didn't see it, and I didn't have to go to the principal or the nurse, so my mom doesn't know."

His eyebrows lifted above his owl eyes. "I am surprised that none of your classmates thought to tell your teacher about your injury."

"No one said anything because Cassie O'Malley told them she'd give them the same thing if they did."

"I see," he said, then it sounded like he hummed. "So this was not an accidental injury."

She shook her head, frowned when she looked up at him. "Do you think I'll end up with a scar? Like you have?"

"It would take more than a child's fist to cause you to scar." He walked back to the chopping block and sat down. She followed. "Would you like to tell me what happened before telling your mother?"

She looked down at the ground because it was easier to look at his feet than his eyes. "Since Cassie's dad doesn't have a job anymore at the Gin & Rummy, some of the kids were telling her she was going to have to sell her iPod and PlayStation. She got all mad and started yelling that her dad would get some kind of . . . *com-pen-sa-tion*, yeah, compensation. Anyway, her dad would get money from the insurance for losing his job."

"It is possible, though I am not certain if that is the case. But you still have not told me why she hit you."

"Oh, I told her that Mr. Vince should've hired you to come fix the wiring like you fixed ours, and she said that if her dad couldn't fix it, no one else could, and I said you could, and she said no you couldn't, and I said yes you could, and she said no you couldn't"—she looked up at him then—"and when I tried to say yes again, she hit me."

Ezra was frowning even though it looked like he was trying to smile. "I do not believe I have ever encountered a situation where a small child was forced to defend my honor."

"I'm not that small, and you weren't there to defend it, so I had to." Emmy Rose moved to the side of the chopping block and leaned against it at his side. "She doesn't know what she's talking about anyway. You could have fixed it, right? Like I told her?"

"There is a good chance that I would have been able to, yes. But that is neither here nor there."

"What does that mean, here nor there?" she asked, tilting her head to look up at him.

"It means that whether or not I might have been able to fix Vince Daugherty's wiring is not important. What is important is your face. You need to have the scratch tended to, and you need to put ice on the swelling to prevent further bruising."

"I'm going to have a real shiner, huh?"

"I believe you are, Miss Maples. And I do not believe you should wait any longer to tell your mother what happened."

She sighed. She knew he was right, but she didn't feel very happy about it. "I was hoping you could come with me to tell her about it."

"Do you not think she will listen to you?"

He must not have ever had a mom. "She'll see my face, and I won't be able to talk or tell her anything. Only to listen. About proper behavior and respecting others and stuff."

"Those are all good things to remember."

"I know." She kicked at the ground with the toe of her shoe and scuffed up a div, a *div-ot*. "And I don't mind all that much really, because when she's done talking and finishes with the sting-y medicine, I always get a treat and lots of hugs."

"I see." He used the toe of his boot to tamp down the dirt into the hole she'd made. "Do you often injure yourself so that you will get a lot of hugs?"

She shook her head. "I don't really do it on purpose, very much anyway, but I don't mind if it happens."

"What if you could find a way to get more hugs from your mother without getting hurt? Would that be something you would like?"

She nodded so hard she thought her head would fall off. But then she frowned because she didn't want him to think her mom was . . . *a-bu-sive.* "She hugs me a lot anyway. Especially at bedtime. And when I do things for her."

"What types of things?"

Emmy Rose shrugged. "Like bring her a flower I picked from the yard. Or load my breakfast dishes into the dishwasher before she tells me to."

"If you know that it pleases her for you to load your dishes without having to be asked, why do you wait for her to ask you?"

"I guess because then I know she needs my help."

"Do you not see all the work your mother does each day?"

"I do."

"Do you not realize that she always needs your help?"

"She probably does, huh?"

"I am quite sure that she does. I am also quite sure that by loading your dishes on your own, you are helping her in two ways."

She thought. And thought and thought and thought. "I can only think of one way."

"Which is?"

"Duh. If I load the dishes, she doesn't have to."

"Correct. But if you load them on your own, you are also saving her from having to ask."

"So that's the second way?" She hopped away from the chopping block and looked at him with a frown. "It doesn't seem like that would help at all."

"Let me ask you this," he said, crossing his arms over his chest. "What if you were on your father's boat and you had hooked a fish, and you needed him to grab it with a net after you had reeled it up to the boat? Would it not save you time and worry if you did not have to ask him to help you?"

"Of course!" She didn't think Ezra knew much about fishing. "If he was somewhere else and I had to wait for him, then the fish might slip off the hook and get away."

"Exactly. And though your mother is not fishing, her situation is similar. If she has to stop to ask you to load your dishes, then one of her other chores might not get her full attention and slip off her hook."

She frowned for a minute while she tried to figure out what he meant. "Is that like another fable with a moral?"

"It is more of an allegory or metaphor." He stood up from where he'd been sitting. "Now, do you think we should go show your mother your injury so she can take care of it?"

Al-le-gor-y. She was going to have to ask Mrs. Counsel what that meant. No, she was going to look it up herself so nothing would slip off Mrs. Counsel's hook.

And that gave Emmy Rose a really good idea. "Maybe I could take care of it myself and not interrupt her. That would be helping, right?"

Ezra laughed. "In this case, I believe the only one that would help would be you."

Chapter 23

On Monday night, Alexa had just finished packing up the last items from her kitchen's lower cupboards when a knock sounded on the door. She glanced at the clock on the microwave. Nine-fifteen. Ugh, how had it gotten so late? She'd been caught up thinking about her pie-and-muffin-baking conversation with Molly and lost all track of time.

It was Ezra, of course, so she called out, "Come in," instead of answering. She'd stayed at his place last night, forcing herself out of bed before dawn to get her act together for the day. She *so* could not wait for the holidays—all those guilt-free late nights with no alarm clock jarring her awake before she was ready . . .

Except Christmas break meant the new year was coming, and the new year meant that Ezra would be on his way, and she hadn't yet reconciled herself to dealing with that fact— even if she *had* gone into this affair knowing it was a short-term thing and that it would end with the holiday season.

No regrets, she told herself. No second thoughts or worries. No *what-ifs* or *should-haves-could-haves* or *if-I'd-only knowns*. Her eyes were wide open. She had only herself to blame if she ended up getting hurt. Living in the moment was a mantra she'd waited too long since her divorce to embrace. And then she laughed because none of that would change a thing. She would miss him. And that was that.

When the door shut behind him, she straightened from where she'd been closing up the top of a box of pots and pans, and watched him seek her out. His eyes went bright when he found her, and he smiled as he headed her way, each step bringing him closer, causing a frantic blip in her pulse and gooseflesh pebbling over her skin.

She no longer looked at his dark boots and fatigues, his short, wiry, corkscrew hair, the scar on his face, and thought *mercenary*. She thought *lover*. She thought *friend*. So what if she didn't know all there was to know about him? He didn't know all there was to know about her. The fact that the secrets he kept brought to mind questions she feared having answered . . . Did any of that matter in the scheme of what they had?

He was her Ezra. That was what she knew. His insight into human nature astonished her. And when he made love to her, the beauty of what they shared tore her apart. His touch caused her heart to ache, to beat, the breath that filled her lungs to burn with all that she felt. Dear God, what was she going to do once he was gone?

"Are you moving?" he asked, cutting into her disturbing musings with a frown.

She gave a brisk shake of her head, dislodging the thoughts that had her eyes growing damp. "No, remember? I'm going to refinish these cabinets during my time off from school. I figured I might as well pack up the things I rarely use now and save myself the time later."

"Ah, yes. I believe you mentioned that you were going to work through your vacation instead of taking the time for yourself."

She stared at him there where he stood with his hip propped against the edge of the counter, one ankle on top of the other, his arms crossed over his chest, drawing the fabric of his long-sleeved black T-shirt tight. She resisted the urge to stop what she was doing and step into his arms.

Instead she bent and slid the box across the floor and up against the wall, then stood to dust her hands and give him a similar look. "This from the man who's spending a month of his sabbatical doing maintenance work?"

"I am spending more than that."

"How so?" she asked, fighting to reclaim the breath that had whooshed out at his statement.

"Comfort Bay is not the first place I have stopped during my travels," he said, lifting his brow to remind her that they'd had this conversation before. "Neither will it be the last. I am only on sabbatical from teaching, not from work."

"Right. I knew that." She turned to double-check that she'd emptied the cupboard, hiding her disappointment and the slip in her façade.

"But you asked me anyway?" he asked, fighting a grin that caused his dimple to deepen.

Hands on her thighs, she pushed up from where she'd squatted, narrowing her gaze and glaring at him with a jesting sort of ire. "Yes, okay? I'll miss you. I jumped at thinking you were going to stay, but I'll get over it. There. Does that answer your question?"

He held her gaze for several moments, his smile slowly dissipating, the humor in his eyes fading away to be replaced by an emotion she found hard to make out.

If they were in a real relationship, a committed relationship, if they were truly a couple and not just temporarily enjoying the physical fruits of their affair, she might call what she was seeing the blossom of involvement. Or perhaps of deep affection, of caring rooted in seeds planted during intimacy.

But under these circumstances? When the only thing they had agreed upon was to have a good time while together? She couldn't call it that at all—even if that was exactly what his expression brought to mind. The heat in his eyes was more than a reminder of what they'd done in bed, though it brought that to mind as well.

And her thoughts especially drifted that direction when he pushed away from the counter and approached without any rush, moving toward her with a lazy regard, but with purpose, causing her heart to thunder, the rush of blood to fill her ears, to ring, and ring—

"Are you going to get that?"

"Huh? Oh." Her phone. Duh. She reached for the cell where she'd left it on the kitchen bar. "Hello?"

"Hey, Alexa. It's Vince."

Her heart lodged in a ball at the base of her throat. Not now, God, not now. "Oh, sweetie. How're you doing?"

"Not so hot. Fucking investigators," Vince said, biting off even more foul words.

"Is there something I can do? Do you need anything?" she asked, turning away from Ezra as if that would keep him from hearing her side of the conversation, too.

"Nah, I just thought I'd pass along some info I got from my buddy in Portland."

"Don't even worry about that," she said, curling the fingers of her free hand into her palm, too nervous to stand still. This was so not the time she wanted to be having this chat. "You've got enough going on."

Vince snorted. "My hands are tied here, Alexa. I can't move for all the red tape. At least this gets my mind off things."

She crossed one arm over her middle to hold herself together. "Okay, then. What's up?"

"Your boy's reference in San Torisco? This Gabriel Corteze? He's legit. Works for some big relief organization, Red Cross or Peace Corp or Greenpeace or some shit. Providing food and medicine, construction, stuff like that."

"I see," she said, a spark of excitement catching as yet more questions flared.

"Yeah, he vouched for the handyman. They go back aways or something."

"That's good then, yes?"

"Sure. I'd say so. Better than having your boy show up out of nowhere with no one knowing a thing."

She wanted to thank him. She didn't want to have to explain what that thanks was for should Ezra ask. So all she said was, "Okay, then. Keep me posted? And tell Rachel I'll call her tomorrow."

"Will do," Vince said.

Alexa hit the button to end the call, and before she could say anything Ezra asked, "That was Vince Daugherty?"

"Yeah." She stared at the wallpaper on the cell phone's screen. A picture of Rudolph with his big red nose glowing bright. "I feel so bad for him. For Rachel, too. Losing the bar was a huge blow for both of them. He has his police pension, but without the bar . . ." She sighed, shrugged. "I don't know how they'll make it."

"I saw Rachel Fine today at the Maples Inn."

Nodding, Alexa returned the phone to the bar then leaned back against the counter, working for a casual outward appearance while her insides roared. "She's going to be doing some work for Molly since there's been a rush of extra bookings lately for the holidays. It'll be good for Molly and Rachel both."

Ezra nodded toward the phone. "Is that what he called to tell you?"

Did she lie? Did she tell him the truth? Did she continue to hedge until he grew suspicious? "No, Molly told me about Rachel yesterday after we talked about Emmy Rose being afraid of her father dying."

She held her breath and waited for his response. What she'd told him was the truth, even if she hadn't answered his question. She wondered if he would realize that she hadn't, if he would wonder why, but he said nothing, only considered her curiously, patiently.

When he didn't press, she breathed a sigh of relief. "I'm sorry. For the interruption. Remind me what were we talking about?"

He didn't argue with the change of subject, but came near, stopping when he had blocked her between his body and the pantry door, not threatening, but still dangerous and dark. "You had admitted that you will miss me. And I had been thinking of asking you a question."

"What question?" Anything would be better than hearing the echo of Vince's voice in her ear; she didn't even have time to process his news and react. She supposed she should at least be elated that she wasn't sharing a criminal's bed—

"Why have you not dated since your divorce?"

Her head came up. She wasn't sure whether to laugh or to frown. That's what he wanted to ask her? About dating? "How do you know that I haven't?"

He crossed his arms, cocked his head to one side. "I learned that yesterday from a man named Tommy Mooney. He was not happy that you and I had become close."

Ugh, she mused, rolling her eyes. "Tommy Mooney is a moron."

"Has he tried to date you?"

"He's tried to date every woman between eighteen and eighty who has given him the time of day," she said, gesturing with both hands.

"Have you given him the time of day?" he asked, leaning against the counter beside her.

She turned to face him, one hand jammed at her hip, the other flat on the countertop. He smelled like the salty ocean breeze. "Why the sudden interest in my romantic past?"

"It is not so sudden," he said, his eyes giving away nothing while his comment turned everything she thought she knew upside down.

"Well, it seems sudden to me. Especially since we already made it clear that I'm not looking for true romance, and that you won't be hanging around." She breathed in, breathed out, trying to pinpoint when the dynamic of their relationship had shifted—and why in this direction.

But the only thing she knew she had to do was set the record straight about Tommy Mooney. "And, no. I have not given Tommy Mooney the time of day."

"Is he not your type?"

"Okay, now this is getting weird." She stepped over his feet and fled the kitchen for the main room and the fireplace, where the fire she'd built earlier was now burning low. She didn't know whether to stoke it or let it die down—much like this verbal exchange. "You've met the man. Why would you even ask me that?"

He walked up behind her then, sure of himself and his purpose, waiting until she raised her gaze from the fire to his face before speaking. His eyes were vivid, his curious expression lacking his usual objectivity, shimmering instead with an inner light defying description.

And his smile, when it came, was just as impossible to define. "Because I was wondering why you were with me."

She stopped herself from asking him, *Why wouldn't I be?*, because that wasn't any answer at all. And because she wasn't sure she was going to be able to find her voice or use it if she did. Her heart was thundering as wildly as a rainstorm battling the ocean's waves.

He wanted more than a simple platitude. What he wanted went deeper, reaching into all those things she'd dismissed earlier as not belonging to what they had. But reaching down and digging there meant opening up, risking the hurt that came with vulnerability.

She wasn't sure she could do that when he would never be a permanent part of her life, when he would, in fact, be gone in a matter of weeks. Self-preservation demanded she keep her emotions buried, that she give him an easier, bearable—if rather shallow—truth.

Chapter 24

She reached for the small box of matches on her mantel, lit the votives and pillars clustered there. "Maybe because you and Tommy Mooney are nothing alike?"

Ezra laughed, a deep, musical sound. "Of that, I am well aware. But that does not answer my question."

She didn't respond except to toss the used match into the fire and stare at the flickering flames. She couldn't give him a suitable reply without knowing what he wanted, why he wanted it, whether she'd been so busy worrying about who he was that she'd missed a change in their rules of involvement.

"Is it because I am a safer choice?"

Safe? He thought he was safe? She backed up, sat on the ottoman paired with her huge leather chair. "I wouldn't say safe, no. More interesting, yes. More intelligent, definitely. More fascinating—"

He laughed again, the sound infused with more lightness than she had ever heard, and she looked up, surprised. "What's so funny?"

"It seems as if I am being sold on my personality," he said, turning his back to the fire, his hands behind him, his fingers spread and seeking the heat. "Which I seem to remember is equivalent to a death knell."

Now this was interesting, this reference to his past and in a context that begged for questions. She scrambled to think of what to ask, but all she came up with was, "A few too many blind dates on the island?"

He looked at her and smiled, the expression seeming to be aimed inward rather than coming as a rejoinder to what she'd said. "I have not always been this old, Alexa. And I have not always lived on the island."

He said it so casually that she wanted to hit rewind and play the tape again, to hear him repeat the words, to make sure that she'd heard him correctly. Instead, she responded with a mild-mannered, "Oh?"

He nodded, came to sit beside her, taking her much colder hands in his, which were warm, and rubbing each of her fingers from the knuckle at the base to the nail. "I hold citizenship in both San Torisco and the U.S. I was born in Virginia, but was returned to San Torisco to be raised by my grandmother when my parents were killed in a boating accident."

"Oh, Ezra. I'm so sorry." She squeezed his hands where he held hers. "What a horrible loss."

"I never knew them," he said, lacing their fingers together and staring down. "So it was a loss, yes, but I did not suffer."

"How old were you?"

"Less than a year."

"And how old are you now?" she asked, because she'd always wondered.

"I am forty," he said, smiling at her nosiness, which had nothing to do with the topic at hand.

Five years older than she was, she mused briefly. She'd always thought of him as ageless. "You were lucky to have your grandmother."

"I was also lucky in that my father had served in the military," he went on, answering more of her unasked questions. "A friend of his took me under his wing and saw to my upbringing."

Alexa frowned. "But I thought your grandmother lived in San Torisco."

He nodded. "She was the one who raised me there, where I have lived most of my life. But I was able to obtain an extensive education in the States because of the intervention of my father's friend."

His explanation was so simple, and cleared up so much. "Do you still see him? This friend?"

"Our paths cross from time to time, yes."

"What an amazing link to your past."

He squeezed her hand. "I have been very fortunate, but this is another truth I do not share with my students, who are less so. Very few of them will have the opportunity to use their education. And no matter the efforts I make, I often wonder if I am doing them any good at all."

After that, he fell silent, and she remained the same, her gaze drifting between the fire and their hands on his knee. She rested her head on his shoulder, studied her inner wrist pressed to his, her skin a creamy porcelain shade, his the color of crushed cocoa beans. The contrast in the pigment was as distinct as were their beginnings.

She had been privileged, upper-class wealthy, a middle child with doting parents and opportunities too numerous to count. Yet here they both were, together in this small coastal town in the Pacific Northwest, Ezra searching for perspective while she sought . . . what? To define herself? Was that the reason she'd stayed in Comfort Bay rather than the loyalty she'd claimed?

She didn't know . . . what she thought, what she wanted, what she felt. Right now, she knew only confusion, and she didn't like it at all. His story should have settled rather than stirred up her doubts, eased her mind, not increased the pressure building at the base of her skull.

But there it was. The truth. She was still wary, itchy, uncertain, wondering about herself as much as about him, and she

shuddered beneath all of it, pulling in a deep breath she
hoped would bring her calm. It didn't work. She found herself
missing something, aching, fearing . . .

As if sensing her unrest, Ezra got to his feet, tugging her to
hers then circling her waist with his arms. She wrapped hers
around his neck and stared into his eyes, where she saw a keen
compassion and an equally violent need, and in that moment
everything else disappeared. He was the only thing that mattered, what he wanted, the ways she wanted him.

He led her to the bedroom, but she was the one who turned
down the bedcovers, turned on the small lamp on the night
table, then turned to watch him undress. He peeled off his
shirt, his muscles flexing, the motion of his body fluid and
powerful, his skin sleek in the lamplight's glow.

His boots were next. He bent to pull them off along with
his socks, then stood and unfastened his pants. He left on his
boxers, left the rumpled fatigues on top of the rest of his
clothes, and then sat on the edge of the bed and leaned back
on his elbows to wait.

It was strange, being here with him now and feeling so
many things she hadn't allowed herself to feel when they'd
been together in the past, things stirred up by what he'd told
her, by what she'd learned from Vince. Hope swirled at the
top of the list, keeping the rest of her disquiet at bay, making
it easier to kick off her loafers and strip.

She started with her pants, tugging her blouse from the
waistband, freeing the button, easing down the zipper, giving
her hips enough of a shake that the fabric slid to the floor. The
silk stockings she wore were a dark salmon pink, the same
color as her bra and panty set, and equally sheer.

Ezra's appreciation was evident, his cock swelling thickly in
his boxers as he took in the length of her legs, his gaze lingering where the shirttail hem of her blouse covered her crotch.
She unbuttoned the first button, then the second, undoing the
third before moving her hands to the tops of her thighs and
beneath the hem of her blouse.

She slid her palms up her hips, to her belly, skating over her panties with the briefest touch before moving higher and cupping her breasts, leaning forward to tease him with her cleavage then turning around, lifting the tail of her blouse over her ass, knowing that he could see everything through the translucent mesh.

She even went so far as to spread her legs, dipping her knees and swiveling her hips as she straightened, as she worked her way around to face him again, breathless and aching and wet. Her arousal was fierce and amazing, made even more so by the near feral hunger, the craving, the thirst shimmering like a wild thing in his eyes.

As she looked on, he shoved one hand beneath the waistband of his boxers, tugged at himself once, twice, then lifted his cock and balls free and started again. He circled his palm over the head of his cock, smearing the moisture he'd released, then ringed his thumb and forefinger beneath the ridge of his glans and widened his legs as he stroked.

Her arousal sizzled, flared, burst. She wanted him in her mouth, in her sex, and grew greedy, slipping her hand into her panties to toy with her clit, dipping lower and pushing into her pussy, squeezing, milking, fingering herself and growing hot, groaning, aching, wanting his cock, wanting his tongue, wanting to bend over, wanting him everywhere . . .

Her chest heaved. His chest heaved, too. His cock was huge, the shaft massive and veined, his abs so tight as he worked himself that she saw his muscles clench and wanted to kiss him there, to feel the weight of his balls on her tongue, to experience again his texture and taste, his heat—

"Stop," Ezra ordered, shocking her into doing just that, into pulling her hand from her panties as if she'd been naughty and caught.

"What's wrong?"

He shucked off his boxers and got to his knees in the center of the bed. "Come here."

She did, peeling off the rest of her clothes and leaving

everything where it fell, caring only about reaching him, lying beneath him, spreading her legs and taking him inside. But he had other plans. Once she was flat on her back, he crawled above her to straddle her chest, his weight on his knees, his balls heavy against her sternum, his cock hot where the tip nudged the base of her throat.

And then he braced his hands on the wall above the bed, and she knew without his having to ask what he wanted. She bunched up a pillow beneath her head and reached toward her night table, finding the lotion she kept there, and spreading it over both of her breasts, the skin between, and his cock.

Her feet planted flat on the bed, she raised her knees, then pressed her breasts together with her hands, creating a deep valley between them to cradle his erection. Above her, he smiled darkly and began to thrust, the head of his cock kissing her mouth with each stroke.

She licked him, caught the ridge of the head with her lips, swirled her tongue over the tight skin and teased the seam beneath, releasing him and watching as he stared down to where the head of his cock disappeared again and again into the tightly rounded O she made of her lips. The strain on his face showed his battle for control, a struggle it didn't take long for him to lose.

Groaning, he tumbled to his back and pulled her down on top. She straddled him, her hands on his shoulders, lifting her hips to take him in. His cock filled her, stretched her. Her clit tingled and throbbed, and she shivered, trembling even more when he pulled open her pussy, slicking her moisture through her inner folds and over his shaft.

And then he began to move, pumping into her and driving his cock deep. She raised her hips, lowered them, ground herself against him, shuddering, clenching, groaning, gouging him with her fingers as she started again, sliding high, coming down, again and again until he pulled himself free and made a twirling motion with one finger, scooting up to slouch against the headboard.

She turned to sit on her knees, her back to his front, and took him inside. He held her close, sliding one hand down to where their bodies were joined, forming a V with two fingers, squeezing them over her clit, playing her while she rode him, while his other hand slipped between the cheeks of her ass to toy with the opening there.

She couldn't take the slow sexy fun anymore, and moved away, settling onto her hands and knees. He rose up behind her, the thick head of his cock probing her, pushing inside, his thumbs playing with the tight ring of her ass, her breasts dragging over the bed with each pounding thrust.

She came then, shutting her eyes and shivering with the sensations that seized her. She surrendered her body to his, unable to feel anything beyond the electrical buzz zinging in her limbs, her breasts, deep between her legs where she contracted around his cock.

And then he increased his speed, his hips driving harder, his balls slapping against her, his fingers gouging her where he held onto her waist. He poured himself into her, releasing a guttural cry that rattled her completely—more so than had her own orgasm.

It was as if he had finally shaken an incredible choking hold, a pent-up pressure, a tightly wound tension that had bound him inside for too long. She wanted to cry with the beauty of deserving that much of his trust.

Instead, she fell in love.

Chapter 25

Ezra was changing the oil in the Maples Inn pickup when Davis Brown and his companion arrived Tuesday afternoon. He stayed beneath the truck as the oil drained, listened to the tires crunch over the shells and rocks in the drive, watched the luxury import roll to a stop.

The engine died. One door opened, then the next. The two men climbed from the car. Both wore dark wool dress pants and expensive leather shoes, but that was all he could see. Neither unloaded luggage, and he heard no conversation, only a set of keys jangling in a pocket with loose change.

The car doors slammed shut, boom-boom, and then the guests whose arrival he had been anticipating for over a week walked toward the inn and out of his range of sight. For several seconds he stared overhead, seeing nothing of the engine above him, seeing only the bitter end of an existence he had endured for too long, an existence that was not a life and had interfered with his having one. Instead he had done the bidding of the basest of men.

Last night he had given Alexa a small piece of his past, enough so that she would have less need to concern herself with what she had learned from Vince Daugherty. What he had not told her—and would never tell her—was how he had spent his time after the military, and especially the last eleven years. He would tell no one about the children he had allowed to be sold into slavery, the drugs he had made certain were delivered to the streets, the funding he had channeled into criminal cartels, the men and women he had killed . . .

The days spent with Alexa had provided him a pleasurable distraction as well as a community connection and cover, but their time had given him more as well. He had needed such an association to reinforce how fully he had lost touch with humanity, with goodness and compassion, with kindness. She had shown him so much, had given him so much, had made him ache to forget where he had been.

This morning, however, he had come awake with nothing on his mind but the day ahead. He had but a singular devotion—making contact with Davis Brown, arranging for delivery of the weapons, then seeing that the information on the transport out of Comfort Bay reached the proper channels.

The authorities would find an arsenal of assault rifles, RPGs, and ammunition, but also an intricate map leading them from the weapons to Spectra IT. He could have provided the same intel any number of times during his involvement with the syndicate, but he was working alone—a situation requiring he have a backup plan should his betrayal fail. The government dossier obtained earlier in the year gave him just that.

The classified documents detailed the illegal manipulation of a military contract for which Cameron Gates, Spectra's founder, had been a principal administrator before disappearing almost twenty years ago. With the dossier as security should his primary plan fail, Ezra finally had the perfect opportunity to deliver the Judas kiss that would topple both the organization and Cameron Gates. Whether or not he would have a life once all was said and done . . .

He shook off the thoughts and returned to the moment, replacing the oil filter and drain plug, then rolling out from beneath the truck. Just as he gained his feet, Alexa's SUV pulled in and parked next to Brown's import. He ignored her, concentrating on pouring clean oil into the crankcase. He had to keep his focus tight. He had no time or emotion to spend on her today, yet felt his body grow tight as she neared.

"What are you doing here?" he asked, checking the level of oil on the dipstick instead of looking up. She stopped far enough away from the truck to avoid the grime, but close enough that the breeze brought him her scent.

"I came to talk to Molly in my official role as her daughter's educator, mentor, and guide," she told him, chuckling softly at her own words.

He breathed deeply, clenching his gut against the sound of her laugh. "About what happened between Emmy Rose and Cassie O'Malley?"

"Molly told you?"

He shook his head, screwing the oil cap in place, disregarding all the things he had no time to feel. "The girl did."

"Hmm. I wonder if she told you what she told me," she said as if probing him, as if wanting him to tell her what it had felt like to learn of Emmy Rose's defense.

"You can find out from her mother." He disengaged the brace; the hood slammed shut. He could not think of the child defending him any more than he could think of having Alexa in his bed, in his life. "She confessed the same story to Molly."

Alexa sighed, turned toward the inn. "I called her during my conference period this morning, but had to leave a message with Rachel."

"Molly has been running errands most of the day."

"And she left you in charge?" she asked, teasing him, flirting with him, seeking a reaction.

All he did was wipe away a smear of oily dirt from the truck's grill, doing his job, vigilant. "I am only assisting Rachel Fine should she need me."

"Is Emmy Rose here?"

"I assume she is with her mother. The bus did not stop."

"Okay, well, I'll grab Molly later then, I guess."

He did not respond, only gathered up the dirty oil filter and plastic jug of used oil, carting them to the recycling tub at the back corner of the parking lot where they would be collected by the Mooney Brothers' Garage for disposal.

He then returned for the trash from the truck's front seat—the oil filter box, the foam coffee cups he had amassed over the last few days, and the wrinkled Maples Inn brochure he had marked up earlier in the day in preparation for Davis Brown's arrival. All of that he carried to the cedar-framed garbage can near the inn's back door.

He left the brochure in plain sight on top of the rest of the refuse. The coded message inside instructed his contact to meet him on his boat tomorrow at eleven. Brown and his man were posing as investors in the nearby Orca Point vacation development. As outsiders, it would not appear unusual for them to be scouting the area at night. And he would have no trouble getting to the docks unseen.

"Are you okay?" Alexa asked, interrupting his train of thought as she walked up the sidewalk to the inn. "You seem so distracted."

"I am fine. I just have a lot of work to accomplish today and tomorrow." He looked at her then, finally, unable to avoid her any longer without seeming bad-mannered. Unable to avoid her any longer simply because. He smiled gently, feeling it too close to his heart. "Forgive my distraction?"

"Sure." Her answering smile was hesitant, though true, as she stepped up to open the back door. "I'm going to check in with Rachel before I leave. I heard she'll be working at the library again tomorrow. I'm going to see if I can grab her for lunch since we missed our girls' night on Sunday."

He backed away, out of her reach, and glanced toward the luxury import in the parking lot before looking back, hating himself for what he was about to say, unable to hold in the words. "I should be able to come by later tonight. If you would like."

This time her smile wasn't hesitant at all, and rang with a truth that leveled him. "Yes. I would like. Very much."

Chapter 26

Wanting to recreate her and Rachel's normal Sunday night dinner—even though they would be eating on Wednesday at noon—Alexa racked her brain, trying to come up with a way to manage a fresh BLT with cheese fries. She had a toaster oven and a microwave in the faculty lounge to work with. That took care of the sandwich part. The bacon would be edible, if not quite as crunchy and greasy as that off Vince's grill.

She refused, however, to believe the claims of "as crispy as deep fried" printed on the bag of microwavable fries. She ended up cajoling the school cafeteria's manager, Patty Mooney, Bobby's wife, to do both the bacon and the potatoes while she made root beer floats, storing them in the lounge's freezer, and carrying an extra one to Patty when she ran back to the kitchen to pick up the food.

She and Rachel had only a forty-minute break each, hers coming while her class went to gym with Mrs. Kelly's third grade students, but sharing forty minutes of near normalcy was better than letting adversity win—especially since nothing would ever be normal for Vince or for Rachel again.

By the time Rachel made it to the lounge, Alexa had spread a picnic cloth over the table, set out their foil-covered food, and dived into her float. "I thought about sneaking you a beer, but decided it wasn't worth risking my job. I really don't want to go work as Tommy Mooney's office girl."

"I don't know," Rachel said, grinning as she settled into her chair, pulling the foil from the food with an appreciatively hungry groan. "You do a good job for Tommy—*job* being the operative word here—and who knows what sort of perks he'll toss your way." Rachel popped a fry into her mouth. "Vince is thinking of applying."

Alexa sputtered her drink, grabbing a napkin and mopping her chin. "Eww, eww, eww. Don't even go there."

"Hey, with all the crap we've got going on, kissing Tommy Mooney's ass, or any body part for that matter, might be worth having a steady paycheck coming in."

The sad part was, Alexa knew Rachel was only halfway kidding. "How are things going at the inn?"

Rachel dragged another fry through the melted cheese then reached for her sandwich. "Damn but Molly has a lot to do. Did you know she used to make her own candy? For the shop? On top of everything else? Thank God she got over that insanity. I don't know how she manages."

"Right," Alexa said with a snort. "This coming from the woman who holds down two or three jobs."

"True, but at least I get to leave it all behind and go home at the end of the day. Or I will until me and Vince can't afford the rent anymore." Rachel reached for her drink, stirred the ice cream and soda with her straw. "I figure we'll end up having to drag our mattress and a hot plate into the back of Second Time Best and camp out in the shop."

"You're not going to have to camp out in the shop," Alexa said, noticing how dark the circles were beneath Rachel's eyes, how stressed and brittle even her hair appeared. "You can stay in my extra bedroom as long as you need to. And if you don't want to do that, you know Molly has plenty of space."

"Please," Rachel scoffed. "Molly has paying guests. She doesn't operate a homeless shelter for freeloaders."

Alexa didn't know what to say. Neither did she know if Molly was mad at her for what had happened, or at herself for being unavailable to her daughter again. "I'm assuming he told her to come talk to you?"

Nodding, Molly reached for a fry, seeming to lose some of her fire as she did. "And here we go again. Since Ezra's been here, my husband has been gone more, my daughter has been turning to him instead of to me, and let's not even talk about a certain friend who I've only seen a couple of times since she started sleeping with him."

Uh-uh. Alexa was not going to let Molly dump on Ezra. And she was certainly not going to go along on her friend's guilt trip. "You forgot the part about Molly having fewer repairs to deal with, fewer errands to run—"

"Seriously, Alexa," Rachel interrupted to add. "You may be here physically, but it's like a big knock-knock hello trying to reach you upstairs."

Alexa turned to Rachel and frowned. "How can you say that?"

"Because it's true?" Molly charged, grabbing a chair from another table and dragging it over.

It wasn't true. She was with her friends one hundred percent when they were together . . . which hadn't been as often lately. Cringing, she sat back down. "I'm always here for you guys. You know that. Yes, I've been spending a lot of time with Ezra—"

"Try all your time," Molly said, snitching a strip of bacon that had fallen to Alexa's plate.

"Not true. I spent all of Sunday in your kitchen."

"Only because Ezra wasn't around," Rachel said, saying nothing about how he had pitched in doing cleanup. "Did he tell you about his run-in with Tommy Mooney at the fire site?"

What, was she suddenly the target of an intervention? "He told me they talked, not that they had a run-in."

"The way Tommy's telling it, Ezra threatened him," Rachel said before biting into her sandwich.

"I'd suggest anyone being told that tale consider the source," Alexa said with no small amount of sarcasm. And that was being kind.

Rachel sat back, crossed her arms. "Do you know him well enough to say he wouldn't make a threat?"

There were so many things Alexa didn't know, but this wasn't even a question. "If he said anything, he felt justified. I don't doubt that for a minute. When he talks, he has something to say. It's not just an exercise in hearing his own voice like it usually is with Tommy."

"How can you know that?" Rachel demanded, gesturing with one hand. "He's been here, what, less than two weeks?"

Obviously Vince had kept the investigation quiet. Alexa wasn't sure what to think about that. All she was sure about was that she'd lost her appetite. "It's been eleven days. And I've learned a lot. We do more than get naked, you know."

"Yeah?" Rachel lifted a brow. "Like what?"

Alexa scrambled. "He's cooked for me. And he's helping me prep my kitchen cabinets to be refinished."

"Whoo-hoo. Sounds exciting." Molly swung a fry in the air.

"It is exciting. Being with him." When neither woman looked convinced, Alexa sighed, shifting her gaze between her two friends. "Think back to when you first started dating Danny. Or when you got together with Vince. Didn't you want to be together all the time?"

Rachel was the one to answer. "Sure, but our relationships had a chance to go somewhere. I just don't get the involvement when you know nothing's going to come out of it."

Alexa ignored the knife blade slicing into her heart. "So, what are you saying? I'm not allowed to have fun while he's here? That I shouldn't enjoy what we have?"

"Of course not," Molly said. "But we don't want you to get hurt. Again."

"Ezra isn't Brett," she reminded them.

"No joke." Rachel snorted, holding her palms up like the pans of a scale. "A computer consultant, a maintenance man."

Alexa only glared.

"Think about it, Alexa," Molly went on to say. "You haven't shown an inkling of interest in dating anyone since Brett skedaddled, and now look at you. It's as if you dived in without ever testing the waters."

First Ezra asking about why she hadn't dated, and now her girlfriends giving her hell because she'd taken the plunge? She lifted a sharp brow at Molly. "I believe you were the one who encouraged me."

"I encouraged you to have a fling."

"I am having a fling."

"No, sweetie. This is way more. A fling wouldn't be so consuming. You'd get a little here, you'd get a little there." Molly waggled both brows. "You wouldn't be spending every minute of your free time with the man."

Alexa thought about the hours she'd spent with Ezra last night, the quiet time, the intensity. She didn't think this was a good time to tell her friends that she was over her head in love. "Do we have to talk about this now? This is supposed to be Rachel's girls' night."

"Don't we usually talk about relationships on girls' night?" Rachel reminded her.

"We don't talk about ours. We gossip about everyone else."

Both Molly and Rachel laughed, Molly saying, "Ah, but today, *you* get the third, fourth, and fifth degree."

Alexa groaned. "You've got five minutes. I've got to get back to class."

"We love you, and we want what's best for you. That means making sure you don't do something you'll regret," Molly said, her eyes bright and concerned, as Rachel added, "Isn't that what friends are for?"

"It is, yes, and you two are the best. But please trust me

when I tell you that you have nothing to worry about. I'm fine. I know what I'm doing. And I'm not going to let myself get hurt," she said, wondering for the first time who she was trying to convince.

Her friends or herself.

Chapter 27

Later that night and still stinging, Alexa held tight to the railing as she descended the ragged steps leading from the coastal highway's sidewalk down the side of the harbor cliff to the docks. The sky was clear, the moon full and bright, the guidepost lamps lighting her way.

When she'd gone out to her SUV after school, she'd found an envelope on her front seat. A note from Ezra telling her to meet him at his boat. He wanted to take her into the bay on a moonlight sail. How he'd gotten into her car, she didn't want to know and didn't plan to ask.

Part of her wanted to hunt down both Molly and Rachel and childishly rub their noses in what she and Ezra had. They wondered why she hadn't dated since Brett? It was simple. No man, Brett included, had ever come close to making her *feel* the way Ezra did.

But the more practical part of her knew that in the scheme of things—and no matter how deeply her feelings for him ran—she and Ezra had nothing ahead of them but a couple of weeks of one another's company and incredible sex. It was a truth that was growing harder to face.

Her friends had her best interests at heart. She knew they didn't want to see her go through the sort of heartbreak she'd gone through with Brett. What they didn't understand—and what she was only beginning to—was that she had never connected with Brett in the way she had with Ezra.

She had never *felt* with Brett as much as she had simply existed, catching up with him in the evening after a day spent absorbed in her world, never a part of his. Yet Ezra seemed to be with her all of the time. All. Of. The. Time. Her heart ached to think of losing that, of losing him.

She probably *had* been thinking of him Monday on the playground when Emmy Rose and Cassie had tangled. And he had *definitely* been on her mind during lunch today with the girls because he was never far from her thoughts.

And her thoughts weren't even specific. She didn't wonder what he was doing, or how he was spending his time. She might picture snippets of their time together. Or think of his smile, the look in his eyes, think of him being close, being here, standing up to Tommy Mooney, coming to her defense, protecting her, caring that much about her—

"Nice night, isn't it?"

She jumped at the deep male voice then turned, finding the owner slouching in the corner of the dock's railing, one fancy cowboy boot crossed over the other. She recognized him as one of the extra guests Molly had put up last week.

She thought he had come about buying property . . . "Yes. It's gorgeous."

"Kinda cold for my southern blood."

She wrapped her leather jacket tighter at his words, trying to place his accent, wondering what he was doing down here. "It can take a while to get used to, but it's nice."

"You're not from this place then?"

She shook her head, laughing. "I'm a SoCal girl. What about you?"

"Ah, no, *chère*. I grew up in the Louisiana swamps." He gestured with a cigarette he held between his fingers. "You wouldn't happen to have a light, would you? I really need to kick this habit . . ."

"Sorry, no." She backed up two steps then turned to head down the dock, calling over her shoulder, "Enjoy the rest of the night."

"You, too," he said, lifting one hand, dropping back into the shadows. She had just reached Ezra's boat when the scent of burning tobacco reached her nose. She glanced back, saw the glowing tip of the man's cigarette, and frowned. Weird. Why had he asked her for a light if he had one?

The sailboat was dark, the windows shut, allowing no light from the cabin to escape. She used that provided by the coastal highway's bridge overhead and the guidepost lamps on the stairway to board near the rear cockpit. She circled the large wheel, finding the steps where they descended into the cabin and climbing down.

Only when she reached the cabin and blinked to adjust to the light inside, did she discover it wasn't Ezra she found waiting for her. It was an older man with a scholarly look. A moment later, a second man who was younger ducked out of the small bathroom. Both were dressed in clothing that belonged in a boardroom, not on a boat in Comfort Bay.

Were they here to see Ezra? Why would they be here to see Ezra? Was the man on the dock waiting for them? Why would Ezra ask her to meet him here if he had other business, she wondered, her nape beginning to tingle, gooseflesh pebbling her skin.

She didn't even try to hide her confusion. "Excuse me, gentlemen, but I think you're on the wrong boat. If you tell me who you're looking for, I should be able to point you in the right direction."

The older man folded down a bench across from the one he occupied and gestured for her to sit. "Good evening, Mrs. Counsel. I hope you don't mind that my associate and I wait along with you for Mr. Moore."

Alarm trickled down her spine to pool in the small of her back. She shivered, but remained standing, realizing too late how much distance she'd put between herself and the stairs.

"I do mind, yes. Who are you, and what are you doing on Ezra's boat?"

The man covered his mouth with his fist before clearing his throat. "I believe you are operating under a number of misconceptions. First of all, this boat does not belong to Mr. Moore," he said, and Alexa thought she might vomit.

"Secondly," he continued, his voice taking on a tone that cut through her nausea and the muscles in her legs. "I don't care if you mind that we are here. We will be waiting with you. Or rather, we will be the ones waiting."

He gestured to his companion. The younger man reached into the bathroom and came back with a roll of duct tape and a coil of rope, heading toward her while the man on the bench said, "You will be biding your time bound and gagged."

Chapter 28

At the end of what felt like the longest day of his life, Ezra arrived at the sailboat to find Davis Brown and his companion in the cabin. The older man sat on the main saloon's bench in front of the navigation station. The younger stood in front of the door to the head, his feet spread wide, his arms crossed over his chest. It was a defensive, shielding posture, and Ezra's senses went to high alert at the tension swirling thickly through the room.

"Gentlemen," he said, nodding at one then the other before moving into the sloop's galley and leaning against the built-in oven and propane stove. "I would like to get our business out of the way with as little fanfare as possible. I hope you have no objections."

"I do, yes," Brown said, crossing his legs and pulling a Browning nine millimeter semi-automatic from inside his coat. He directed the barrel toward the center of Ezra's chest. "I have several objections, and I plan to detail each one."

"Weapons are not necessary, Mr. Brown," Ezra said, feeling the weight of his own Walther beneath his pea coat at his waist. He kept his hands in his pockets. "You would not be here to complete this transaction if you felt you were in danger or that I was a threat."

"Oh, I am not the one in danger, but I *am* the one who's a threat," Brown said, giving a nod toward his companion. The other man stepped aside and pushed open the door he'd been guarding.

Alexa sat inside on the head, her ankles bound, her hands tied behind her, her mouth covered with tape. Her eyes were wide with fear, asking questions, leveling accusations. Her chest rose and fell with her terrified breaths.

Ezra kept his expression passive, returning his attention to the motherfucking dead man sitting in front of him. "If you are here to make some sort of bargain, Mr. Brown, I have no authorization to change the terms of this deal."

"My name is not Davis Brown," the man said as he got to his feet, and Ezra felt his world crumble. "It is Giles Shore. Two years ago in a Manhattan parking garage, you killed my brother, Oliver. I've come to return the favor by taking your lover's life before I take yours."

Chapter 29

Ezra remembered Oliver Shore. He had worked with the Spectra agent closely, assisting him two years ago in a transaction with the Smithson Group. While Shore had retrieved data on Spectra's diamond smuggling operation stolen by a member of SG-5, Ezra had held an innocent woman hostage. And because it had suited Ezra's own purpose, he had released her after putting a bullet into Oliver Shore's brain.

The SG-5 operatives who had witnessed Oliver Shore die no doubt suspected Ezra was responsible for the Spectra agent's death, but they had not seen him pull the trigger. And even had they discovered proof that he was the shooter, they would not have leaked or shared the information. Hank Smithson's team of covert operatives functioned as far outside of the law as did Ezra himself.

So how this man who claimed to be Oliver's brother could possibly know what had transpired in that Manhattan parking garage all those months before . . .

"I see you are at a loss for words," Giles said, cutting into Ezra's silent scrutiny of the incident from the past and continuing to hold his weapon at the ready.

Ezra moved to the corner of the small galley and leaned against the door to the aft berth. The shift in position removed

Alexa from his line of sight. "I was working with your brother when he was killed, but I was occupied elsewhere at the time of his death." Lies came as easily as the truth and caused no concern. "Since you are here, I assume you are aware of the identity of the group I work for? The same one who employed Oliver?"

"Yes, I am," Giles said, adjusting his position to rest his left arm along the back of the bench, his right hand holding his weapon on his knee. "Over the last several months, in fact, my associate Josef and I have become well acquainted with my brother's employer. It seems Oliver had a young . . . shall we say companion in Switzerland, an attorney to whom he often sent sealed envelopes to be stored in his lockbox and opened by me upon his death.

"I was given these documents eighteen months ago once Oliver's estate was settled. He had many things to say about his employer and about you, Mr. Moore," Giles said, gesturing with the weapon as he spoke. "He also repeatedly made mention of an organization called the Smithson Group. Much of this information I have kept confidential, but there were certain revelations I deemed best shared with Oliver's superior. A Mr. Warren Aceveda."

While Giles talked, Ezra assessed the situation. He did not care how things had come to this point. He only cared about getting Alexa out of here unharmed. But hearing the other man speak Warren's name brought Ezra up short. He pushed off the door and faced his adversary, his hands in his coat pockets, holding the garment close. "I know Warren Aceveda well. If you had given him cause to doubt my loyalty, I would no longer be in his employ, much less alive."

Giles shared a quick smile with Josef, glancing at the younger man where he blocked both the door to the head and Ezra's view of Alexa. It was a brief exchange, but it conveyed a startling degree of confidence. It also caused Ezra's nape to tingle with the awareness of how extensively his position with the syndicate had been compromised. Turning back—an option which had never crossed his mind as viable—was now without doubt an impossibility.

"Think about it, Mr. Moore," Ezra heard Giles saying. "If I was able to take my brother's revelations and piece together the extent of your duplicity, no doubt your employer has been able to do the same. Did it not seem strange that you were allowed to undertake this assignment on your own instead of being attached to another agent? Do you now understand that this exercise, this trip, has all been a game?"

It had not seemed strange at all. The level of Ezra's true autonomy within Spectra was known only by Aceveda and Cameron Gates—a fact of which Giles had no reason to be aware. It was also apparent that he was unaware of being the true pawn in whatever game Ezra's superiors were playing.

Their reason for allowing Oliver Shore's brother to pose as the imaginary Davis Brown, however, was inconsequential, and Ezra wasted no time trying to divine their intent. He had time for nothing but finding a way out of here while inflicting the least amount of collateral damage and saving the one innocent life that mattered.

Giles picked that moment to get to his feet, reaching into his coat pocket and withdrawing his weapon's silencer. "Josef, would you rid our captive of her tape and ropes? It is time we finish here. Oh," he continued, turning to Ezra again. "Do not worry about your cargo falling into the wrong hands. I will see that the weapons are returned to their rightful owner."

Warren Aceveda could not afford the risk to Spectra Giles would present were he to remain alive, and returning the weapons was tantamount to walking into the mouth of the lion. But Ezra kept that information to himself. Instead, he focused on Alexa as Josef freed her from her bonds, bracing himself against the emotions precipitated by having her in his arms.

But she did not rush toward him. She did not move at all.

She remained standing between Giles and Josef, her eyes cast down, her crossed arms hugging her body as if doing so was what kept her upright. A jagged bolt of pain seized him, catching him off guard and ripping into his heart. He took seconds too long to shake it—seconds Giles used to his advantage.

The other man pulled Alexa in front of him, using her as a shield when there was no need. Ezra had not made a threatening move since entering the cabin. And then, above Alexa's soft, fearful whimper, he heard what Giles must have heard moments before. The thump-thump-thump of footsteps on the deck overhead.

The older man placed the hand holding his weapon along Alexa's neck. "Josef, take Mr. Moore up to the deck and see that he dispatches whomever it is that has come to visit. And Mr. Moore, be warned. If you do not do as I say, I will end Mrs. Counsel's life here and now."

Heat began to melt the cold façade Ezra had forced himself to maintain. The heat of anger. The heat of fear. The heat of hatred for this man who dared make threats. The only thing that kept Ezra from killing him now was the fact that he had no clear shot with Alexa in the way. He pulled in a deep breath and prepared to move—just as the visitor made himself known.

"Hey, ho, hello down there, anyone? The lady I spoke with on the dock earlier? I have something that I think may belong to her."

Alexa shook her head, shuddering as she shrugged, her skin bleached white, her voice hollow. "I don't know him. We only talked briefly. I can't think of anything I might have dropped."

Giles backed her toward the bench and shoved her down, sitting beside her, his gun beneath his coat and aimed at her side. "Make it quick," he ordered her in a hiss of a whisper before calling out, "Certainly, sir. Please, come in."

"Be right down," the man answered, moving one foot onto the first of the four steps.

Nerves bristling, Ezra watched him descend, taking in his cowboy boots and jeans, his hip-length rain jacket, and when he turned, the black T-shirt beneath it. He was large, fit, with the air of someone who had more of a purpose than returning whatever he proposed Alexa had lost.

"Don't mean to interrupt your evening, but after the lady here and I spoke, I found this on the dock . . ." He frowned, patting one jacket pocket then the other, finally reaching inside and finding what he was looking for.

His expression sharpened as he pulled his hand free, and with it a semi-automatic. He turned away from Ezra, leveled the weapon at Josef's head and fired. A circle of blood blossomed between the young man's eyes.

He crumpled to the ground, and Alexa screamed. Ezra whipped his weapon from his waist, took aim at Giles. The stranger did the same. Giles shoved Alexa to her feet and took cover behind her, the barrel of the silencer digging bruisingly into her neck.

He was cornered. He had no way out. His eyes went wide. His forearm tightened across Alexa's chest. His gaze lashed from Ezra to the second man. His laughter chilled. "Well, gentlemen. It seems we find ourselves in a rather uncomfortable situation. Since I know neither of you wishes to see harm befall Mrs. Counsel, it seems I hold the upper hand."

The stranger coughed and cleared his throat. "No, boo. I don't think so."

Giles turned his attention to the stranger, exposing but a few inches of his neck. It was all Ezra needed. He fired. Alexa screamed. Giles fell, taking her with him. She kicked, flailed, scrambling away from his body and the blood pooling beneath what remained of his head.

Gun raised, Ezra spun toward the other man defensively— only to find the stranger returning his weapon to the shoulder holster beneath his coat. It took several seconds for the man's withdrawal to register, but when it did, Ezra rushed forward and grabbed up Alexa, backing both of them toward the closest bench where they collapsed. He held her close while she sobbed, while his own heart thundered, while he tried to make sense of what had happened and determine where to go from here.

Finally, he met the other man's steadfast gaze and held out his hand. "Ezra Moore."

"Simon Baptiste," said the other man as he shook it.

Ezra gave a slight frown, feeling his way. He had assumed the man had been sent by Spectra to monitor his confrontation with Giles Shore and return to Aceveda with a report . . . but now he was not sure. Simon did not seem interested in any of what Giles had learned about Ezra's past actions.

He waited until his own pulse had calmed and Alexa's crying had quieted before asking, "Warren sent you?"

"Hell, no, boo." Simon flipped open a lighter and fired up the cigarette he'd pulled from a box in his pocket. He took a deep drag, blew smoke rings overhead, looked back at Ezra, and grinned. "Hank Smithson did."

Chapter 30

Alexa sat huddled in the corner of the sailboat's deck, her knees drawn tight to her chest, her arms wrapped around them, her head buried between. The subtle vibrations of the motor rattled her body as Ezra steered the boat out of the harbor and into the quiet waters of the bay. She was freezing, shaking, her bones aching with the horror of what had happened—or so at first it seemed.

When she examined what she felt more closely, she realized she didn't feel a thing. Nothing. Not internally. Not externally. And no wonder. The man she loved had just killed two people. Or killed one and sanctioned a second's death. The fact that she was cold and wet and quivering like a leaf barely registered. She was too numb to feel anything but the pitch and roll of the boat.

Even the fear that had consumed her while sitting alone in the tiny bathroom and unable to move her hands or her feet was gone. She had been confined for what felt like forever, but couldn't have been more than thirty minutes. The room had been dark, sterile, and tiny, suffocatingly close. She had rocked her body back and forth, praying for Ezra to come for her quickly, then praying he not come at all.

She'd been torn, wishing the Ezra she loved out of harm's

way, wondering who in the hell the Ezra was that those men had been waiting to see. The minute the younger one had pushed open the bathroom door after Ezra arrived, she had her answer. He had looked inside, his expression blank, his eyes disinterested, his stance relaxed.

The entire package was a sham.

In that moment, all she'd been able to do was think back to the first time she'd seen him walking up the grassy slope from the coastal highway to the Maples Inn. That man, the one whose aura of danger had enveloped her there, who had frightened her by doing no more than existing, who she'd been certain meant harm to the girl walking with him, he was the man who had spared her a five-second glance before turning away.

Sea spray spattered her arms and her head, and she shivered, suddenly furious at how gullible she'd been. Molly and Rachel had encouraged her to enjoy herself with Ezra while warning her not to get seriously involved.

And hadn't she played the fool, telling them not to worry, swearing that she wouldn't get hurt, insisting that she knew Ezra well, and above all, ignoring her intuition when it told her to dig deeper into what Vince had found?

She could not believe she had spent all this time since her divorce alone, protecting her heart, trusting the instincts that told her she would know when it was time to dive back into the dating pool, only to end up so royally duped.

There were illegal weapons onboard this boat. Two men had lost their lives and would shortly become fish food. A stranger with no name had stepped into the fray as if the goings-on were nothing but a day in the life.

And Ezra hadn't blinked at any of it.

What kind of man could be so brutally cold?

She felt the weight of his gaze, but couldn't bring herself to look at him. Not yet. And especially not when she knew what lay ahead, how he was using the diesel engine to take the sailboat into the open waters, how while he did that, Simon Baptiste was down below securing the bodies of the two men for disposal . . .

Her stomach roiled as she pictured the blood, and the smell came back to haunt her, warm and metallic and heavy, settling into her clothing, her hair. She would never get it out of her skin. And she would never again enjoy the scent of the salty sea air. She would have to move. As soon as she could resign her position, she would go, she didn't know where, she didn't care, she had to go, go, get out—

"Alexa."

Ezra's voice interrupted her panicked thoughts. He sounded so calm, so unaffected. She kept her head down, only raising one hand, a stop sign to keep him from saying another word. She didn't care what he wanted to tell her. She didn't want to ever hear anything he had to say again.

But he paid no attention, stepping away from the wheel to kneel in front of her. "Alexa, listen to me. What has happened is unfortunate and extremely unpleasant. But we have more here to do, and you may prefer to go below and wait for me in the forward berth."

She shook her head. She couldn't go back down there. Didn't he get that? How could he not get that? Was he so used to murder that he didn't understand how repugnant his actions were? How his attitude was unfathomable?

He waited beside her for several minutes. She sensed the heat of his body as he crouched there, sensed the worry that radiated from him, but she refused to say a word, to acknowledge his existence. Moments later, he was gone, throttling back the engine, leaving the boat to rock in the waves, a nauseating standstill as he headed down below.

She knew what they were doing, he and the man named Simon. She knew they were carrying the bodies to the deck. Bodies wrapped in blood-soaked bedclothes, secured with tape, tied with ropes, the bundles weighted down with the assault rifles she'd seen them unload from the storage space beneath the bed in the aft berth.

She heard the heavy tread of their footsteps as they struggled beneath the dead weight they hefted up the steps. She couldn't look. She felt the shift in the tilt of the boat. She heard the first splash, the second. The boat rocked to and fro.

She surged to her feet, spun around, leaned over the side, and threw up.

Chapter 31

Leaving Alexa on deck under Simon's watch, Ezra went below to clean up the cabin, covering the blood-splattered benches with the blankets from the beds, mopping up the blood that had not previously soaked into the dead men's clothing and the sheets with which he had wrapped their bodies.

Her reticence to return to the murder scene with so much of the evidence remaining was understandable, but he had many things he needed to explain to her before they docked and very little time before they did. To that end, he headed back to the deck where he engaged the autopilot.

He requested Simon remain on deck. The other man agreed, huddling deeper into his rain coat and lighting a cigarette, humming a Grateful Dead song under his breath. That Ezra recognized the tune caused him to smile for the first time all day. The smile quickly faded, however, when he was forced to grab a unwilling Alexa and haul her to her feet.

Once they made the climb down the stairs and reached the cabin, she jerked away and whirled on him, raising both of her hands to keep him at a distance. The loathing in her expression shocked him, as did that in her voice. "Stay away from me. Do not touch me. Do not speak to me. Just take me home and then get the hell out of my life."

Her hair was a wild mop of damp curls framing her face. Her skin had grown sallow, her dark eyes pained, her lips taut and bloodless. He swallowed hard against the anguish rising to choke him, and took an intimidating step forward. He needed her to sit down, to calm down, but she remained standing, unmoving, hating him passionately, the malevolence in her eyes unshakeable and bone-chillingly deep.

"Sit down," he ordered her gruffly, once he was able to speak. "I will make you a cup of tea."

"I don't want—"

"Sit down."

She backed into the bench and sat, her hands shaking so violently she pressed them between her knees. He wanted to go to her but knew she would rebuff any gesture of comfort. So he stepped into the galley, filled a mug with water, and set it in the microwave, taking a teabag and a sugar packet from the small tin stored in the cupboard, staring down as he asked, "How did you come to be on my boat this evening?"

"You left me a note that you wanted to take me on a moonlight sail. I found it in my front seat after school." She laughed then, the sound lacking any of her usual humor. "This wasn't exactly what I was expecting, but then you weren't the one who left me the note, were you?"

He shook his head, removing the mug at the microwave's beep. He poured in the sugar and let the bag steep, staring at the brown eddies swirling in the clear liquid, looking for the words he needed to say. "Alexa, you must know I would never wish for you to have seen what happened."

"Oh, like that's some big surprise," she said, bold with her sarcasm, refusing his contrition. "If I hadn't been here, you could go right on doing your dastardly deeds by day, and doing me by night."

Knowing no response he could make would assuage her, he kept silent, disposing of the teabag and bringing her the mug. He held it out for her to take, thinking she planned to slap at his hand and scald him with the liquid.

Instead, she took the tea and inhaled the fragrant steam, closing her eyes as she did. "All I can smell is the blood. And the gunpowder. I'll never get the stench of either out of my nose."

He knew olfactory memories had the strongest sensory recall. But he knew, too, that she would eventually have less of a reason to remember. "Alexa, I want to explain to you who I am, but I can only share with you so much."

"As always, a man of few words." She shuddered, kept her gaze on the tea. "How long till we get back?"

"As long as it takes me to explain," he said, still standing in front of her.

That was what it took to get her to lift her head, to bring up her chin and pay attention. "So now I'm your hostage instead of that other man's?"

"You are not a hostage." He sat down on the bench across from hers, braced his elbows on his knees, laced his hands, and met her gaze. "But I cannot let you walk away without knowing the truth."

"Don't bother," she said sharply. "I know more than enough already. All I want to do is forget that I ever met you and wash off everything about these last few weeks." Trembling, she inhaled deeply, blowing out her breath with a grimace. "God, I need a shower."

He knew she was feeling used and betrayed. She had every right; he had no defense. Still, her words stung. He had thought . . . He shook his head, shook it off. "Whether or not you forget about me, washing away what you have seen is not quite that simple. There are . . . repercussions to be considered."

She was sipping at her tea when he spoke, both hands wrapped around the mug. She held it in front of her mouth for several seconds, unmoving, staring at him as she digested his meaning, her eyes growing wide once she had.

"You killing those men," she began, clearing her throat. "I'm not out of danger, am I? I heard too much. Whoever sent them to find you . . . He'll come here now, right? To finish what they didn't? And he'll come after me, too?"

Ezra met her gaze squarely, directly, saw the return of her fear as it swept away the revulsion that had moved in once she had been freed, once she had seen him at work. "I will not let anything happen to you."

"Like you didn't let anything happen tonight?" One hand quivering, she pointed out the bruise on her neck where she'd been gouged by Giles' gun, the rope burns on her wrists, the welts on either side of her mouth from the tape Josef had used to gag her, the droplets of blood on her clothes.

Fury rose up to engulf him, a raging storm spawned by his inadequacy. He had never been in a position of having to protect any life but that of the Spectra agent to whom he was assigned. Bringing an innocent civilian, bringing *Alexa* into this operation . . . He had not thought through the consequences.

He had been too arrogant, believing things would go according to plan, that he would meet no unexpected resistance. And now he felt impotent, caught in the center of a maelstrom from which he could not fight his way free. "I will not let it happen again. Ever.

"And I will get you something else to wear," he added, taking in the state of her clothes. She had been close, the one to feel the sting of the spray, the sharp whiz of the slug, and only now had the rush of adrenaline subsided, allowing him to focus on more than saving her life.

"Can you answer a question for me?" she asked before he had a chance to move. "Or maybe what I should say is will you answer a question if I ask it?"

He nodded. "If I am able, yes."

She twisted her mouth at his response, then sipped at her tea before she spoke, the liquid close to sloshing over the mug's rim. "This man's brother. Oliver Shore. Were you lying when you said you didn't kill him?"

She hadn't asked if he had committed the deed. Only if he had lied. "Yes."

"Why?" she asked, her head cocked with curious consideration. "Why would it matter, him knowing, if he was going to
die anyway?"

Ezra arched one brow. "When he made his accusation, he
was the one with the gun."

She took a minute to think, returning with, "So you lied to
save your life? To buy more time? To find out what else he
might know?"

Smart questions, all of them. "I lied because it was in my
best interest to do so. For all the reasons you mentioned. And
also as a delay tactic."

"Delay?"

"I needed time to assess the situation in order to find a way
to extract you safely."

A silence thick with the weight of what lay ahead hung over
the room, rippling with Alexa's next words. "Have you killed
many other men?"

"I have."

"This organization you work for, is it attached to any country's government or military?" She changed the subject without reacting to his admission. There was no shift in her
expression, or in the way she held her body.

Here was where he had to decide what to reveal. He would
be gone soon; how much explanation did he owe her, did he
want to leave her with? And when had revealing anything entered into the picture?

He was exiting this life, never to look back, yet he had
much to take with him, so many atrocities binding him to the
past. His actions made him a heinous criminal. He scrubbed
both hands over his face, looking for an answer. All he found
was Alexa, waiting.

He sat up, leaned back against the padded bench and
crossed his arms. "I left the military a long time ago. I operate
independently, and I have for many years."

"But this organization that employs you . . ." She didn't finish the sentence, letting it die as pieces of tonight's puzzle

tumbled into one whole. "You're working against them, aren't you? That thing about your duplicitous activities and your employer finding out."

She sat back, too, shaking her head, the mug in her lap her only anchor to reality, her knuckles white with the force of her grip. "You had to kill that man to protect yourself. You weren't thinking about me at all."

"You are right that I am working against them," he told her before telling her what was even more important for her to hear. "But you are wrong if you believe for even a moment that I was not thinking about you."

She stared at him, studied him, considered him for so long that he felt an uncomfortable need to squirm. And then she broke the spell, freeing him from the urge by asking him, "Who are you?"

"I am who I have told you. A schoolteacher from San Torisco, educated at a military academy in the States. I am in the employ of an organization that is not aware I am working against them. All of those things are true."

"And you kill people."

"I do, but it is neither something I enjoy nor anything I do lightly. I do it because sacrificing a single life in many cases saves countless others."

"The end justifying the means?" she asked, her voice rising, her tone growing shrill. "That's no defense for murder. And that's what you're doing, operating on your own, no matter your intent."

"I am not defending what I do. I am only explaining—"

"You think there's a difference?" she asked, railing at him. "In defending what you do and explaining it? There's not. You're just wrapping it up in nicer words."

He waited a moment, fighting the urge to tell her there was nothing nice in what he would say. "Would you like me to tell you more about my employer, Alexa? What they do and why I am working against them?"

"Why bother?" She fluttered one hand, waving off his offer. "Nothing will get me to change my mind about you, or think better of you for your noble deeds. Besides, why should I believe anything you tell me when lying is so easy for you?"

"I only lie—"

She snorted. "Yeah, yeah. I know. When it suits your purpose or is in your best interest. I got that."

"No, Alexa. You have nothing. You have no idea." He surged to his feet and loomed over her, his chest heaving as the horrors of the last eleven years rushed over him. "I work for an organization which supplies weapons to terrorist groups. I work for an organization which delivers illegal drugs to city streets in huge quantities.

"I work for an organization which has no qualms about kidnapping young girls, many of whom are runaways, and forcing them into prostitution. I work for an organization which has technology allowing them to access classified transmissions between governmental agencies. I work for an organization which makes a great deal of money smuggling conflict diamonds out of Sierra Leone."

He struggled to breathe, struggled to keep from tearing apart the room, from ripping himself to shreds in front of her. "You may think what I do deserves no defense. But I believe with everything I am that working against my employer, no matter what I have to do in order to destroy them, is in far more interests than my own."

Chapter 32

"Where is your vehicle parked?" Ezra asked as they reached the coastal highway, having climbed the incline of jagged rock steps from the dock.

"At the inn." She pulled away when he reached for her arm to guide her across the road, but he held tight, refusing to let her shake him off. He had too many things yet to say to her, too many things left undone.

The death of Giles Shore and Josef settled nothing. What Oliver's brother had known and revealed about Ezra's dealings with Spectra had set him on edge. Even if Ezra felt it wise to postpone what he was going to do, the syndicate would never allow him to walk away. Neither would they let him return. Not after he had dumped a valuable cache of weapons overboard into the Pacific. Not if they knew everything Giles had implied. And not with Alexa in the picture.

They would not believe her capable of silence, assuming instead that she would speak of what she had learned, that she would dig for more information about what she suspected. Giving the benefit of the doubt was not how they operated—a fact Ezra knew well. He was the one they sent to take care of such threats.

"Who is he?" she asked, bringing Ezra back to the present

as she nodded toward Simon Baptiste driving away. He had left the boat ahead of them, and was now nothing but taillights in the distance. "Does he work for the same people you do?"

Ezra slowed their steps as they made their way up the grassy slope to the inn. "He works for a group I have assisted on occasion."

"And he condones what you do? Wait, let me guess," she said, taunting him but with less rancor than previously. "He does the same thing."

"Not exactly, though we are on the same side." When he heard her snort, he continued. "Nothing here is a case of black and white, Alexa. There are more shades of gray than you can imagine."

She raised a hand, halting further discussion. "Right now, all I want to imagine is a shower. I smell. I'm soaked. I've got to be at work in, what, five hours? I'm fucking miserable if you want to know the truth."

He shrugged out of his pea coat and draped it over her shoulders, pulling her into the curve of his body, leaving the weight of his arm where he thought she might need it. That she did not push him away gave him hope that she was still within reach. He needed her sharp and focused. He needed her close. He was not letting her out of his sight until he knew what Aceveda and Gates had planned.

They avoided the main drive and circled the inn from the rear, coming up on his quarters from behind. Alexa kept going, heading for her car. He stopped her. He did not want her traveling to her cabin in the woods alone. "Stay here. It's late. You can shower and sleep. I'll take you to get clothes in the morning."

"I'm fine," she insisted, pulling away. "I'd rather sleep in my own bed."

"Then I will go with you," he said, and started them walking again.

"I want to sleep alone."

"I will sleep in the chair."

"Ezra, please—"

"No, Alexa. I am not leaving you to stay by yourself. Not tonight, not tomorrow night, not the night after." He ground his jaw, stared down at the frown on her face, seeing her eyes by the light of the moon. "I have little choice during the day, but I will not leave you alone at night."

It took several moments for what he said to register, for her frown to deepen from annoyance to fear for her life. She didn't say a word when it did. She only turned and headed for the door to his quarters, waiting for him to unlock it, bolting inside when it swung free.

He closed and secured it behind them, switching on the small hanging lamp that cast a warm glow in the corner of the main room. The warmth did not reach far enough to take the chill from Alexa's complexion. Her lips appeared to be the color of parchment, the circles beneath her eyes that of the night sky.

He removed his coat from her shoulders and tossed it across the kitchen bar. Then he guided her through the bedroom to the structure's small bath, closing that door behind them, too. She stood with her arms crossed, her hands tucked close to her body seeking heat, keeping herself apart.

But she was not as defeated as she seemed. "I can shower by myself."

"I know you can."

"You're not going to let me do that either, are you?"

"Tonight? No. I am not."

"Fine," she said, toeing off her shoes. "This is just a shower, okay? Getting warm. Getting clean. Dear God, I smell like dead fish."

"You do not smell," he said, shucking his shirt overhead and dropping it to the floor, unable to avert his gaze when she did the same. He cared for her so very much. The idea that he was responsible should anything happen to her struck against his ribs like a punishing fist. "I am sorry, Alexa. For everything."

"I don't want to talk anymore. Not now, okay?" She took a deep breath, still not looking at him. "I can barely deal with what's going on in my head, much less put it into words."

She lowered the zipper on her jeans, tugged them down, and stepped out of them. And then she stood there in bra, panties, and socks, all of them sheer, all of them the color of the blue-green waters from his home.

He turned away, reached into the tub, and started the water, adjusting the temperature and pulling open the plastic curtain. She kept her gaze cast down as she removed the things she was wearing and stepped beneath the spray.

He took another moment or two to finish undressing, giving her time alone, giving himself the same amount, and burying the urge to seek absolution in her body, fighting the accountability cutting into him like a garrote for bringing violence and the ugly truth of his life into her world.

But she was the one who needed solace tonight. The one who had witnessed what no one ever should, what he had become too used to. He had grown hard, his protective shell thick, limiting his movements outside of his insular world, barring all emotion. And now here came Alexa into his life . . .

"Are you coming in?" she asked, pulling the curtain aside and peering out. Her hair was slicked back, a dark fall around her shoulders. She sputtered as water dripped from her brow into her eyes, shaking her head as if dislodging those few drops would make any difference.

He didn't want to move. He wanted to stand there for as long as he could, frozen and caught by her eyes. It was as if this moment had been what he had been moving toward all of his life. She was waiting for him, his Alexa, waiting even after telling him she wanted him gone.

He removed his briefs, feeling as if he were baring more than his body when he did. She stepped back and he stepped in, closing the curtain behind him, breathing deep of the scent of her skin and her hair, of the bar of soap she held.

He moved beneath the shower head and lifted his face to the sting of the spray. He couldn't look at her without wanting her, without aching to feel her arms around him, holding him, touching him, her skin on his skin.

She stood behind him. He didn't want to turn, to reveal his arousal. He had agreed they were here only for the shared heat and to get clean. But then he felt her soapy hands on his back, the fingers of one massaging him while the other scrubbed him briskly with a cloth.

He braced his palms on the tiled wall, hung his head, and groaned. He had no memories of anything ever feeling so good, of anything he had needed more, of anything else that had made him forget how long his life had been empty.

She washed his neck, his shoulders, and his arms, pressing her body against his in order to reach his elbows, then his wrists. He spread his fingers, and she cleaned each one before returning his palms to the wall.

He ground his jaw as she attended to him, as she knelt behind him to wash his legs, his heels, the crease of his knees, her hands sliding up to cup and knead his buttocks, her fingers slipping between. His cock was board stiff, his sac heavy in the heat. He hurt with wanting her, he ached liked he never had before.

"Turn around," she told him, and driven by both reluctance and desire, he did, lacing his hands on top of his head and staring down to watch her work her way from his toes to his ankles to his knees to his thighs. She urged his legs apart, and he opened them, giving her access to his penis, his scrotum, the erect ridge behind.

She washed him, but she didn't linger. Instead, she moved her soapy rag and hands up his torso to his chest, washing his armpits and his throat, finishing with his face. This was where she took the most time, tracing his chin and his jawline, fingering his scar, his brow, the bridge of his nose.

He kept his eyes closed, and she touched his lids lightly, returning to his mouth, running her fingers over his lips and stopping there. He leaned back to rinse his face and clear his eyes, and then he opened them and looked at her, unable to speak beyond the thick swelling in his throat.

"There." Her voice was so soft he could barely hear her over the water's roar. "You're all clean."

She had no idea what she was saying. How deeply her words pierced him, a jagged slice tearing through his shell. His eyes burned. His chest tightened. He reached for her, his hands cupping her shoulders, her neck, tilting her head, his thumbs on her jaw, his fingers sliding into her hair, holding her still as he lowered his head. As he kissed her.

He kissed her, and she tasted like fresh water, like the toothpaste he kept on the shower's shelf, like his salvation. Her lips were sweet and soft, pliable beneath his, and then she kissed him back.

She kissed him back, and he froze, standing there with water and soap suds swirling around his feet and down the drain, washing away the dirty, ugly façade of his life, freeing him to move, to move . . .

He stepped into her fully, pressing her back to the wall and the front of his body to hers. She was so small and so beautiful and so giving, and he felt like an oaf, like he would break her, like he didn't deserve anything this good.

That didn't stop him from tightening his hold and opening his mouth, asking her with his tongue to do the same. She parted her lips and welcomed him, sweeping her tongue over his, her fingers gripping his biceps with bruising strength.

He was so afraid of hurting her, but he was unable to hold back, crushing his mouth to hers, needing her kiss more than he needed to breathe. But then Alexa's hands began to roam, and the tenor of the kiss suddenly changed.

She let go of his arms and pressed her palms to his chest, kneading his muscles, playing with his nipples, massaging him until he groaned, moving her hands lower, her fingers walking over his abdomen toward his groin where she gripped his cock with one hand, cupped his balls with her other.

Though she had been the one to set the limits of this shower, he had no intention of stopping her, or of asking her for what he needed most. He took it instead, sliding his hands down her back, over her buttocks to her thighs, slipping his fingers between her legs, then lifting her up.

She wrapped her legs around his waist, her arms around his neck. Her kiss begged him to take her. He did so with no niceties or foreplay. Even knowing there would be no later for those pleasures, he did not take his time. He pushed into her, driving as deeply as he could, burying his cock inside of her all the way to his balls.

He slammed into her again and again, purging himself, not caring about taking his time, needing to empty himself of guilt for all the times he had closed his eyes when he should have kept them open, for all the ways he had justified the things he had done as righteous.

She was so hot and so tight, gripping him inside while holding on for his journey. Her heels urged him on, gouging into him. Her fingers did the same. And then her mouth was at the base of his neck, her teeth nipping, her tongue healing, her lips sucking away his pain.

He exploded, bursting from the inside out, pouring himself into her, unable to hold back the anguished sounds surging up from his gut. He pounded her over and over, losing the world around him, knowing only that she was his, she was his, she was his . . .

"Stop," she told him softly, breaking into his haze, sliding her feet to the floor when he finally did.

"You didn't—"

"It's okay." She wouldn't look at him. She refused. "It doesn't matter."

"It does matter. It matters to me."

"No. It doesn't. And this doesn't change a thing," she said, her words crushing him, even though he had not thought to hear anything else.

He nodded slowly, replying, "I will leave Comfort Bay as soon as I am able."

And then he left the shower, giving her the time alone he didn't want her to need because of loving her as much as he did.

Chapter 33

Emmy Rose Maples sat cross-legged on the auditorium's stage next to Mrs. Counsel's chair. She was going to die from being bored. Any minute now she was going to melt into a puddle like the Wicked Witch of the West and leak all over the floor. All she had to keep her busy was her math homework, and she didn't want to do that until she got home and had a snack, but she might have to since she didn't even have anything to read while she waited.

Her Harry Potter book was too big to fit in her backpack and too heavy to carry around. If she had a Gameboy or PS2 she could be playing that, but she didn't. And now her mom was late in picking her up, which wasn't so bad since she might get to skip her dentist appointment, except she was stuck here with her homework while everyone else on the set crew had fun.

Well, everyone but Cassie O'Malley. Cassie had gone home on the bus. Of course, Emmy Rose would rather have gone home on the bus than have to go to the dentist for a cleaning or have to sit here dying of boredom *forever*! The only good thing about waiting was thinking about all the kids making Cassie so mad that she got into another big fight and into even more trouble than she already was.

It made Emmy Rose want to laugh, but she didn't. Or at least she didn't laugh very loud. If Mrs. Counsel heard, she would want to know what was so funny, and Emmy Rose really didn't want to have to tell her teacher the stuff she'd been thinking about Cassie.

Not when Mrs. Counsel had been so cranky today. Right now she was mad about the lights little Bobby Mooney had messed up. Emmy Rose was glad she was sitting where no one could hear her, even though doing her homework still sucked.

"Are you enjoying your mathematics, Miss Maples? Or is there something else that you find entertaining?"

Wow. She hadn't even heard him climb onto the stage. How did he walk without making any noise when his boots were so big and heavy and looked so loud? "I was laughing about . . . my own private thoughts."

"I see," said Ezra Moore, squatting down beside her. "Why are you sitting over here instead of working with the other students?"

"I'm being disciplined." She frowned. *Dis-ci-pline* was one of those words where the letters didn't make any sense. She never could remember where the "C" went.

"Why are you being disciplined?"

"Duh. For my black eye and the fight. Me and Cassie both got kicked off the pageant crew."

"Do you still get to perform in the pageant?"

She nodded. "Yeah, next Tuesday. Then we only have half a day of school on Wednesday, and it's time for Christmas break." She closed her math book and looked over at him. "Are you coming to the pageant?"

"I will do my best to be here," he said, turning away from looking at Mrs. Counsel to look at her when he said it. "I will do my very best."

She shrugged, though it was nice the way she felt like a balloon rising into the sky. "It just makes me so mad not to be able to help anymore. I didn't even get to finish painting my reindeer."

Ezra Moore dipped his head. "Your teacher seems to be unhappy."

"Yeah," she said, squirming around to tell him. "Little Bobby messed up the lights he was supposed to straighten out for the stables. But she's been pretty grumpy all day."

"Perhaps she is not feeling well."

"She's probably tired. She's been yawning a lot. She should've called and then Miss Fine could have substitute teached for her."

"Your teacher is presenting an example of strength under adversity," he said, looking back toward Mrs. Counsel again. "And the word is taught."

Taught. She knew that. "What does that mean, strength under *ad-ver-si-ty?*"

He shifted on the floor so that he faced her, leaning closer with his elbows on one knee. She heard the squeak of his soles on the wood, and was afraid Mrs. Counsel would look over and get mad, so she opened her book up again and pretended to read about fractions.

"Do you know what adversity means?" Ezra Moore asked.

"I think so," she said, nodding. "It's like when something bad happens."

"Yes, it can be, though it is often a case of being faced with an uncomfortable situation or unfavorable circumstances instead."

She thought for a minute, looking at the spots of brown paint dotting his boots. "So, if Mrs. Counsel is tired but she still came to school to teach, that would be showing strength in adversity?"

"That is exactly right."

"Would it be the same with me if I was doing my homework instead of sitting here being mad about not getting to work on the set?"

"Yes, it would."

She guessed that made sense, though she always thought only adults had to act that way. "And if I miss my dad a lot but I'm patient about waiting to see him? That's the same, too?"

"You are a very bright young girl, Miss Maples."

She frowned, thinking more, then took a deep breath. "So, if something really bad was to happen to my dad, I would probably have to be strong then, too, huh?" she asked, squirming again.

Ezra Moore moved in front of her, sitting cross-legged the same way she was, and reached for her book so she didn't have anything to do with her hands and had to pay attention. She should've just done her homework and ignored everyone else and then she wouldn't have been laughing, and he wouldn't have stopped to talk to her, and she wouldn't feel like the balloon she'd been riding in was going to crash.

"Emmy Rose, why do you believe that ill is going to befall your father?"

She liked the way he talked to her like she wasn't a kid and understood everything. Except sometimes she didn't understand at all. "What do you mean, ill? Like he's going to get sick?"

"You seem to have convinced yourself that something bad will happen to your father. I am curious as to why."

She reached for her backpack, which was on the floor behind her, and pulled it into her lap. Then she unzipped it and waited for him to put her book inside, but he didn't. She guessed it was because he was waiting for her to answer him, except she couldn't. She didn't know why she felt like she did.

She shrugged. "I don't know."

"Is it because he is absent so often that you are preparing yourself should he never come home?"

Her eyes started getting all watery, and her throat felt like she'd swallowed too much bread all at once. "I don't know. Maybe."

"A man's work often takes him away from those he loves. Many soldiers serve their countries overseas and are unable to return for months. Businessmen travel to distant destinations and are away from their families for extended periods. Your father comes home every day, does he not?"

She nodded. "But I never ever get to see him. He might as well be dead. Even Cassie O'Malley gets to spend time with her dad after school since he's not working anymore. She said they play video games together all the time."

"Would you rather play video games with your father, or would you rather talk to him about your days at school and hear about his days spent as a fishing guide?"

"Talk to him."

"Then that is what you should do."

"I can't," she said, the tears finally spilling from her eyes. "He's not there."

"How do you think the children of soldiers tell their fathers about their days?"

"On the phone?"

He shook his head. "On occasion, but not often."

"Maybe they write them letters or e-mails?"

"I am quite certain they do. I am also certain that you could do the same."

"Write my dad letters?" That was the dumbest thing she'd ever heard, except then she started thinking about it and got excited about all the things she could say. "I could do that. Like when I'm doing my homework?"

"Or after you do your homework?"

"Yeah, I guess. At bedtime or something. I could tell him about school and about what's going on with Harry Potter."

"I think that sounds like a very good idea. You could start tonight."

"I could," she said, scrambling up to her feet, wondering if she could get her mom to buy her a new set of colored pens since she didn't know what she'd done with the ones she got for her birthday. "Can we go home now? I've got a lot of stuff I need to do."

"Yes, Miss Maples," said Ezra Moore, smiling. "We can go home."

Chapter 34

Alexa hadn't seen him when he walked in, which didn't surprise her. He was like that. A cat. Stealthy. Quiet. Using no more motion than he had to. Making no noise at all. But she'd known he was there. It wasn't anything she was able to explain. It was just the way things were because of everything that existed between them.

She tried to ignore him, keeping her back turned as she dealt with the tangled mess little Bobby Mooney had made of the tiny white Christmas lights to be strung on the reindeer stables. But her trying failed because she could sense him there, watching her, aware of her, even while he crouched down to talk to Emmy Rose at her level.

Still, she kept her focus on the set, rubbing at her forehead to get rid of all the thoughts he brought with him. They followed him into the room, a swirling cape of all the things she wanted to forget, gunshots and ropes and screams and blood and threats, the splash of dead weight hitting water, of the diesel engine motoring back to the dock.

There were other thoughts, too, ones harder to ignore because of how swiftly her body reacted, her pulse pounding, her skin growing flush, her nipples hard as her breasts swelled. A little more than twelve hours ago she'd been naked in his shower, his body driving into hers, his kiss branding her, the sounds he made those of a tortured man.

How could she still want him the way that she did, still love him as much now as she had before? She'd told him in the shower that what she had given him there didn't change a thing. She still wanted him gone. The words had rolled off her tongue so easily they might as well have been true, and she'd kept the tears at bay until she was out of the room.

Lying in his bed later, curled up on one side facing the wall while he stretched out on his back on the other, all she'd wanted was to take them back, to tell him that the thought of him leaving Comfort Bay was unbearable. But how could she ever make a life with a man who pulled a trigger so easily? A man who disposed of bodies as if he were dumping chum?

A man who had chosen a road she couldn't imagine anyone taking, who had traveled it for so long she didn't know if she could trust him to turn around, didn't know if he was able, didn't know if that was what he wanted to do. And until she had an understanding around which she could wrap her tired mind, she didn't want to see him.

She wasn't going to get her wish, of course, because he insisted on staying with her at night, and because she had to let him. She'd be stupid to insist on staying alone after the things she'd witnessed and the position she was now in with the people who employed him.

She had hoped that at least her days would be her own, that she'd have those hours for sorting things out, for thinking about where she was going to go from here, and deciding if she could live without him. Even now she was doing her best to forget that he was here, separating the horrors of last night with the mundanities of today. But then Emmy Rose got to her feet as if to leave.

Alexa sighed. Even if Molly was her best friend, she couldn't let the girl go without the proper permissions, and so she steeled herself for the unavoidable encounter, shoring up her defenses and leaving little Bobby Mooney to straighten out the strings of lights as she crossed the stage to where Ezra stood with Emmy Rose.

"Hi," she said, keeping her distance, her arms wrapped tightly over her cardigan beneath her breasts. She knew the posture was telling, but better the truth than more lies. "Is Molly not coming?"

His eyes never leaving her face, Ezra dug into his pocket for a note Molly had written, handing it to her. "I believe she had a request from one of her guests for a surprise birthday dinner for her husband."

Alexa read the note, turned to the girl. "You're free to go, Emmy Rose. Don't forget you have math homework due tomorrow."

"Does that mean I get to skip my dentist appointment?" Molly's daughter asked, ignoring Alexa and looking up at Ezra. "Or are you taking me to that?"

"Your mother asked me to bring you home. That is all that I know."

Emmy Rose bent to zip her math book into her backpack. "I hope that means I don't have to go. Do you think she's going to need me to help? I have other important things to do."

"She has help from Rachel Fine, but it might be nice for you to offer and do those other important things later," he said, glancing down at her with an expression that had her nodding in agreement.

Amazing how easily he seemed to have fallen into the role of the girl's mentor. Amazing because of the other things Alexa had witnessed him do. "Emmy Rose, would you please wait for Mr. Moore in the chair by the door while I talk to him?"

"Yes, ma'am. I'll wait." The girl, having been dismissed, lumbered toward the steps as if carrying the weight of the world. "I'll sit there and have strength in adversity."

"What is she talking about?" Alexa asked, once she and Ezra were alone. "Such drama."

He gave a soft laugh. "She and I were talking about being strong during hard times."

Why was she kidding herself? There was no ignoring anything about him. His presence was too compelling, his understanding of human nature too pure. Of all the men to get involved with, she'd chosen a killer.

She swallowed, wanting to choke on the reality. "If that's a course I can sign up for, tell me when and where."

"I am sorry this time for you is hard."

She shook her head, kept her eyes on Emmy Rose, tightened her arms around her middle. "Don't. Please. Don't. I'll be fine."

He stepped to the side, into her line of sight, forcing her full attention as he came closer. "You will be, but I still want to know how you are feeling."

"Besides dead on my feet?" That one was easy. "Dead on my feet."

He reached up to tuck stray curls behind one ear. "You need more sleep."

She waved one hand, brushing off his concern, turning to check on her students and breathe, waiting for the impact of his simple touch to fade because she felt it like a blow to her heart. She was doing her best to compartmentalize her emotions, to face the facts as analytically as she could.

She wasn't doing a very good job of it, obviously, but his empathy and compassion derailed her further. "I'll sleep tonight. In fact, I may sleep sooner. Once we're done here"—she glanced at her watch—"maybe thirty minutes, I'm going straight home. If I'm already in bed when you get there, don't wake me up." If he didn't wake her up, she wouldn't have to talk to him. She could go on with her real life, keeping him where she kept everything she needed more time to handle. "If you're still coming, that is."

He nodded, slid his hands into his pockets as if that was the only way he could keep them to himself. "I am. And I may be there soon as well. I have only one pressing task to take care of once I get Emmy Rose safely home."

Safely. As if she thought he wouldn't take care of the girl? She backed away to return to her own pressing task. "Okay, then. I guess I'll see you when I see you."

"It will get better, Alexa," he said softly, his voice coaxing and comforting, his words proving his devotion and making her eyes burn with tears. "It will not always be so hard."

"For you, maybe," she admitted, all of her fears on the tip of her tongue, battling to be heard. "I don't see how it won't always be this hard for me."

"Tonight. I will do my best to help you through any questions you have."

She sniffed, swallowed, swiped a finger beneath both eyes and turned, leaving him with, "I'm not sure either one of us has that much time."

Chapter 35

Ezra had only just taken the pickup out of gear in the parking lot of the Maples Inn when Emmy Rose opened her door and jumped down. She barreled toward the back door as if unable to wait another moment to start writing her first letter. By the time he had climbed down and locked up the vehicle, another was pulling into the drive—the Shelby Mustang belonging to Simon Baptiste.

Ezra made his way to the rear of the pickup, lowering the tailgate to unload the crates of fresh food he had picked up for Molly from the grocer's loading dock in Newton before going to the school to get Emmy Rose. He reached for the crates, sliding them forward, only looking up when Simon walked over.

"Shore's car's out of the picture. Sad to see such a fine machine meet such a nasty end, taking a header over the cliffs off the coastal highway . . ." Clucking his tongue, Simon dug for a cigarette, lit it, inhaled, and blew smoke rings overhead. "Hard for any body, human or auto, to survive that kind of fall."

Meaning authorities would assume Shore and his companion had failed to heed the highway's warnings and had taken a dangerous curve at too high of a speed. Ezra nodded his thanks.

"I am quite certain Aceveda will send someone for me now. It is only a matter of how soon."

"You don't have to do this alone, boo," Simon told him, lowering his voice, leaning his forearms on the edge of the truck's bed. "And you don't have to do it from here."

Ezra shook his head. "I cannot leave and draw Spectra from Comfort Bay until I know Alexa is safe."

"I'll take her off your hands," Simon said, and Ezra's gut tightened, his brow drawing down, causing the other man to chuckle. "We can relocate her. You, too, for that matter. A new identity, a new start. After all this time? Tell me that isn't the best offer you've had in awhile."

He could not deny the temptation of having Alexa to himself with this life behind him, with nothing but a clear future ahead. He wasn't, however, sure she would share his view. "I have business to attend to before I can accept. But with Alexa out of harm's way . . ."

"It would make it a hell of a lot easier to do what you have to do," Simon said, dropping his cigarette butt and grinding it out with the toe of his boot.

She was so loyal to her friends and her students. She had made her home here and was set on improving her living space. Would he be able to convince her to leave? "I will talk to her tonight."

"All right, then. I'm heading out. I figure I've seen enough property to convince anyone I'm looking to buy." Simon slapped the pickup's side panel. "I won't be far. And you know how to reach me."

Ezra finally looked up, meeting the other man's gaze as an equal—not as an employee of the Maples Inn conversing with a guest. He looked at him instead as a man who knew well that walking away from this life they both lived would never come easy to either of them.

"I do. And thank you, Simon Baptiste. You are a good man to have as a colleague. And as a friend."

Chapter 36

Alexa had planned to do nothing after school but go home and sleep. She'd been through hell the night before, and dared anyone to say she didn't deserve those hours in bed—a dare aimed primarily at her overachieving and overcommitted self. This was when she most appreciated living alone and as far as she did from town. Very rarely did anyone drop by unannounced.

Of course as mice and men knew, it didn't take much for plans to go awry, and hers ended up giving way to the stress of her stress. She tossed and turned in her bed for thirty minutes before moving to her big leather chair. She sat there for another fifteen, then curled up in the corner of her sofa where she tried afternoon television, soft music, and a book she'd put down ten times so far. Nothing worked.

Which was why when Ezra arrived around seven, she was in the kitchen wearing a T-shirt and coveralls, standing on the countertop, an electric screwdriver in hand, removing the doors from her cupboards and stacking them at her feet. She didn't even stop to answer when he knocked, because he gave the glass one rap and walked in. They'd gotten that cozy and comfortable, and she was getting to used to both.

Shaking his head, he crossed the main room toward her, setting the brown paper bag he carried on the stove. Whatever he'd brought with him smelled like it had come from Molly's kitchen, and her stomach noisily rejoiced. She hadn't eaten a thing since scarfing down a muffin with her coffee on the morning drive to school.

"I thought you were going to sleep," he said.

"I thought so, too." Her eyes felt like toothpicks were keeping them open while her brain spun around a track at two hundred miles per hour. "It seems I thought wrong."

He hefted up the cabinet doors and set them on top of the boxes into which she'd packed her pots and pans. "Would you like some help?"

She glanced around, surprised to find all of her cupboards bare of doors as well as contents. There was something to be said for this autopilot thing. But then her stomach growled again, reminding her it was way past time to be fed.

"I guess you can help me down. Or else get out of the way so I can jump. And find me a fork while you're at it."

"I will help you first, then I will find you a fork." He reached up and grabbed her by the waist. She slipped the screwdriver into her bib pocket and braced her hands on his shoulders. He lifted her effortlessly and swung her down, but he didn't release her.

He held her there in front of him instead, staring down into her face, his eyes dark with more emotions than she could count, the scar on his face a jagged reminder of why she shouldn't be standing here letting him get to her. Forget the food. All she wanted was to kiss him.

With no small amount of reluctance, she shook off the urge and forced her feet to move, stepping around him and peering into the bag. "Mmm. Italian. And garlic bread. I think I have a bottle of wine in the fridge."

While she unloaded the containers of food, he found two glasses she hadn't yet packed, two plates she had, added forks, and somehow came up with a corkscrew. And since her small table was cluttered with newspaper and tape and paint chips as well as dishes waiting to be packed, he led her to the main room. She settled on one side of the coffee table, he sat on the other, a small fire burning in the fireplace at his back.

She reached for the corkscrew and the bottle of wine. "I thought Molly was doing a special birthday meal tonight or something."

"This is it," he said, dividing the salad of tomatoes, onions, and greens, and the chicken marsala between their two plates. "One of the guests checked out today. Two others did not attend the meal. When I told Molly you were not feeling well, she had me bring the rest to you."

"Mmm," Alexa murmured, digging in. "The guests' loss, my gain. At least three or four pounds worth. I could eat garlic bread morning, noon, and night."

"I am not so sure I would enjoy kissing you if you did," he said, stabbing up a forkful of salad.

She halted with her wineglass halfway to her mouth and stared at him, dumbfounded. "Ezra Moore. Did you just make a joke?"

"I made an attempt," he admitted, his tone sheepish. "I am not so sure it held any humor."

"I'll bet beneath that tough guy exterior you're blushing," she said, swirling her wine in her glass.

"If the heat I feel on my face is any indication, I believe you are right."

He tickled her, so proper in his communication, yet so very human and personable, not the least bit distant. At least not with her, not the Ezra she had come to know. That didn't negate the fact that he was still the one who knew how to pull a trigger, who knew how to kill a man who was using her as a shield without harming a single hair on her head.

She wished she could keep the two of him separate, but she would never get over that, seeing the barrel of his gun pointed in her direction, seeing the calm hatred lighting his eyes when he did. She drank down half of her wine, setting the glass on the table before asking, "How did you know you wouldn't hit me? When you fired your gun on the boat?"

Her question unbalanced him, if only briefly. But he did keep his gaze down when he answered. "I would never have fired if I did not have the shot."

"But how did you know?" She toyed with a chunk of chicken, pushing it back and forth on her plate. "Is it a practice makes perfect kind of thing?"

He didn't want to answer. His silence was the obvious giveaway, but there was more to his avoidance. A hint of shame or remorse; she couldn't be sure of either, though she suspected both. He hadn't said anything to make her think he was examining his life, that he was seeing himself as an outsider would rather than as he'd seen himself all this time. But something inside of her knew.

"You scared me. The look in your eyes. It was like you were someone I didn't know at all. And then to see the gun barrel glaring at me." She left her fork on the edge of her plate, pulled her knees to her chest and wrapped her arms around them, making herself small, too small to be a target.

"How can you live like that? Putting other people through that? I mean, I understand wanting to rid the world of evil, but I can't even imagine what that's done to you as an individual. You, Ezra Moore."

He, too, abandoned his food, sitting with his forearms on the table. "I cannot say what it has done to me. I do not know who I would be if I did something other than this."

"What about what you did before?" she asked, cocking her head to one side. "What were you like then? What did you do before you became . . . ?"

"An assassin?"

She swallowed hard, her chest aching. "Is that how you think of yourself?"

"It is what I do. I act as bodyguard to my employer's agents, and I remove any individuals who get in the way of whatever they have set out to do."

"And since the people you kill are bad guys, you're okay with it?"

He studied her face, his gaze moving from her mouth to her eyes as if he thought he might find a motive for the question other than her need to know. But he couldn't, because that was all there was. She needed to know, to understand.

"I have never been okay with any of it, Alexa. I have done it because no one else will."

"And when you leave here? You can't go back to that life now, can you? What are you going to do? Dear God, what am I going to do?" His words from last night came back to haunt her. It was time to face the reality of the danger she was in.

"I want you to relocate."

"What?" Her head came up sharply. "Like witness protection?"

"In a way, yes. I have contacts who can help you."

No doubt he had contacts who could do just about anything. "Is this a forever thing? Changing my name, leaving my job, my friends? Starting over, alone in a place where no one knows who I am or what I have been through?"

"I will know."

"But you won't be there with me, will you?"

"Not right away. I have things I must do first."

"I'll take that as a no," she said, pushing to her feet, pacing, rubbing the band of stress squeezing her forehead. "You'll go off and continue being the man who conquers evil, and I'll be the woman with no name and no life."

"You will always be who you are," he said, still sitting in front of the fire.

She crossed her arms over her chest and faced him. "I started over here with my ex after we left L.A., and then I started over again after he left me. I'm not the same person now that I was either of those times. Is the third time supposed to be a charm?"

He didn't answer her. He only sat there, staring, his eyes dark, his mouth a flat grim line.

Dear God, she couldn't do this. Not alone. Not without him. "Do you want to be there with me? If I go? Not will you, but do you want to."

"I want to, yes. And I will. I just cannot say when."

"When? Or if?"

"I am sorry that I cannot be more specific."

"I love you." She blurted it out, not understanding where the words came from, not the least bit sorry she'd set them free. "Did you know that? Did you have any idea?"

He nodded slowly, simply said, "I love you, too."

Her heart gave a blip, but she couldn't process any of what she was feeling. "Yet here we are talking about never seeing each other again."

"I did not say we would never see one another."

"You didn't say that we would."

"You are important to me, Alexa. I do not want anything to happen to you. I want you safe."

"Safe so you can be out there putting your life on the line, leaving me alone to worry that I'll never see you again, or that you're dead, or that if you are killed, I won't know because there's no one to tell me. I can't live like that, Ezra. I don't know anyone who could." She stopped, laughed harshly. "I guess that's not true, is it? I know you."

He got to his feet, circled the table, settled his hands on her shoulders. He was so calm, so . . . calm. How in the hell could he be so calm?

"All of that can be settled later," he told her. "Right now, the only thing that matters to me is that you are safe. I cannot be effective if my mind is on you. I cannot afford the distraction."

"Right. I'm a distraction."

"You are the best sort of distraction, Alexa," he said, his voice breaking as he took her in his arms. "The only sort I have ever allowed. I want you in my life. I am trying to make that happen. But there are many things I have started that I must finish before I can devote my time and attention to anything else. And that includes you."

She wanted to admire him, and she did. But there was still a selfish part of her that wanted a normal relationship, a life with the man she loved where they lived in the same house, where their travels were shared, where neither was but a text message away from the other.

Right. Things had worked out so well for her before when she'd had exactly that. She breathed deeply, smelling him, the sea, the soap. "I have to think. I can't decide on something like vanishing off the face of the earth without giving it more thought than this."

"I know you would like time, but you may not have it," he said, holding her cheek to his chest, his hand stroking over her hair. "I fear that whoever comes after me will want to cripple me as a threat by doing harm to you."

"The pageant," she said, because she couldn't think of anything else. "At least give me until then."

Chapter 37

When they crawled into bed an hour later, nothing was the same. They'd spent the night together as many times at her place as they had at his. They'd slept, talked. They'd lain together silently, wrapped in each other's arms. They'd made love until both were sweat-drenched and exhausted and close to being used up.

But tonight there was a new tenderness there. A sharing of souls and emotions, as if they were no longer two strangers engaged in an affair but true lovers in love, reaching for all the things that came with that truth. It frightened her deeply, but she didn't turn away.

She couldn't turn away. Not from Ezra. Not tonight. No matter where they went from here, in body or in spirit, what they shared now would always be with them, reminding them how easy it was for brutal reality to steal away joy, for evil to drive off innocence.

Lying on her stomach with her arms spread wide, she stretched her fingertips toward the sides of the bed. Ezra sat behind her, straddling her thighs, kneeling there and massaging her back. His fingers gripped her hips as he pressed his thumbs against the bones above her buttocks.

She groaned at his touch, groaned more as he continued the

circular pressure up the length of her spine. Once his hands reached the base of her skull, he rubbed her neck and shoulders, kneading the taut muscles there, working her upper arms before making his way to her wrists.

She couldn't remember any massage she'd ever paid for feeling so good. Then again, a lot of the good part was due to the fact that she was naked beneath him, his skin on her skin, trapped between his spread thighs, the weight of his testicles warm against her legs.

When he rose up on his knees and ordered, "Turn over," she did, finding his gaze on her hands as he took them in his. He manipulated each of her fingers, squeezing the joints and the tips, compressing her palms. She swore she could stay there forever, never moving, ecstatic with a pleasure that was close to being better than sex.

No. It was closer than close. It was right there, edging into orgasmic. She thought she might die a little death. "Do you know how good that feels?"

"Yes, I know exactly," he said, placing her arms at her sides and returning his hands to her shoulders, this time rubbing pressure circles along her collarbone.

"In this case?" She shook her head, groaned, held her breath against another. "I'm sorry, but there's no way giving feels half as good as receiving."

"Perhaps not to you." He arched a teasing brow. "But you forget where I am sitting."

She hadn't forgotten at all. She had felt his cock thicken between her legs, felt the tip of the head seek out the moisture she'd released, felt him come close but stop shy of entering her each time he moved. The sensations of waiting were as amazing as those brought on by his hands.

"How could I forget anything when you keep poking me like you have something important to say?"

He poked harder, his cock sliding inside of her an inch before sliding back out, causing her to whimper, causing her to groan. "Everything I say is important. Have you not learned that by now?"

If his hands had been elsewhere, if they hadn't slipped down to cup her breasts, if her sex wasn't tingling and aching and begging him for more, if none of that had been the case she would've come back at him with another playful barb.

As it was, she could barely breathe. She certainly couldn't think to find words, and locating her wit was out of the question.

"Could we stop talking now?" she asked, arching her neck and curling her fingers into the sheet. "If I agree that you are the master of all conversation?"

"We can stop talking even if you do not. But it is nice to know that you recognize the superiority of my skills."

She gave him a look. "I can't recognize what you're not demonstrating."

That was the wrong thing to say, of course, because he stopped touching her at all. He planted his hands on the mattress on either side of her head and did nothing for several seconds but stare down so intently that she fought against gathering the blankets around her and crawling away.

She wanted to ask him what he was looking for, what he saw, if any of it was what he expected, if she pleased him, if he wasn't quite satisfied, what he was thinking about, what she made him feel. But she didn't ask him anything. Neither did she relate to him any of the myriad thoughts falling over one another, tumbleweeds in her mind. There were so many things she didn't think she could tell him . . .

When she looked at him she saw exactly what she wanted, even though he'd come to her in such an unexpected way. He was a man who cared for her, who cared about her, who could not go about his business without knowing she was safe. He pleased her greatly, satisfied her in equal measure. He made her feel as if she was the most important thing in his life.

And though she loved him beyond belief, she pushed her

emotions aside. She would deal with her heart later. Right now she only cared about the stirring ache in her body.

"If you're waiting for a go ahead, please," she said. "Go ahead."

He lowered himself over her, his elbows taking his weight, and nudged her legs apart with his knees, settling between. His gaze locked with hers as he probed and prodded and pushed against her opening, finding himself where he wanted to be and sliding deep.

And then he stopped—but only because she had closed her eyes. She opened one. "Worn out already?"

"If I am," he began, his mouth twisting against a grin, "I have been made so by your jokes."

She smiled, and then she opened her other eye and brought up her hands to cup his face, her eyes filling with the tears she'd been trying so hard to keep at bay, her throat swelling with all the things that she feared. "Right now, joking is all that's keeping me sane. If I get serious, I'll think too much about the world outside of this room. I don't want that right now. I don't want to think about you being hunted down, or about losing my own life."

"What would you like to think about?" he asked her softly, turning his head to nuzzle his lips against first one palm then the other.

"Do I have to think about anything at all? Can't I do nothing for this one night but feel?" She took a deep breath to stave off the sobs threatening to ruin this time she would never get back. "Please, Ezra. Please make me."

His eyes were glittering when he lowered his head and kissed her, when he brushed his lips to hers with the lightest touch. He didn't linger there, but kissed her cheek and her chin, her jaw and her neck, finally settling his mouth near her ear, whispering words she didn't understand in that musical voice she loved hearing.

And then his body began to move, sliding in, pulling out, a

slow easy rhythm that set her skin on fire. His chest grazed her breasts, teasing her nipples as he stroked over her, as he filled her, the base of his cock grinding against her clit and bringing her up off the bed.

She gasped, groaned, wrapped her legs around his and hooked her heels over his thighs. He raised up onto his elbows, his hips still driving, the strain showing in his face and in the veins on his neck, sharp with rigid relief. She wanted more, and so she came up with him, forcing him to arch his back as her forearms took her weight.

She used the leverage of her body to pull him in, looking down to where they were joined, watching the tangle of their hair, the slick slide of his cock in and out, the way she opened for him, the way he stretched her. She was mesmerized, seeing the very thing she was feeling, her arousal heightened with every long, slow stroke he took.

She'd been wrong earlier. Nothing came close to being better than sex. "Do you know how good that feels?"

"I know exactly."

"This time I'm not even going to argue. It's impossible to separate the giving from the receiving."

"I thought you didn't want to talk," he said, grunting as he adjusted his position, as he came at her from a new angle that had them both breathing hard, had them both struggling to stay afloat, tensing against coming too soon.

She dropped her head against her shoulders, felt her hair tickle her back. "What I don't want to do is come. I don't want this to be over. If I go away, if I leave and become someone else, I might never have this again. I can't imagine giving this up. Giving you up."

"You will not be giving me up. You will only be waiting until I can be with you."

She looked at him, at his eyes, heavy-lidded and glazed, at his mouth, which showed his struggle for control. "How long? How long will I be waiting?"

He shoved forward, expelled sounds sharp with the pain of his pleasure. "I cannot say. Only that it will be no longer than necessary. I do not want this to be over either. And I do not ever want to give you up."

"Promise me that you won't," she said, dropping to the mattress, digging her heels into his thighs and lifting her hips to meet his thrusts. "Promise me that you'll come to be with me. That you won't leave me alone to wonder if I'll ever see you again."

"I will be with you physically the moment I am able. I will be with you spiritually every moment until then. But for now, I am finished talking."

That was fine with her. She reached for him, wrapped her arms around his back, her legs around his waist, and took him in as deeply as her body allowed, keeping him as close as she could. The storm of their passion swept her away. She gave in. She gave up. She came in a fury of sensations and emotions, all of them tangling too completely to peel apart.

He followed her into the tempest, driving into her again and again with brutally lashing thrusts. She stayed with him, came with him, gave herself up to this powerful thing they shared and returned from the journey exhausted and drained. He collapsed on top of her, his body as hot and damp as hers, the air around them thick with their shared scents.

"Did you mean it when you said that you loved me?" she asked a long time later, still holding him against her, still holding him close.

"I did," he said, and nodded, his hair tickling her cheek.

"I'm glad." She stroked his back with her free hand, her other crushed beneath him. "It makes me happy."

"It makes me happy to love you."

"Does it make you happy to be loved?"

This time he didn't answer right away. Instead, he pushed up onto one elbow and looked into her eyes, his chest expanding with each ragged breath he drew. "It makes me happy, yes. But it does so much more," he said, his voice breaking. "Being loved by you humbles me, Alexa. You bring me to my knees."

And after that, she didn't bother to hide her tears or her sobs when she cried.

Chapter 38

Sunday night ended up being a combination of Alexa's girls' night with Rachel and another one of Molly's bake-a-thons. None of it had been planned, but the habit of spending the last hours of the weekend with friends was hard to break. Thoughts of the decision she was going to have to make were weighing heavy, and she wanted normalcy. She needed normalcy—a reminder of what her life was like now, all the things she had and what she'd be losing, what she'd be giving up if she left.

The three women gathered in the kitchen of the Maples Inn, where they dove into the pie crusts and bread dough and muffin mix like a bunch of rowdy bakers, creating a monstrous mess and laughing through all of it, their merriment fueled by a bag of tortilla chips, a bowl of salsa, and an extra large pitcher of frozen margaritas that they somehow managed to keep from spilling into any of the various pastries.

For once, Danny had made it home early and had retreated to the family's upstairs living quarters at the insistence of Emmy Rose. She had forcibly dragged him out of the kitchen, chattering on about some letters she had written before switching gears and telling him every detail of the upcoming Christmas pageant—and making him swear on her Harry Potter book that he'd be home Tuesday night in time to go.

Alexa loved seeing the rapt devotion on the girl's face as much as she loved seeing the smile on her girlfriend's at Molly finally having her husband home to enjoy before passing out from exhaustion. Of course, if she passed out from the margaritas, she wouldn't be enjoying much of anything—a fact of which Alexa decided to remind her.

"Uh, Molly, sweetie?" Alexa gestured with a measuring cup coated with the thick corn syrup she'd poured into a mixing bowl of chopped walnuts and mincemeat. "I know lowered inhibitions make for really great sex, but I'm pretty sure you've gone about as low as you can go. At least if you want to remember any of it tomorrow."

Molly snickered, glancing at Rachel. "One little fling, and suddenly she's the house sexpert," she said, the two women cackling until neither one of them could breathe.

All Alexa could do was roll her eyes. "That might be funny if I hadn't lost my virginity when I was—" She stopped, clamped a hand over her mouth, her eyes wide as she looked from Rachel to Molly before reaching for her drink.

Molly cupped a hand to her ear. "When was that? I didn't hear what you didn't say."

"And you're not going to hear it either," Alexa said after she'd swallowed. "I was way too young and even way more stupid and not half as discriminating as I should have been."

Rachel shuddered. "First sex is horrible. Horrible. It hurts, and it's messy, and forget teen boys even knowing where to find the good parts, or anything like an orgasm happening. Hell, I knew how to do that myself before I ever slept with guy number one."

"Okay, you two," Molly said. "I've been with Danny forever and been married more years than I was ever single. He was my first, and we waited for our wedding night. So, please. I'm begging." She clasped her hands together as if in prayer. "I want names and numbers and ages. Anything you've got that's good and juicy."

"Sorry, no can do. I save all my good and juicy stuff for Vince," Rachel said, her eyes growing wide as if she'd shocked even herself, her cheeks puffing up like Dizzy Gillespie before she let the laughter go.

Alexa shrieked, watching Rachel bury her face in her hands, her long blond ponytail falling over her shoulders. "I can't believe you said that. And please don't say anything else. My stomach muscles can't take any more laughing."

Rachel sat back up, tossed her hair behind her. "You mean all your recent bedroom gymnastics keeping you too busy for your friends and you're still not in shape?"

Alexa giggled as she shrugged, though the alcohol-induced laughter felt forced. Her friends had no idea of the hoops she'd been jumping through. Even worse, she couldn't tell them. She couldn't share her fears, or talk about any of what had gone on, or even ask for their advice on the decisions she faced, and she hated it. Hated it. She didn't want a life shrouded in secrets, or to spend any more time in hiding . . .

And that's what she'd been doing, wasn't it? Hiding out, avoiding the risk of hurt, squirreling herself away in the woods where she was physically safe and emotionally invulnerable? Was she really using isolation as a barrier to keep out the world? Was that what Ezra had seen that first day when he'd told her she wasn't happy living here at all? She loved him, but dear God, she couldn't live like a prisoner . . .

"I was just wondering," Molly said, interrupting Alexa's elucidative musings and frowning as she fluted the edges of a crust. "What would you guys think if Danny and I closed up the inn for a week and took a real vacation?"

"When? Where would you go?" Rachel asked on top of Alexa's distracted exclamation of, "Are you kidding? I think it's exactly what you need to do."

Molly straightened on the barstool where she was sitting, arching her back to stretch. "I have no idea when or where, but I do know we need it. I'm just not sure we can afford to give up the income from guests and Danny's charters while we're gone, plus pay for whatever trip we might take."

Alexa got up to refill all of their glasses. "If you can work it into your budget and find the time, you should do it. I mean, I've lived here for five years, and I can't count on my fingers and toes the number of days you've taken off."

"I know, but choosing between mental sanity and financial stability? Who can make a choice like that when there are so many ramni . . . ramni . . . oh, you know . . . ramifications," Molly finally got out as Alexa chuckled, saying, "Sounds to me like someone is beyond overdue for time off."

Molly leaned forward and slowly pushed her glass to the center of the kitchen's island. "More like overdue for cutting back on the margaritas."

"Well, this isn't as much fun as vacation talk or getting drunk," Rachel put in. "But I have an announcement to make."

"You're getting married?" Alexa and Molly said at the same time, exchanging looks and then laughing.

Rachel shook her head. "Vince has decided to move back to Portland."

"What?" Alexa immediately sobered.

Molly followed suit. "You're kidding. Why?"

"Are you going with him?"

"I might. I haven't decided." Rachel shrugged, reached for a chip and cracked it in half, staring at the two pieces as if she didn't know what to do with them. "He just doesn't want to deal with rebuilding the bar."

"The Gin & Rummy has been here forever." Molly pressed her hands to her rosy cheeks, blowing out a breath heavy with disbelief. "It's a landmark."

"And Vince says anyone who wants the property is welcome to rebuild it." Rachel gestured with half the chip, popped the rest into her mouth. "He'll sell it for pennies on the dollar. He just wants out."

Alexa shook her head, stared solemnly into her drink. "I

can't imagine how hard it hit him to lose the bar. Especially thinking this was it, that he was settled and would be here for the rest of his life. And be here with you."

"I know." Rachel climbed down from her stool and headed for the sink, leaning against it and staring out the window there at the woods behind the inn. "I hate having to make a choice. I can stay here where I grew up, or I can start a new life with the man I love."

All three of them fell silent at that, time ticking by loudly on the stove's timer as the truth of impending change settled over them. Molly finally shifted on her stool, glancing at Alexa as if expecting more bad news. "What about you, missy? Are you going to head off into the wild unknown with your man when he leaves next month?"

"I just started stripping my kitchen cabinets," Alexa said, biting back the admission that she might be leaving them sooner than that, and that her reasons had less to do with her man than saving her own life. "Why would I go to all that work if I was going to skip town?"

"Better resell value on the cabin?"

"Who's going to want to buy my cabin with the development going up at Orca Point?" Alexa really, *really* did not want to have this conversation when she was too tipsy to hold onto her tongue. "Besides, this is just a fling, remember?"

"Uh-huh. And that's why all the kids from your pageant crew are buzzing about him coming to see you." Rachel hopped up to sit on the edge of the counter. "They're all saying he touched you on stage."

Alexa gasped. "What?"

"Emmy Rose told me," Molly said, nodding. "He tucked your hair behind your ear and touched your face."

"Oh, good grief." Heat rose, no doubt turning said face a nice bright red. "If he did, I don't even remember."

Molly raised a brow. "Doesn't say much for your love life that you can't remember."

"Yeah, guess he's not all that," Rachel said and snorted.

"My love life is just fine, thank you," Alexa said, pouring the pie mixture from the mixing bowl into Molly's crust.

The other woman smoothed it out with a spatula, saying, "I think someone is protesting too much."

"And I think that your guests are going to need more than one pie tomorrow," Alexa said, deciding then and there to change the subject before she revealed all the things she had to keep to herself, hating, hating, hating the secrecy, and suddenly wanting to cry.

"Hmm. You're probably right," Molly said, reaching for Rachel's hand to pull her down from the counter so the three of them could get back to work.

Alexa's mind began to whir. If she left as Ezra wanted her to do, as he insisted she needed to do if she wanted a guarantee that she'd reach the ripe old age of thirty-six a few months down the road, she would be leaving all of this behind. Yes, she'd left behind friends and coworkers when she and Brett had moved from Los Angeles to Comfort Bay, but Molly and Rachel were more.

Since Brett's abandonment, they'd become her family; she couldn't imagine abandoning them in return. Would they think that was what she'd done if she vanished without a trace? If they never heard from her again? If she walked out of their lives as if she had never existed? Would they think she'd only used them when she'd needed them?

How could she do that to them? How could she make a choice between these women, the men in their lives, Molly's daughter, and the rest of the place she called home, and the man who had come out of nowhere to bring her back to life?

Chapter 39

Ezra arrived at the school auditorium for Tuesday night's pageant after the play had begun. He had wanted to avoid drawing anyone's attention, knowing many parents would think it strange for him to attend. He had no children enrolled in the district, and no permanent ties to the town. What he had was a young girl counting on him, and she was the one he was here for.

He also wanted to avoid causing any trouble for Alexa. He was not aware of any gossip Tommy Mooney had spread following their encounter at the site of the fire, but he did not discount the possibility that people had talked. After tonight, however, the gossip would be of no importance. After tonight, Alexa would be out of harm's way and Tommy Mooney's reach.

Standing next to the exit door, Ezra looked over the audience toward the stage. He saw Rachel Fine at the curtain's edge giving directions, and he caught a glimpse of Alexa rushing by. He knew from Alexa that the pageant would be presented in segments by each student level, her second graders closing the production with their runaway reindeer tale.

And since he was only here because of the promise he had made to Emmy Rose, he allowed himself to become distracted—

and eventually entertained—while waiting, watching parents with video cameras claiming choice positions along the wall and down the center aisle.

He grew so engrossed in their competition, in fact, that it took him several moments to realize that the crowd had grown restless, that several members of the audience were on their feet as if something on the stage was awry.

Something indeed was. The children were looking at one another curiously, peering toward stage left as if waiting for instructions. But no instructions came, and the music that had been playing was suddenly switched off.

That was when he heard the first scream.

A second followed. The children began to whimper in alarm. Family members called out to them, pushing their folding chairs aside, making for the front of the room. His nape tingling, Ezra shoved away from the wall and stepped into the fray.

Teachers herded the student actors toward one corner of the stage. An administrator requested the audience to calm down, but the parents refused. The crowd grew animated, demanding an explanation.

Moments later, Rachel Fine ran out onto the stage, scanning the faces in the room, cupping her hands to her mouth and calling, "Ezra? Ezra Moore? Are you here?"

The group came alive, turning this way, turning that, those who might know him searching the room as the level of noise rose higher. He broke into a run, pushed his way through the people milling uselessly, waving a hand to gain her attention. She jumped down and met him halfway.

"Two men. I didn't really see them. They grabbed Alexa and Emmy Rose. They left you this." Her chest heaving as she struggled to breathe, she handed him an envelope with his name scrawled across the front.

He ripped it open and unfolded the sheet inside.

You say you value the lives of your people.
But whose life do you value the most?

The note was unsigned, but he did not need a signature to know who had written the words. A terrifying anger swept in to boil his blood.

He pictured Alexa, pictured Emmy Rose, shoved the paper into the pocket of his pea coat, and dug into the lining for the phone he rarely had cause to use, striking out against hands that grabbed to hold him, blocking arms that tried to prevent him from completing his task.

He dialed the number by memory, knowing the call would be routed directly to the man he needed to reach no matter where in the world he might be. It took only two rings before the phone on the other end was answered.

"Hank Smithson, here. State your business."

"Aceveda has taken two hostages. He wants to make an exchange."

"I'm assuming that exchange would be the two of them for the one of you?"

"Yes. I am the one he wants."

"Well, then. Let's see what we can do." Hank paused for only a moment. "Jackson just flew the bird down from Portland to fetch Simon. They're not far from you. I'll send 'em your way. Shouldn't take too long."

"I am at the elementary school."

"I'll let the boys know."

Ezra ended the call. Aceveda's men could be motoring away from the docks by now. Or they could be halfway to Newton by car. The helicopter was his only chance of reaching the kidnappers before they left the state, but that would not happen if Hank's men took too long to arrive.

He turned for the door, stopped by the silent faces of Comfort Bay's residents staring at him, and by Bob Calendar, the chief of police, barreling his way through the crowd. He was the first to speak. "Mr. Moore. Do you mind telling me what's going on here?"

"I need you to have the parking lot cleared."

"Do you mind telling me why?"

There was no time for confidentiality or finesse. "Alexa Counsel and Emmy Rose Maples have been kidnapped."

"Let me see that note," Chief Calendar demanded, pulling his radio from his belt and calling to his dispatcher, giving orders to contact state agencies and the FBI.

The man was wasting time. Ezra headed for the door. "They have been gone for twenty minutes. To you that may not seem like any time at all, but to the men who have taken them it is endless. I need you to have the parking lot cleared."

Just then, he heard Danny Maples yell his name. "What's going on here, Moore? Someone said my daughter's missing, that she's been kidnapped. Where the hell is Emmy Rose?"

"I'm on top of this, Danny—"

Ezra stepped in front of the police chief, cutting him off. "I am going to get her back. A helicopter is on the way. I need the parking lot—"

"A helicopter?" Danny Maples's face grew flushed, his eyes wide and panicked. "You just phone up a helicopter like you're ordering a pizza? What're you involved with? What the hell kind of crap have you brought to our town? And where the fucking hell is my little girl?"

"I will explain when I am able. But I will not waste time." He turned away, his pulse pounding, seeking out the police chief. "The parking lot. Please have it emptied of the cars."

"I can't just—"

He waved one hand, stopping the other man from speaking before stepping nose to nose, drawing gasps from those gathered. "I need the parking lot cleared. Now."

"Do it, Bob," Molly Maples said with a bitter softness, Danny beside her, his anger bulging behind his eyes. "Just do it. That's my little girl out there. If he knows how to get her back . . ."

Nodding, Chief Calendar gave the order to his men who made their way through the room, sending drivers outside. Unable to face what he had caused them, Ezra did not look at the Mapleses again. He slammed through the doors, pacing the sidewalk wedged between the parking lot and the building.

This was taking too long. Taking too long. Alexa was already too far away. He should not have allowed her to wait. He should have taken her away the night of the murders. He should have seen to her safety—

A large body moved into his way. Tommy Mooney glared down at him. "I don't know who you are, but I know enough to tell you that we don't want you here. You pack up your stuff and you get the hell out, and let us take care of our own. We don't need your helicopt—"

Ezra lashed out, drawing his weapon and leveling it at the other man's nose. His other hand closed around Tommy Mooney's throat in an immobilizing grip. "One more word and you will never draw another breath."

"Now look here, Moore," Chief Calendar said, moving closer. His hands were held up as if to ward off danger, though Ezra recognized the signal. He watched one of the deputies move up on his side, a second into position beside the chief. Both men had their hands on their holstered weapons, ready to draw when ordered.

"There's no call for violence," the chief went on to say. "We seem to all be wanting the same thing here. Getting back Alexa and the girl—"

But that was all he got out before chopper blades began to slice the sky overhead. The crowd dispersed, backing away as the big bird set down in the parking lot, whipping the playground bark and the landscaped beds into a frenzy of flying debris.

Ezra shoved Tommy to the ground with no mercy, then jogged toward the chopper, his gun drawn as he tracked the area, searching for threats. He saw none, only a sea of shocked faces as he climbed into the cockpit beside Jackson Briggs.

Chapter 40

Jackson Briggs set down the helicopter at a private hangar near the Portland airport. Ezra and Simon pulled off their headsets, scrambled down, ducked away from the rotor's blades, and hoofed it across the tarmac, where they boarded the private jet that Hank Smithson had called to have waiting.

There was only one logical place where Aceveda's thugs would have taken their hostages. Spectra IT's western U.S. headquarters sat beneath a concrete bunker in the New Mexico desert. The organization had no other secure location this close to the Pacific Northwest. That was where he would find Alexa and Emmy Rose—if they were still alive.

He had to consider that they might not be. Aceveda and Gates both knew he would come after them whether the hostages were dead or alive, that he would want proof either way, that even with proof he would not abandon his objective to annihilate the syndicate. That left him to face his biggest fear—arriving to find Alexa and Emmy Rose dead.

He had not done due diligence in taking care of them. He had known of the threat to Alexa; he should also have suspected that to Emmy Rose. His precautions had not been thorough. He should never have left them alone, never let either of them out of his sight, forced both of them to leave

Comfort Bay with Simon Baptiste until it was safe to return. He had failed them, and his heart ached, growing heavy with dismay and dread.

It seemed to take forever to reach the abandoned airstrip near the Texas/New Mexico border, and he paced the cabin for much of the flight, remembering when he had last been at Spectra's desert compound eighteen months before.

During the operation that had taken him there, he had made a deal with one of Hank Smithson's operatives, exchanging a young trespasser who had been detained for the military dossier that would bring down Cameron Gates.

The dossier would do the job, but Ezra would not use it except as a last resort. He did not want to send Spectra's septuagenarian founder to prison for treason he had committed two decades ago.

He wanted Spectra wiped off the face of the earth, the reach of their long arms stunted, their satellite facilities left floundering. He wanted the rank and file desperate to survive, cannibalizing one another while watching the syndicate's structure disintegrate into sand.

Right now, however, all he wanted was the plane to touch ground and to have Alexa safe in his arms.

Moments later, they banked a wide circle around a grass fire and landed, the jet taxiing to a small private hangar where Simon appropriated a Jeep for the drive. Being familiar with the compound's maze of tunnels and access shafts, Ezra would have no trouble getting them inside sight unseen . . .

Except as they drew closer, he realized the black smoke billowing into the sky was not a grass fire out of control. It was the bunker, blown into oblivion, the compound beneath burning as if a hole had opened into hell. He stared, disbelieving, fear and fury knotting his gut.

Aceveda had guaranteed any authorities Ezra sent would find not evidence but ashes. He knew that all the computer equipment and digital files would have been destroyed remotely, and all paperwork, fingerprints, and other physical evidence rendered useless. He could not bring himself to care.

All he could think about was Alexa and Emmy Rose being left behind to burn alive. His stomach clenched. His head pounded, a countdown to detonation. He pinched the fuse, not ready to blow. There was one other place the hostages would be—if they hadn't been left to die in the fire.

Staring straight ahead, he spoke to Simon at his side. "We are going to the Caribbean."

Chapter 41

Alexa pulled her knees to her chest and leaned against the wall behind her, looking over to where Emmy Rose sat on a bunk identical to hers. She had no idea where they were other than locked inside a room with no fixtures, no furniture other than the beds, and a single bulb in the ceiling. The square concrete box reminded her of a prison cell appropriate since she and Emmy Rose were prisoners.

They'd been moved from car to boat to plane to helicopter in what she thought was a space of a few hours, but now she wasn't sure how much time had passed since they'd been scooped up so brutally and taken from the school. It was hard to keep track of anything when blindfolded.

She did know that she'd fallen asleep on the longest leg of the flight. She'd tried to stay awake, listening for even the smallest clue that would tell her where they were going. She'd heard whispers, caught a couple of words, but nothing specific and no telling details.

Whoever the kidnappers were, they had to work for the same organization that employed Ezra. He'd warned her that she was in danger, but she'd never thought they'd take Emmy Rose, too.

The two men had walked up while she was straightening

the antlers on the girl's costume. Since she'd seen them only peripherally, she'd thought they were parents offering to help with the stable lights that had started blinking in the middle of the play.

She'd started to turn, grateful, only to have a hand clasp a foul-smelling cloth over her nose and mouth, an arm across her chest dragging her toward the stage door. When she'd regained consciousness, she'd been bound and blindfolded, lying on her side and rocking as if on a boat. She'd called out, hearing Emmy Rose answer. They'd been inseparable since.

"Are you okay, sweetie?" Alexa asked the girl now. They'd been given sandwiches and bottled water earlier, and escorted down a short hallway for a bathroom break. That took care of the physical necessities. She was more worried about Molly's daughter's state of mind.

"I'm fine. I just wish I had something to do." Emmy Rose threw her arms wide before falling backwards onto the bunk. "Do you think someone could find me a copy of a Harry Potter book? I haven't finished the one I was reading, but I can read one of the other ones again."

The girl was as resilient as her mother. "You're not frightened?"

"Not anymore," she said, tucking her chin to her chest and toying with the strings on her sweatshirt. "I felt like I was going to throw up on the boat, but when you started talking to me it helped."

Emmy Rose might not be frightened, but knowing what their kidnappers were capable of, Alexa was downright scared. That night on his sailboat, Ezra had given her a clear demonstration of what she and the girl were now facing. Sure, he was on the right side—if there was such a thing—but he was just as hard and calculating when he had a gun in his hand.

She remembered it all, every sound, every scent, the splash of the water, the gunshots, the spray of blood, the thud of bodies falling. She would never forget a single moment of that night. And here she and Emmy Rose were in the belly of the very same snake, being swallowed alive like tiny white mice. She didn't know whether to laugh or to cry.

"Do you think they finished the play after we left?" Emmy Rose asked, cutting into Alexa's thoughts.

God, but she wished she shared the girl's innocence. It would be so much easier than fighting the fear clinging like sweat to her skin. "I doubt it. It would've been hard for the show to go on without you there to play your part."

Emmy Rose huffed, pulling the strings tight around her neck. "Miss Fine could've gotten one of the kindergartners to do it. It's not like it was a big part or I had a lot of lines to learn or anything."

Alexa couldn't even imagine what Rachel must be going through, being so close to what had happened, but not knowing what was going on. Or why. "Well, the big parts had to go to the older kids. It's their last year in elementary school. You'll get to do something next year."

"I won't if we don't get out of here." Emmy Rose sighed, flopping over onto her stomach. "I wish Ezra Moore was here. He'd figure a way to get us out."

"I know he would, sweetie," Alexa said, believing every word that she spoke. "I know he would."

Chapter 42

The trip from New Mexico to the Caribbean took too long for Ezra's comfort. As he had on the flight from Portland, he paced the chartered plane's cabin, chafing when forced to strap himself in for the landing, the plane setting down at a small airstrip near Smithson Engineering's construction site on the island of San Torisco. He would much rather have maintained a position at the door.

While in the air, he contacted his former employer, demanding to know the fate of Alexa and Emmy Rose. Aceveda assured him the hostages were safe, an assurance Ezra did not take too closely to heart. Until he saw them both, he could not afford to relax his guard, or assume the story he was given to be true. Aceveda and Gates were not above using a lie to lure him, hook him, and reel him in.

He did, however, pray that the two remained unharmed, that they were not overly frightened, that they believed he would see to their safe return. Whether or not they trusted that he would, he was not so presumptuous as to think it wise to attempt this rescue alone; the hostages were too important for him to rely solely on his own skills and strategic knowledge of Spectra IT. To that end, he had arranged during the flight for members of Hank Smithson's SG-5 team to help.

His return to Spectra's Caribbean headquarters marked the end of the very long road he had traveled. He was not going to risk having things go afoul due to any inadvertent failure on his part to follow protocol, and so he agreed to Aceveda's instructions that he come by sea and come alone, using the other man's commands to formulate his own strategy.

Once grounded, he commandeered one of Smithson Engineering's Jeeps and headed for the Rio Verde, where the company's speedboat was docked. Traveling to Cameron Gates's private island by water was not Ezra's preference, but Aceveda's directives were clear. Ezra knew that his approach would be monitored by the patrols on the perimeter of the compound. What they would not know was that he was only a decoy.

While the guards focused on his imminent arrival, Hank Smithson's dive team would make landfall on the island's far side. Their job was twofold: take out any Spectra agent who had not already jumped at word of their ship going down, and rescue Alexa and Emmy Rose. Ezra's job was more personal. He had eleven years of pent-up animosity fueling him on. And if the final step in the annihilation of the crime syndicate cost Ezra his life, so be it. The hostages would be safe.

He docked the boat as instructed, allowing the two Spectra sentries who met him to pat him down and rid him of the one token weapon he carried. Knowing he would be required to pass several checkpoints before reaching Aceveda and Gates, he had not come to the meeting armed with more than the small knife strapped to his boot. Most of what he would need had been strategically placed over the years.

Arming himself along the way, he climbed the exterior staircase that was built into the wall of the compound, certain both men would be watching him from the building's rooftop terrace. His presumption was confirmed when he reached his destination.

Cameron Gates sat in a chair beneath a patio umbrella,

pitchers of ice and lemonade, bottles of rum and tequila, and a handgun all on the table beside him. Warren Aceveda leaned against the barrier wall behind him, his legs and arms crossed, his suit as impeccable as always.

"Ezra Moore." Gates crossed his legs, nodded, lifted his lips in a smile that did not reach his eyes. "I've been counting the minutes, waiting for your arrival. I trust your trip was comfortable? And that our requirements for this meeting weren't too stringent?"

Ezra was not here to exchange pleasantries. Neither did he believe that Cameron Gates was sincere in his welcome. He knew the man's mind too well, and had only one thing on his own. "Where are the hostages?"

Gates waved him off, reaching for a tall frosty glass that he filled with lemonade and offered to Ezra "The hostages can wait. Let's talk about what matters. You must be thirsty."

"The hostages are the only thing that matters."

"To you, perhaps. Not to me." Gates paused, took a sip of the drink himself. "As you've no doubt surmised, their only purpose was to make sure you and I had this opportunity to discuss several pressing matters."

Ezra didn't care what Gates thought pressing. He did, however, need to buy time for the SG-5 team to penetrate the compound using the schematics he had supplied. "Provide me proof that the hostages are well, and I am all yours."

At that, Warren Aceveda snorted, pushing off the wall. He moved to stand behind Cameron, adjusting the fit of the sunglasses on his face. "If I didn't know you as well as I do, Ezra, I'd say that was a weak attempt at humor. You're not the one calling the shots here. You're all ours whether your girls are alive or dead."

Ezra fought the fire in his belly, battled the roiling boil of his blood. He fisted his hands at his sides. "I want to see them."

"I'm sure you do, but it isn't going to happen," Warren said.

"In fact, if you don't listen to what Cameron has to say, I'll make sure you die without ever knowing their fate."

Ezra lunged. Gates jerked back, toppling his chair. The umbrella table crashed to the terrace. Warren scrambled for the weapon skidding across the flagstone and fired into the air. Ezra slammed a shoulder into the retaining wall, shrugged off the pains shooting into his back, and pushed slowly to his feet.

"Let's not act like uncivilized thugs." Aceveda returned the gun to the older man. "That won't get any of us what we want."

"What is it that you want?" Ezra asked, circling the up-ended table to stand in front of them again.

"Answers, Ezra. That is all." Gates righted his chair and settled down, legs crossed, and tweaked the crease along the knee of his pants.

"What are your questions?" The Spectra founder was taking too long to make his point, and trying Ezra's patience. He had heard nothing yet through the earpiece of his comm unit from any member of the SG-5 team, a circumstance which added to his troubled state of mind.

Cameron Gates frowned, his thick gray brows drawing together. "Why would you do what you've done, Ezra? We brought you here when you were struggling to put food on your grandmother's table and gave you everything you could ever want. And you turn on us like a rabid dog."

Ezra could not hold back any longer. He stormed forward, feeling the comparison to the canine in his bones. "What I have done has not been about me. I came here a grown man. But I came because of what you had done to my home. Because of how you deceived the young boys who thought working for you meant they would have a better life. You turned them into criminals, or you treated them like slaves."

Aceveda pushed away from the edge of the wall where he had returned to lean. "We did give them a better life. You think staying on that shithole of an island, sleeping on the ground in filth, and drinking water from the same river where cattle wallow is any way to live?"

"It is an honest way to live."

"It is a hellacious way to live."

Ezra turned his attention from Warren to Cameron, and felt the muscles in his jaw grow taut. "No, hell is to serve in your employment."

"You have seemed to enjoy the perks enough over the years," Cameron said, cocking his head to the side curiously. "You have never wanted for anything. And you are hardly an innocent man."

"I have wanted for my entire life," Ezra said, his voice rising, grating in his throat, his chest heaving with every fiery breath he took. "I have wanted for the lives of the young girls you forced into prostitution. I have wanted for the lives of the children on the streets who have been destroyed by your guns and your drugs. I have wanted for the lives of the San Toriscans you have ruined."

"Worthless lives," Gates said, dismissing them so easily Ezra knew there was no longer any discussion to be had, any argument to be made.

All he said was, "I have returned the TotalSky dossier to the authorities."

Gates laughed. "I can't imagine that is all you have done, though it is enough."

"You are right. On both counts."

"And no doubt CIA agents or Interpol or James Bond will be here soon," Gates went on to say, picking again at the seam on his knee. "Though I must say you were quite quick on the draw disseminating your information."

"I was not working alone."

"Do you know what I have learned over the years, Ezra? That working alone is second only to working with a right-hand man you can trust." He lifted the gun from his lap, turned the weapon on Warren Aceveda, and pulled the trigger.

The shock on the other man's face twisted into a rictus of horror before he tumbled off the roof and down the rocky cliff to the sea below. "Now can we discuss a future that will benefit you and I?"

Ezra heard crackling in his earpiece, but he could not make out any words. He focused on Gates, the last man standing, the man with no soul. "You have no future. There is nothing left. Every outpost has been compromised. There is no place you can go. Spectra IT ends here and it ends now."

"There is a future. There is always a future. Ah, the youth of tomorrow." Cameron looked beyond Ezra's shoulder. "But I believe our discussion will have to wait."

Ezra turned to see three SG-5 operatives in full camo gear crossing the terrace. He turned back to his former employer, the founder of Spectra IT. "Spectra is no more."

"I wanted you back here for this. I knew taking your lover and the child was the only way to make it happen. You and I are the only ones left, Ezra." Gates's expression grew accepting. "No one else knows how much we have done."

Ezra did not want to think about what he had done. He was not proud as this man was. He held many levels of shame. "The authorities know."

"Ah, but the authorities are only working with the evidence they have gathered. They do not have the experience of having been at the helm of such an organization. We ruled the world, Ezra. You were there the entire time."

"I was only there to stop you."

"Unfortunately, I cannot be stopped. Other wheels have been set into motion . . ." He paused for a moment, a wistful and strangely tender look crossing his face. "But I do recognize that I am an old man. I won't be here to see where things take you. In fact, I won't be here long at all."

And then Cameron Gates put the gun barrel into his mouth and pulled the trigger, his chair falling backwards, his life blinking out before Ezra's eyes.

Ezra stood there and watched the dark red blood seep into the pool of tequila, rum, and lemonade, the swirling mess mesmerizing, his daze finally broken by the sound of approaching footsteps.

"Fucking hell. All this way to watch an old man off himself?"

Ezra turned to Kelly John Beach, asking the only question he wanted to have answered. "Alexa and Emmy Rose. Did you find them? Are they safe?"

It was Simon Baptiste who slapped him on the shoulder, lifting the heaviest worry he had ever carried from his mind.

"They are indeed, boo. They are indeed."

Chapter 43

"In case you didn't know it, son, I thought for a lot of years that I'd lost you."

Hearing the true heart behind Hank Smithson's words, Ezra pulled his gaze away from a sleeping Alexa and turned to the older man who sat opposite him in a half-moon section of seats—and who had played the vital role of mentor during the early years of his life.

Both of his charges were safe and cared for and on their way home. And though the ongoing cleanup of the syndicate's remains would spur on territorial conflicts, other organizations claiming Gates's and Aceveda's industry as their own, Spectra IT was no longer a threat.

The battle between good and evil would never see a true victor, but Ezra had done his part. He now deserved to salvage what he could of his existence and move forward, and with any luck he would have a forgiving Alexa at his side. He could only pray that Hank would forgive him, as well.

Ezra sat forward, his forearms on his knees, his hands clasped, his head hung low. "I was not able to let you know what I was doing. I knew of your concern, but I had to keep myself apart. I am sorry for the worry I caused."

"Hell," the older man said, rolling the unlit stub of a cigar from one side of his mouth to the other. "It wasn't worry so much as just what the hell was going on, and not being able to get an answer."

Ezra found himself nodding. He had feared the loss of Hank's faith because he could not explain the full extent of his actions. Having that faith now confirmed brought an unexpected relief. "I will be glad to answer any questions you wish to ask. I do not see any harm in you knowing the things I have done, or knowing of my regrets."

Hank sat back, hooked the cigar with his forefinger and removed it from his mouth. "Well, see, here's what I'm thinking. If you fill me in on the last eleven years, that means you'll have to go back to some pretty damned dark places that you may not want to spend time revisiting. It's no skin off this big schnozz of mine if you'd rather stay in the here and now. It's enough to me that you're back."

Ezra shook his head. "I live in those places every day. At no time do I leave them, and I do not believe that I ever will." He did not make the admission lightly. Neither did he make it without drawing on the strength of what he felt for the woman sleeping across the aisle. "I can only hope that speaking of them will rid them of their hold, and that removing myself from similar situations will help their memories fade."

Hank gestured toward Alexa. "Help in the same way that little lady over there does?"

Ezra closed his eyes, picturing her in his shower telling him that he was all clean. He found speaking difficult, and almost choked when he said, "I do not believe anyone has ever helped me more."

"She's a tough cookie, that girl. She reminds me of my Madelyn, God rest her soul," Hank said, making the sign of the cross. "I sometimes wonder how I've managed to make it this long without her."

After a long moment of silence, Ezra asked Hank to see to the rebuilding of Vince Daugherty's Gin & Rummy bar. That taken care of, he began to speak softly of the thoughts that were the strongest, the ones he feared would be the hardest to shake, those that recalled the worst of his crimes. The words poured out like water over a falls, crashing around his feet only to rise in a cleansing spray.

Chapter 44

Fighting off her groggy exhaustion, Alexa woke as the plane began its descent. She'd only been gone from home for a couple of days, but she still felt like she'd been denied food and water, beaten with a stick, and forced to run a hamster wheel marathon. Her tattered nerves were in serious need of repair, her clothes, hair, and body in serious need of washing. She did what she could with her tongue and index finger to clean her teeth.

When she opened her eyes and focused on the plane's cabin, the adrenaline finally began to flow. She was safe. She was free. She and Emmy Rose both, she realized thankfully, glancing at the girl sleeping in the seat across from hers. She owed her life to Ezra. He'd come after them. He hadn't let the bad guys win. It was such a silly B-movie cliché, but that was where her mind went.

And why wouldn't it go there? She'd seen those men in action, been a victim of their villainy. Nothing Ezra had told her about his employers had prepared her for the truth. To kidnap an innocent child and use her as bait? What kind of twisted mind could even think of doing such a thing, much less follow through? Yes, she'd listened to him, but words were poor substitutes for deeds.

None of that mattered now, however. She was safe. She was free. And she would never be able to pay the debt she owed Ezra for saving her life. She swung her legs to the floor and sat up, stretching her arms overhead as she yawned, twisting side to side. And then she looked out into the cabin, her gaze settling on the man she loved so completely.

He sat across the aisle in a sectional seat, his elbows on his knees, his head in his hands. He didn't move when she turned to face him; he inhaled and exhaled at a slow even pace. He had to be sleeping, and no wonder. With all he'd endured? And not just over the last days and hours but through so much of his life? She couldn't even imagine the totality of his mental exhaustion, or of the emotional strain.

She curled up in the corner and watched him, thinking of the guilt he must have suffered when he realized she and Emmy Rose were gone. She wanted to go to him and hold him, to reassure him that she didn't blame him for anything, that she understood so much better now the things he had done, and why he felt he was the one charged to do them.

And then he raised his head. It was as if he had been listening to her thoughts, waiting for her to mentally voice the exact things he needed to hear, that she would never hold that life against him.

He didn't say anything. He didn't even move beyond lifting his head. All he did was drink her in, his gaze roaming over her face, her torso, her limbs. She wanted to be uncomfortable, knowing she had to look like microwaved death, but honestly? She didn't care. How could she when everything she saw in his eyes told her that he'd never thought anyone more beautiful or loved anyone more?

Her eyes welled with tears, and her heart ached with all she felt, but they would have time later to explore where these emotions would take them, time she hoped would go on forever, time when they were alone and not about to land. Right now there were other less vital points of interest stabbing at her curiosity.

And so she asked, "What happened after we were kidnapped?"

"I do not want to talk about that."

His firm tone of finality did not stop her from pressing for an answer. "Did Danny Maples try to take your head off with his bare hands for endangering Emmy Rose?"

"I did not let him."

"Did Tommy Mooney try to ride you out of town on a rail for endangering the town?"

"I did not let him."

"Did Chief Calendar try to arrest you for . . . whatever he could come up with?"

"I did not let him."

She cocked her head to consider him, fighting a smile at his matter-of-factness. "Did you do all that not letting with persuasive speaking? Or did you blast the lot of them with both barrels?"

He straightened, sat back, laced his hands on top of his head, and studied her. "I did not blast anyone. Though I did have my gun drawn when I climbed into the helicopter."

Another day in the life of her spy. God, she wished she'd been there. "Where did it land?"

"In the school parking lot."

"I wonder if anyone caught it on videotape."

"Someone may have, but their tapes will have since been destroyed."

That didn't mean they wouldn't be talking about the day at every Elk's Lodge gathering for years to come. "Party pooper. I wanted to see you in action."

He arched an imperious brow. "I believe you did see me in action."

She shook her head. "I didn't see you at all. Only your friends."

At that, he finally got up, his hands on his knees as he pushed to his feet and crossed the aisle to sit in the seat at her side, warming her, comforting her. "You saw too much. So did Emmy Rose."

"She thinks you hung the moon, you know," she said, and when he didn't respond, she reached for his hand and held it between hers. "What are you going to do now? Ride your white Lear into the sunset?

"The Lear is not mine," he said with a smile.

Mr. Literal. She knew that. "When the plane lands, what are you going to do?"

He gave her a nod. "I will disembark along with you."

"To stay?" She laced their fingers, staring at the contrast between the size of their hands, the color of their skin. "Or just to walk me to my car?"

"What do you want me to do?"

"I want you to do what is safe," she said, looking up, her chest tight, aching, fighting to breathe normally and not let him see her panic. "I don't want you to end up in the county jail."

He brought their joined hands to his lap. "I have broken several laws while in Comfort Bay."

"I know. You were doing what you had to do."

"Do you believe that the end justifies the means?" he asked, raising his solemn gaze to meet hers.

"Do you?"

He didn't answer, and after several moments of holding onto her gaze, he looked back at their hands, flexed his fingers tighter around hers.

She wished she knew what he was thinking, or how to reach him to tell him that she loved him no matter what he'd done in the past. She was so afraid that somehow she was going to lose him, that he wouldn't be able to stay.

It was so hard to say what she had to. "Once we land, if you have to go, I'll understand."

"If I do not stay, will you come with me?"

Her heart tripped at the question, at the soft desperation in his voice. "To where?"

"Wherever I decide to go."

"Just like that?"

"Yes." He nodded, his eyes bright. "Just like that."

"What would I do there, wherever there is? What would I do about my obligations here?" she asked, wondering when she'd grown so stodgy, so set in her ways.

"What you do there would be anything you want. What you do here, I cannot say."

"The cabin is a mess. I just started redoing the kitchen. School starts up again on January the fifth. I've promised Molly that I'd help her as much as I can with the inn's holiday festivities—"

He placed his fingers against her lips to stop her. "That is why I cannot tell you what to do. There is only one thing I can say."

"What?"

"I love you," he said, his eyes warm and honest, so very very sincere.

She swallowed hard, wanting him so much that she hurt. "That's not fair."

"I did not say it was fair. I said it because it was true. I have never loved a woman before."

"Never?"

"Never. I have slept with many—"

"Too much information—"

This time he stopped her with a kiss, a soft, soulful press of his lips to hers before pulling away. "But I have never involved myself at a deeper level with anyone before meeting you."

"We've only known each other for three weeks." She swore she would never again bash the idea of love at first sight. "It's all happened so fast."

"I do not care about the time, Alexa. I know what I know."

"And what's that?"

"That I love you. That I want to be with you wherever that may be."

"If I wanted to stay here, you'd stay with me?" she asked, tears rolling down her cheeks.

He wiped them away with his thumb, kissed away those that followed. "Yes."

She couldn't let him do that. Not with the threat of imprisonment for the things he'd done hanging over him. "Will it be safer for you elsewhere?"

He nodded again.

That was all she needed to know. Well, that and the fact that she'd hate herself forever if she didn't take this chance. "Then we'll go. Will I need a new identity? Will I have to change my name?"

His eyes grew misty, his voice breaking when he answered. "Only if you want to change it from Counsel to Moore."

It took a minute for what he was saying to sink in. It took her a nanosecond to reply.

"I do," she said, knowing it would take a lifetime to finish what they'd started, and even longer to give him all of her love. "I do."

Chapter 45

Emmy Rose sat on her knees with her seat belt holding her in place as the plane made a circle over the small airport in Newton where her parents were waiting. She pressed her nose to the window but couldn't really see them yet. There was a whole crowd of people down there jumping and waving, but from this high up they really did look like ants.

She had never been in a plane before. Well, she'd been in the one she'd ridden in after the bad guys had grabbed her and Mrs. Counsel at school, but that didn't really count because she'd had to wear a blindfold and sit still or else they would've tied her up and killed her or something.

Of course, she had known she would never really get killed, just like she had known Ezra Moore would come to save her. She couldn't believe that he was a spy! A real spy! Knowing someone in real life who was a spy was even cooler than stories about boys who were wizards and flying dragons and bad guys who could not be named.

The bad guys who had taken her had names, but she didn't know them. She'd been kept away from all the adults who had to do stuff about arresting people and putting them in jail, but that was okay because she got to hang out with another spy named Simon, and he had showed her the coolest computers she'd ever seen. They even fit in his pocket.

Now that would really be something to make Cassie O'Malley jealous. Cassie thought her PlayStation and iPod made her so special, but those were just toys. They couldn't find anyone who'd been kidnapped, or signal to other people coming to the rescue, or save the world like the things—the *gad-gets*— Ezra Moore and Simon had could do.

She couldn't wait to tell her dad about them. She couldn't wait to tell him and her mom about everything she'd seen. She never went anywhere much away from Comfort Bay except to Newton, and she'd never seen an ocean that was so calm and so clear and aqua-colored like the one near where Ezra Moore lived. She just wished she'd had time to see some of the jungle, too, and all the animals that lived there.

Oh, man, was Cassie ever going to be mad when they went back to school after the holidays. No one would pay attention to her ever again. All the kids in *all* the classes were going to want to hear Emmy Rose's story over and over. She couldn't wait to tell them about flying in a plane *and* in a helicopter. This was the best Christmas she'd ever had, she thought before she felt a big sigh come over her.

It probably wouldn't be very nice to act like a big shot in front of the other kids. Ezra Moore never acted like a big shot, and everyone thought he was a hero. Maybe she would be like a hero, too, except she hadn't really done anything except what she'd been told to do.

"I am very proud of you, Emmy Rose Maples."

She looked over at Ezra Moore. He was putting on his seat belt, and she hadn't even known he was there. She'd been busy looking out the window at the people who were getting closer and closer. She thought she could even see her dad, and she jumped up higher on her knees and waved really hard as the plane went by to land, bumping against the ground and bumping her back against her seat.

She waited a minute until her stomach settled back to where it was supposed to be, and then she asked him, "Are you proud because I had strength in adversity?"

"Because of that, yes, but also because you are smart. You trusted your instincts. You did not panic. You were able to see what you needed to do, and you did it."

"That's because I was thinking about what you would do, and about the pink frog and other things you told me."

"Then I am glad I was able to advise you as I did."

"I was pretty scared some of the time," she finally told him, keeping her voice very small.

"You had every right to be so."

"I think Mrs. Counsel was scared, too, but she acted pretty brave."

He looked across the plane to where Mrs. Counsel was talking to the old man with the cigar, laughing at something he said. "I am very proud to know her, too. Not everyone could endure what both of you had to."

She was pretty sure Cassie O'Malley wouldn't have *en-dured* it at all. "I'll probably be pretty popular when I go back to school, huh?"

"I'm sure you will be," he said, looking down at her with serious eyes. "But the important thing is not being popular, but what you do with your new fame."

Yeah, she'd already thought about that, too. And then she thought about something else he'd said earlier. "Did you *advise* me because you knew I might get kidnapped and would need to know what to do?"

"No. I advised you because it is my responsibility as an adult to share what I have learned through my life."

"But not everything, right?" she asked, thinking it would be extra cool for him to show her more about computers. "Just the stuff that will help me make good choices and not make mistakes?"

"I hope that is what I have shared with you, Miss Maples. I hope that indeed."

"You won't be staying to work for us anymore, will you?"

He shook his head.

"Is Mrs. Counsel going with you?"

He nodded.

She sighed. "I was afraid of that."

"Do you understand why we must go?"

"Something like you need to go where your skills are most needed? And Mrs. Counsel likes you a lot so she wants to go, too?"

"That is it precisely."

"I guess that's okay," she said, though she knew she was going to miss him.

The plane stopped then, and this time when she looked back out the window she did see her mom and her dad. She waved again, and they waved back, and she undid her seat belt and ran toward the front of the plane.

She had to wait forever for the pilot to open the door and unfold the steps. Once everything was in place, he gave her permission to exit as long as she was careful going down the steps and waited until she was on the ground to run.

She could hardly walk down, her legs were shaking so hard and her stomach was tumbling everywhere. She could hear her mom and her dad calling her name, and hear their shoes as they ran toward the plane, but she kept looking at the steps so she wouldn't fall from being so excited.

When she got to the bottom, she looked back over her shoulder, waving at Mrs. Counsel and Ezra where they stood together in the doorway of the plane. And then she frowned when he motioned for her to check the pocket of her sweatshirt.

She thought it felt kind of heavy when she reached in, and then she pulled out an iPod. She couldn't believe it! She turned back and waved even harder, and when he winked at her, she knew that the best friend she'd ever had in her life was Ezra Moore.

Please turn the page for a preview of
I ONLY HAVE FANGS FOR YOU
by Kathy Love.
Available right now from Brava!

"Why are you so scared of me?" Sebastian asked softly. She shifted away as if she planned to move down a step and then bolt. He couldn't let that happen, not before he understood what had brought on this outburst.

"Wilhelmina, talk to me." He placed a hand on the wall, blocking her escape down the stairs.

She glared at him with more anger and more of that uncomfortable fear.

"You can bully your mortal conquests," she said, her voice low. "But you can't bully me."

Sebastian sighed. "My earlier behavior to the contrary, I don't want to bully you. Or anyone."

"You can't seduce me, either," she informed him.

"I don't . . ." Seduce her? Was that what all this was about?

"Do you want me to seduce you?" he asked with a curious smile. Maybe that was the cause for her crazy outburst. She *was* jealous.

She laughed, the sound abrupt and harsh. "Hardly. I just told you that you *didn't* want to seduce me?"

"No," he said slowly. "You told me *I can't*. That sounds like a challenge."

Irritation flared from her, blotting out some of the fear. "Believe me, I'm *so* not interested."

He raised an eyebrow at her disdain. "Then why do you care about me being with that blonde."

"That blonde?" she said. "Is hair color the way you identify all your women? It's got to be a confusing system, as so many of them have the same names."

He studied her for a minute, noting just a faint flush colored her very pale cheeks.

"Are you sure you don't want me to seduce you?" he asked again, because as far as he could tell, there was no other reason for her to care about the identification system for his women.

She growled in irritation, the sound raspy and appealing in a way it shouldn't have been.

Sebastian blinked. He needed to stay focused. This woman thought he was a jerk, that shouldn't be a draw for him.

"Why did you say those things?" he asked. "What have I done to make you think I'm so terrible?"

Her jaw set again, and her midnight eyes locked with his. "Are you going to deny that you're narcissistic?"

He frowned. "Yes. I'm confident maybe, but no, I'm not a narcissist."

She lifted a disbelieving eyebrow at that. "And you are going to deny egocentric, too?"

"Well, since egocentric is pretty much the same as narcissistic, then yes, I'm going to deny it."

Her jaw set even more, and he suspected she was gritting her teeth, which for some reason made him want to smile. He really was driving her nuts. He liked that.

He was hurt that she had such a low opinion of him, but he did like the fact that he seemed to have gotten under her skin.

"I think we can also rule out vain, too," he said, "because again that's pretty darn similar to narcissistic and egocentric." He smiled slightly.

Her eyes narrowed, and she still kept her lips pressed firmly together—their pretty bow shape compressed into a nearly straight line.

"So you see," he continued, "I think this whole awful opinion that you have formulated about me might just be a mixup. What you thought was conceit, which is also another word for narcissism," he couldn't help adding, "was just self-confidence."

His smile broadened, and Wilhelmina fought the urge to scream. He was mocking her. Still the egotistical scoundrel. Even now, after she'd told him exactly what she thought of him. He was worse than what she'd called him. He was . . . unbelievable.

"What about depraved?" she asked. Surely that insult had made him realize what she thought.

"What about it?" he asked, raising an eyebrow, looking every inch the haughty, depraved vampire she'd labeled him.

"Are you going to deny that one, too?" she demanded.

He pretended to consider, then shook his head. "No, I won't deny that one. Although I'd consider myself more debauched, then depraved. In a very nice way, however."

He grinned again, that sinfully sexy twist of his lips, and her gaze dropped to his lips. Full, pouting lips that most women would kill for. But on him, they didn't look the slightest bit feminine.

What was she thinking? Her eyes snapped back to his, but the smug light in his golden eyes stated that he'd already noticed where she'd been staring.

She gritted her teeth and focused on a point over his shoulder, trying not to notice how broad those shoulders were. Or how his closeness made her skin warm.

He shifted so he was even closer, his chest nearly brushing hers. His large body nearly surrounding her in the small stairwell. His closeness, the confines of his large body around hers, should have scared her, but she only felt . . . tingly.

"So, now that we've sorted that out," he said softly. "Why don't we go back to my other question?"

She swallowed, trying to ignore the way his voice felt like a velvety caress on her skin. She didn't allow herself to look at him, scared to see those eyes like perfect topazes.

"Why are you frightened of me, Mina?"

Because she was too weak, she realized. Because, despite what she knew about him, despite the fact that she knew he was dangerous, she liked his smile, his lips, those golden eyes. Because she liked when he called her Mina.

Because she couldn't forget the feeling of his fingers on her skin.

She started as his fingers brushed against her jaw, nudging her chin toward him, so her eyes met his. Golden topazes that glittered as if there was fire locked in their depths.

Once again she was reminded of the ill-fated moth drawn to an enticing flame. She swallowed, but she couldn't break their gaze.

"You don't have to be afraid of me," he assured her quietly.

Yes, she did. God, she did.

And we don't think you will want to miss
THE ULTIMATE ROMANTIC CHALLENGE
by Katherine Garbera.
On sale now from Brava.
Here's a sneak peek.

Sterling parked his car on the street and followed her up the walk to her town house. She glanced over her shoulder at him. He had a quiet intensity that made her more aware of her body; she could feel his gaze on her with each step she took.

"Nice neighborhood," he said as she unlocked her door and stepped inside.

It would have been easier if they'd been swept away with passion, kissing frantically and making out in her foyer, the way frenzied couples always seemed to mate in movies, but they weren't young, impassioned lovers. They were mature—

Sterling caught her hand, drawing her into his arms as the door closed behind them. "Ah, that's better. No martini shaker to keep us apart."

He lowered his head, rubbing his lips lightly over hers as his hands slid lower on her back and drew her tightly against his body. She shifted against him, angling her head to a more comfortable position under his.

He teased her with nibbling kisses but didn't kiss her full on the mouth. She waited for it, tensed each time he drew near, but he always pulled away. And the anticipation was driving her wild. She sensed he was doing it on purpose, making damned sure that she knew he was in total control here.

She plunged her fingers into his hair and held his mouth still on hers, opening her mouth, and inviting him to taste her. He thrust his tongue deep in her mouth past the barrier of her teeth.

She was overwhelmed by Sterling. Held in his strong arms, one hand around her waist, the other smoothing a trail up and down her back. His scent surrounded her. Something masculine raw and earthy—and salty from the sea breezes. She tunneled her fingers deeper into his hair, holding onto him as if that would let her control him. Keep control of him. Make this crazy night about nothing but hot and wild sex.

She pulled back from him, caressing his jaw as she trailed her hands down his neck to rest on his shoulders. Her lips tingled from contact with him. Her fingers rubbed over his stubbled jaw. His dark hair was tousled from her fingers, his lips swollen. He looked like a fallen angel ready for sin, and she wanted to be the one to lead him down the path.

"That was . . . unexpected."

"I wanted to make sure that you understood why I was here," he said after a few minutes.

She doubted he knew why he was here. Maybe he thought the way to get her cooperation with the merger was to seduce her. Or maybe experience had taught him that dinner automatically translated into an invitation into the lady's bedroom. She didn't care what his agenda was. She had her own and she wasn't afraid to go after what she wanted. What she needed.

She needed to figure out what made this man tick and then use it to drive him away. Away from Charleston, away from Haughton House, and most definitely away from her.

And here's a quick look at
THE SEX ON THE BEACH BOOK CLUB
by Jennifer Apodaca.
Available in January 2007 from Brava!

Holly was sure that Wes knew Cullen's last name. All she had to do was convince him to tell her. She hurried through the cool night and reached the bookstore just in time to see Wes come outside, turn around, and lock the door.

Slowing her pace, she walked up. "Hi." Damn, he was still sexy in that overbearing male way.

He pulled his key out of the lock, then turned his gaze on her. "Change your mind?" He glanced down at the book in her hand. "Want me to return Cullen's book?" He added a grin that should be labeled as dangerous.

Holly leaned against the side of the bookstore and shrugged. "I have time to kill. Thought I'd see if you still wanted to get a drink. Unless" she opened her eyes wide, "you really are afraid that I'm a stalker with murder on my mind."

A small smile tugged at his mouth as he shoved his keys into his pants pocket. "If not murder, then what—sex?"

Oh yeah. Wait, no! God, she was weak tonight. Maybe it was her bad week. She decided to change tactics. "I asked you out for a drink, Brockman. All you have to say is that you aren't interested." She turned and started to walk away.

"Does that work?" he called after her.

She'd only gone a couple feet and turned back. "What?"

"The offensive. Does it work?"

She couldn't help smiling. "Usually. But then I don't often have to beg men for their company."

He directed his gaze in a slow examination down her body, clad in a burgundy tank top and form-fitting jeans, then back to her face. His green eyes darkened. "Tell me more about this begging."

Down, girl. What was it about him? She shot back, "For that, you'd have to buy the drinks."

He stepped closer, throttling his voice down to a dangerous rumble. "Sex on the Beach?"

She swore the ocean roared in her head. Her hormones surged up into huge waves of longing, washing over her. "You're offering me sex on the beach?"

His grin widened, crinkling his gorgeous eyes. "The drink. What did you think I meant?"

Her thighs tightened in response. *Get a grip, Hillbay—it's just a reaction to a handsome man and a long dry spell of no sex.* Holly was all for sex, but on her terms. She always kept her emotions in check. She was the cool one—the one that walked away when the relationship had played out. It was time to take back the power. She said, "That information will cost you more than the price of a drink."

He didn't hesitate. "Name your price."

"Steak." She was hungry. And food might keep her from thinking about sex.

"Done. You can follow me in your car."

She was practically dizzy from the pace he set. Or maybe that was pent-up lust breaking free. "Follow you where?"

"My house. On the beach. I'll make the drinks, and we'll grill some steaks out on my deck and watch the waves. Or maybe listen to the waves since it's dark out." His grin suggested more than wave-watching.

She thought about that, but in the end Wes had what she wanted. Information on Cullen.

Not sex.

She lifted her chin. "I'll follow you. I can spare an hour or so."

He nodded like it was no more than he expected.

Annoyed, she said, "I'm not sleeping with you."

He moved up to her until she felt the brush of his breath. "No?"

She felt a tremor in her belly that spread wet heat. *Keep control of the situation,* she reminded herself. "I don't go to bed on the first date."

He reached down and picked up her free hand in his larger one. "Kiss on the first date?"

She should put a stop to this. But the feel of his hand wrapped around hers was warm and sensual. She opened her mouth to tell him they weren't dating, but ended up saying, "If I like the man."

He ran his thumb over her palm. "You like me. Make out?"

Regaining her wits, she jerked her hand away. "Ain't gonna happen, book boy."

His face blanked at the nickname, then a grin spread out over his face. "Why don't we go to my house and take these rules of yours for a test drive?"

She was playing with fire. She knew it but couldn't stop herself. Wes was not the man she expected when she had walked into his bookstore. There was so much more, and she had a strange compulsion to peel back the layers and find out just who this man was.

Could she do that and keep her clothes on? Or maybe do it naked, but keep her emotions in check?

She was going to find out. "Lead on, book boy."

 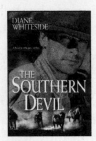